FAIRY BONES & A DRAGON'S EYE

—·—

LEXI LOPEZ

Copyright © 2026 by Lexi Lopez

All rights reserved.

No portion of this book may be reproduced in any form without written permission from the publisher or author, except as permitted by U.S. copyright law.

To Nydia Lopez Marrero. You always loved your stories.

Contents

1. Dead Man Talking — 1
2. An Unexpected Visitor — 8
3. The Phoenix Feather — 17
4. Is it Foreplay or Torture? — 34
5. Beware the Jungle Road — 41
6. Not Dead Yet — 49
7. Partners for Now — 57
8. To the Heart of the Jungle — 63
9. Darkthorne's Domain — 72
10. An Invitation to Dinner — 80
11. Quill & Dagger — 87
12. Dragon Bones — 102
13. Smite & Gash — 109
14. She's One of Them — 116
15. A Burner for the Gate — 120
16. You Know What I Want — 123
17. The Dragon Eye — 132
18. Part Two — 138

19.	Worst Blow Job Ever	139
20.	Gloriana's Choice	146
21.	The Helpful Prince	151
22.	A Rescue Mission	157
23.	She Has Me	162
24.	Part Three	166
25.	On the Road Home	167
26.	The Den of the Huntress	172
27.	Manticore Toenails	180
28.	Rosadela	183
29.	Your Secret's Safe with Me	187
30.	Never Trust a Succubus	191
31.	It's Complicated	195
32.	The Dragon in Me	202
33.	Telaraña	211
34.	Mythics & Madness	221
35.	Gloriana's Trap	225
36.	His Heart is Mine	229
Epilogue		235
Acknowledgements		238
About the Author		239

1

Dead Man Talking

NYIA

The fairy's wings are dry and withered. I bite the inside of my cheek as I pull them off the decaying body with trembling fingers. I almost drop the delicate things, and they crumble as I shove them past Martin's lips. He doesn't swallow.

Dead men can't swallow.

I try to ignore the stiffness of his body, left out to harden and rot in the island's harsh tropical climate. His skin, once so tan and youthful despite the decade he held over my own twenty-six years, is now sallow and pale. His lips, once full and eager to laugh, are now pulled back in a harsh sneer. It is a face I once loved, a face I grew to hate, and a face I now scarcely recognize. Martin, my lover, my villain, and my only hope of leaving this island—gone. I can't tell if there's been a struggle, though the jagged wound that opens his throat tells me enough of the story. Martin is dead. Murdered.

I have only seen two other dead bodies in my life. My parents—and they seemed almost peaceful in their death bed, their faces nothing like this strange imitation of Martin.

"Who did this to you?" I whisper. I think of his gambling debt, of the collectors that will inevitably show their faces later this evening. When he left last night with the eye and hadn't asked me to join him I assumed he planned to meet with one of his clients. This wasn't the first time I woke without my husband in our bed, and I blink my eyes in rapid succession to clear the thought that it would be the last.

The dragon eye. I swallow against the sudden rush of bile. I need some space, some distance between me and . . . this thing. Not Martin. This mass of flesh isn't Martin. The dragon eye is missing. I take a deep breath, allowing the information to slowly sink in. *You're in shock, Nyia.* Just breathe. The dragon eye is missing, likely stolen away. It is too big to be hidden in any of Martin's pockets. It didn't roll to rest along the jungle carpet. It's gone. I try to wrangle any fleeting moments of hope that Martin hid the eye at home, but instead the cold realization sinks into my gut like a stone. That's it. I'm stuck here forever now.

The dragon eye is gone. Martin is dead. I'm never leaving this island.

I press my fingers against his lips and push the magic of the crumbling fairy wings as deeply as I can down his throat. The stench of him is nearly unbearable. I squeeze my eyes shut in a desperate attempt to ignore the insects crawling over him, to block the smell, the image of his broken body.

"Martin." His name is a strangled croak that escapes my lips. I only have one opportunity, one question. "Where is the eye?" His body convulses. Once, twice. And then a single word stretches from his thin lips.

"Darkthorne."

I shove the scorched fairy's remains into my satchel and rise to my feet. Ruben, our single remaining servant, hovers behind me. He is worried about me—urged me not to see Martin in this state. But I insisted. I think I knew, had always known, it would come to this. I flinch away from Ruben's steady hand on my shoulder. He says something, but I can't hear him over the screams inside my head.

Gone. Martin is gone. I will never again suffer another sleepless night waiting for his arrival. Never again feel his hands on me. Gone.

Thank the forgotten gods.

"Make the arrangements to move the body." I close my eyes against the sight of my husband's lifeless form. I force myself to take a single shaky step back toward the road. Then another. "I have much to plan before this evening."

***

It's not the worst brothel I've ever been in. The Den of the Huntress at least has a pleasant lemon smell, and the employees all appear healthy and willing. I throw down a few brass coins in exchange for a mug of ale and thank the barkeep with a halfhearted wave.

I don't usually drink this early in the day, but I need to blend in with the other patrons, and if any day called for warm beer in the morning, it is this one. The brothel is bustling with business, despite the early hour. Those who have yet to make their way to one of the private rooms upstairs are cloistered around tables in small groups, intoxicated, their voices loud as they leer at the scantily clad women serving drinks and those dancing on the narrow stage. I don't need to bring any attention to the fact that I'm a lone woman. Some might be inclined to think I am looking for trouble, though I very much am.

I take tiny sips from my copper mug as I study the room. The ale is warm and bubbly but still good. If I wasn't here on official business, I might allow myself to indulge a bit, to continue drinking until the pain washes away and I feel nothing. I'm so tired of feeling everything, and more than anything, I want to disappear into the comfort of my bed, hiding away from the world and the ceaseless troubles growing around me. Mama was right, Martin was more trouble than his worth, even when he was alive. And now there is the burial I can't afford and the navigation of the endless pile of debt he left me to deal with. I take another careful sip of my ale. I want to disappear, but it's too early in the day for that.

Heads turn when she enters. Even in her human form, Sienna oozes sensuality—she can't help it. Such is the cost of being a succubus.

She saunters toward me, hips swinging with purpose until she reaches the bar. A shot of something dark appears beside her and she snatches it up, downing the glass in one swallow.

"Huntress." I dip my head in deference.

A slow smile spreads across her lips.

"Nyia. Always such a *pleasure*." Her eyes rove over my dark corset top and tight leather pants. "Are you here on business or have you come to play?"

I inhale her intoxicating scent, not caring her musk is part of her power, and she leans closer, her breath hot against my ear. "We just got a shipment of your favorite fairy wine."

"Martin. My husband—"

"Ah, business." She leans back, assessing me with her dark eyes. "The rumors are true then. I'm sorry for your loss."

I down the remainder of my ale in a single gulp, relishing the burn it leaves in my throat. I will not cry. Martin doesn't deserve my tears. Whatever pieces of my meager life remain, Martin doesn't deserve them. And I won't cry for myself. Not when I have to keep fighting for the one thing I need. My freedom. I need it more than air. And so long as the key to my freedom is linked to the damned eye, I am hopeless. The Huntress was loyal to no one but herself, but she owes me a favor—more than one. If she leads me to Martin's murderer, I can find the eye. I play her words over in my head, her apologies for my loss. Empty words that mean nothing but are the only solace outsiders can offer to those who lose their entire world. But Martin wasn't my world. He was merely my asshole husband who'd gotten himself murdered and stranded me on this island.

"It was Darkthorne." I spit out the name with venom. "I know it." I don't need to elaborate on how I know this—Sienna is well-versed in my methods. I know she doesn't take my request lightly. *I* don't take it lightly. Darkthorne has a dark reputation, and Martin believed he worked with King Ernesto as a parts dealer, perhaps even as a Burner like me. He is wealthy and holds the sort of power on this island that makes a man dangerous. If he truly is a Burner, then the threat of his danger only multiplies.

The Huntress raises two fingers and another, larger shot appears. She takes her time sipping this one, studying me over the rim of her glass. Her eyes are large and luminous, honey-brown pools that stare into my own. On the surface, Sienna is simply a young woman, stunning in her beauty. Even those who can't sense magic might be aware of the depth of her power masquerading as simple magnetism and not the strength of a succubus. But she is more than just a brothel owner, more than simply a succubus. Just as I am more than a grieving widow.

She presses her full lips together, frowning in thought before she asks, "If you already know it was Darkthorne, then what do you want from me?"

"Information. I need you to tell me who he keeps in his circle—where I can find him. Who is he?" I keep my voice low, my tone even despite the breath that hitches in my throat. I need more ale. My nails bite into the meaty flesh of my palm. I need this. I need *her*. The Huntress and the information she can bring me.

"Say I do give you this information. What will you do with it then?" She tilts her head. "Will you kill him?" There is amusement in the question. I know what she sees when she looks at me. The weak human girl, desperate for answers, desperate for a way back to a home I have never known.

"It will be justice. Will you try to stop me?" I reach for her, my fingers scrambling to take hold of hers. "Or will you help me?" I bite back a desperate sigh. *Please.*

"I won't stand in your way." Sienna shakes her head, long, dark hair falling artfully over her exposed shoulders. "But, Nyia, killing him won't get you off this island."

She wouldn't say that if she knew what I planned to do with the dragon eye, if she knew how desperate I am.

"That's for me to worry about. If it's about money, I—"

"It's not about the gold." Sienna sighs. Her warm eyes meet mine in that devouring way of theirs. "But I can't help you in this folly. Going after Darkthorne is suicide, Nyia. Don't do this. My advice is to stay far away from the likes of him. And if he is someone your asshole of a husband wronged in some way, then he had it coming."

My fingers itch with the need to slap her. How dare she. Martin isn't even in the ground yet. And yes, he was an asshole, but no one deserves to be murdered and left in the street to die. I know better than to consider the Huntress a true ally, but I convinced myself she would help me with this. With Martin gone, she is my only connection to the mythics, and silly girl that I am, I convinced myself that a bit of information tossed my way between random nights of passion gave us some kind of connection to one another. I convinced myself she was a friend.

"I've upset you," she acknowledges. "Come, let me make it up to you." She presses herself against me, sliding her soft lips against my collarbone. "Come upstairs with me and I'll help you forget."

I want to. I lean into her for just a moment, considering it. She can make me forget the pain of Martin's betrayal, the insurmountable debt, everything . . . and then she can make me literally forget. Forget that I am all alone in this foreign land, trapped. Forget the loss of my family and the recent loss of Martin. That I had a husband at all. Succubus feed on more than lust. No. Not yet.

"Another time, perhaps."

She steps back, crossing her arms under her chest and pouting slightly.

"He'll kill you, you know. There won't be another time." She lifts her brows, and for just another moment, I consider taking her up on her offer.

"Then I guess this is goodbye." I press my cheek to hers and she grabs me, pulling me closer and bringing her mouth to mine. She tastes like honey and sugar cane. The kiss is lingering, sweet, and tinged with a hint of regret. A goodbye instead of a promise.

"He'll be at the king's ball in three nights," Sienna says.

My eyebrows rise at the admission. The trip to see her was not a waste after all. Not that I have an invite to the palace, but that is future Nyia's problem. A time and location are all I need to come up with a plan.

"I'm sure getting in won't be a problem for one with your talents, but here." In a single fluid movement, she snatches the dagger at my hip and slices off a lock of her hair. She hands it to me and the silken strands hum with power. "Take this. In case you run into any trouble."

"Thank you."

She shakes her head. "Goodbye, Nyia."

2

An Unexpected Visitor

I've never been to the king's ball. The event is reserved for the court and elite families of the island. An opportunity for those in power to flaunt their wealth. Martin and I were once comfortable, before his gambling and seedy deals with the underbellies of society stole our future. Before I realized who I'd married, before Martin discovered what I am. But even in those early days, we were never invited.

This year is no different, but I'm not about to allow something as silly as a lack of invitation keep me from attending. At least I have a few days to come up with some sort of plan.

I decide to walk home from the brothel. We don't live very far, and it is still early enough that the sun has yet to reach the full heat of the day. I stroll through the crowded street, pausing to look at various bolts of fabric and other wares being peddled to me, though I have no coin to spare. Clothing myself for the ball will be a challenging enterprise, but I will use the last of my fairy remains if needed. The center square is bustling with its usual business, the markets now so full that one district blurs into the other. The odors of various smoked meats and fresh baked fruits assault my senses, and I shiver at the sudden thrum of magic in the air as the booths blend from simple human wares to those made from mythics.

"Fingers, toes, and claw clippings! Fresh-pressed pixie powder, squeeze your own," a gruff voice shouts in my ear. I keep my head down, only nodding once to Carmen waving from her stand where she peddles hair dye made from troll urine. I don't stop for the idle chatter. I wonder if she's heard the news about Martin. Most likely she has, and I don't think I have the energy to suffer through her condolences.

I feel my shoulders sag with relief as I leave the outskirts of the city, and I'm grateful for the solace of the long winding footpath that leads home. I don't have the energy to talk to anyone else, though I doubt the evening will bring me the peace I so desperately seek. It isn't much longer before I reach the narrow walkway leading up to our home.

Like most of the city's homes, ours is a tiny, sturdy structure made of stone. Although the colony has stretched to cover over a third of the island, the city proper remains close to the dock and fringes of Ernesto's castle. He isn't a proper king, merely the son of the pirate who discovered the island and its magic. His father didn't proclaim himself king until decades later, when my parents first arrived on the island.

My childhood home is only a few streets away, though a new family lives there now. The streets are lined with these houses, all living in the shadow of the king's castle. Beyond the walls of the city and my tiny village, there is some farmland parceled for crops, but even those are controlled by the castle. I've lived my entire life within the perimeters of the city's streets. I've never left the kingdom, no matter how much my heart longs to. And, like many, I've never dared to leave the colony. It isn't safe beyond the borders. Not when the remainder of the island belongs to them. The mythics.

The house is quiet upon my arrival.

I call out for Ruben, but he doesn't answer. Most likely he's soliciting a burial for Martin. Or perhaps he's left me too. He knows I can't pay him. I haven't returned to our bedroom since Martin's disappearance yesterday. Yesterday, when I assumed my husband's absence meant he'd fallen asleep at another games table or perhaps stayed the night with one of his favorites at Sienna's brothel. Yesterday, when my husband was still alive. I flinch at the involuntary memory of his body lying on the side of the road to town. He was so close to home . . .

I shake my head. Martin's death was no accident, but who murdered him? Darkthorne? Was it because of the eye? The eye would bring fortune to anyone, but it would be priceless to another Burner. I still remember the utter shock I felt when Martin revealed it to me. It was the most impressive mythic part he'd ever brought home. How could we have let it slip away? I know it is a futile effort, but I tear the house apart in my search for it, in hopes that I was mistaken and Martin hid it safely. Hours later, when our home looks to have suffered a hurricane and I am dripping in sweat, I admit to myself the dragon eye is well and truly gone. It isn't possible for anyone to have burned the eye in its entirety—no, that would take weeks, years if used sparingly. The amount of magic it would take to burn the eye in a single use is inconceivable, and that only means one thing: it still exists somewhere out there, waiting for me to reclaim it.

So how did Martin lose it? Is it possible he was set upon by some petty thief? Martin was known to have a few too many ales and waste the evening away telling tales and bragging about his accomplishments. Did he make a spectacle of the eye? But then why did he name Darkthorne, if not to claim him as both murderer and thief?

I need to reclaim the eye. It is the only inheritance Martin can offer me. It is my passage to freedom. With the eye I can afford to get off this island, to sail far away and live a life of my own in a place where magic isn't real and Burners don't exist.

I take several deep breaths, blowing hard to release the maelstrom of emotion and nervous energy rumbling inside me. Then, I set about tidying the disaster I made of our home. Even when we had a full staff, I didn't need more than two women to assist me, and I was forced to let them both go last summer after Martin lost big in the ogre pit fights. I was accustomed to handling my own cleaning, and the mindless chores took my mind off Martin for a time.

I'm just finishing up when Carmen arrives. Outside of Martin and Sienna, Carmen is my only true friend. She arrived on the island a little over four years ago, the last time the gate to the veil opened. Carmen had recently lost her husband, and the young widow had leaped at the opportunity to explore this new world. I'm not sure how she learned to alter the properties of troll urine to transform it into a colorful dye for humans—she's not a Burner like I am—but her business is booming. Today, her hair is streaked in aqua blue and glittering gold. As usual, she doesn't bother to knock, just bursts in and hugs me and cries about Martin until I am forced to serve her the last of my fairy wine so she can calm down. She takes the wine and sniffs and prods for answers. I listen to her condolences for as long as I can stand it and then practically shove her out the door. I am exhausted by the time she leaves and wonder how I can handle seeing anyone else.

"You pitiful thing. Get some rest, Nyia. You need it."

I slam the door after her final departing remark and trudge toward our bedroom. It isn't even close to my usual bedtime, but the thought of sleeping until tomorrow sounds wonderful, despite the source of the suggestion. *Get some rest. You need it*. I scowl as I replay Carmen's words.

The house holds a single full-length mirror. A monstrous thing Martin brought home shortly after our wedding. He was delighted with himself—claimed it was enchanted—though neither of us were ever able to discern how it worked. It's leaned against our bedroom wall for years now, collecting dust. I frown in front of it, picking apart the image before me and finding her wanting. I look as though I haven't slept in a week, the circles under my eyes evident in the harsh afternoon light. It will probably take the last of my fairy remains to make a suitable disguise for the masquerade ball. The succubus hair might work, too, though I've never burned it before. Like every new mythic part I encounter, I have to test the results on myself before I can learn what the burning will bring. I consider testing out a single strand when there is a knock at the front door.

I frown at the interruption but make my way to the door to greet my guest. It seems Carmen was only the first of Martin's mourners. The remainder of the evening is spent receiving Martin's old gambling buddies and business acquaintances. Some to share condolences and others nudging for a payment on debts. It is hours later when I finally manage to push out the remaining guests and reclaim the solace of my home. I should sleep now, I think. But instead I find myself climbing into Martin's chair by the hearth. I thumb through his ledgers, squinting at his poor penmanship and shoddy equations. How could it have gotten so bad?

I must have fallen asleep because I am jolted awake by a sudden pounding from my front door.

I frown at the mounted clock on the wall, it is well past the civilized hour for guests, so who would dare show up so late?

I meet Ruben in the foyer. He looks as exhausted as I feel, and I make a mental note to find the funds for his severance, I'll sell anything I can—and to write him a letter of recommendation. He deserves that much at least.

You have the succubus hair in your pocket, I remind myself against the sudden jolt of panic and nod at Ruben. He opens the door and I force a reluctant smile.

My visitor is easily the most beautiful woman I've ever seen. She must be burning fairy because only a glamour could produce hair this shiny, a face this perfect, a body this divine. She is flanked on either side by two massive men. If you told me they were part giant or ogre, I wouldn't bat an eye.

She smiles at me, full red lips stretching over brilliant white teeth. It somehow makes her even more beautiful. Her tawny skin practically sparkles, and her eyes are a mesmerizing color between green and gold.

"Nyia Marre, I presume?"

"Y-yes." I want to keep looking at her, but I'm distracted by both of her escorts drawing daggers the length of small swords. They each point one toward me, and the one on the right grins, revealing a mouth full of gaping holes. The teeth he does have are all filed to sharp points.

"Excellent. I'm sorry to meet under these circumstances, but surely you understand how difficult it is for a woman to make her way in this world. Now, I'm assuming you know why I'm here?"

I have no clue. Her voice drips honey, but there is venom flashing in her hazel eyes. I have a feeling she could order both of these men to attack with a mere snap of her fingers, and I don't want to give her any reason to make such demands of them. She wears an expensive gown and enough jewelry to fund a small kingdom. There is no reason for someone like her to be at my house, which can only mean one thing. This is Martin's fault.

"I'm sorry. I have yet to get my husband's affairs in order." That is a stretch. The king's guards haven't had any interest in investigating Martin's murder. Once I identified Martin, they called it an unfortunate side effect of his bad habits. In other words, no one cared. Unless they were concerned about the gold he still owes them.

"I'm here for my payment, dear. Now do you have it, or does Smite get to eat you?"

At her words, the giant man I can assume is known as Smite starts toward me. I plant my feet and search my memories for anything I might have learned about burning succubus hair. It doesn't seem I can seduce my way out of this one. That leaves reasoning with her. Or, at the very least, stalling her until I come up with a better plan.

"Payment? Who are you? I don't know anything about a payment." Martin had someone he unloaded the goods on. After taking our cut, of course. Did he give a portion to her too? For what? Or did he owe this woman some other debts? Gambling or—

"Easy." She holds up a hand and Smite stops mid-stride, stepping back behind her. She inhales deeply, sniffing at the air between us. "She's telling the truth, and she hasn't burned anything significant in over thirty minutes."

My mind reels with the implication. What is she burning that allows her to know all that?

"I apologize Señora Marre. Coming to your home, under such strenuous times, must be especially difficult. Please, call me Doña Gloriana. May I come in?" She doesn't wait for an answer and sweeps by me, assailing my nostrils with a heady rose perfume.

I strangle back a cough but can't help the sneeze.

The woman who calls herself Gloriana dusts at Martin's favorite armchair before gracefully sitting down.

Ruben's panicked eyes meet my own. There is a question there, and I quickly shake my head. There is little the two of us can do against two armed men.

I swallow as Smite and the other large man take their place beside their mistress, who somehow looks regal as a queen despite her humble surroundings. Is she related to the king? His mistress, perhaps? Their weapons remain pointed at me, daring me to run. I clear my throat. "You, umm, mentioned a payment?"

Doña Gloriana smiles again. "Yes. Normally I wouldn't feel the need to collect in person, but with the changing of hands in the family business, I thought it prudent. You did work with your husband as his Burner, did you not?"

I will my expression to remain neutral. How does she know that? We were so careful. Or rather, I was so careful. I've always remained in the shadows, for my safety. The less I knew, the better—that's what Martin always said. But what did he manage to keep from me? Magic smuggling without the king's approval is dangerous work. Did we pay Doña Gloriana and her goons for protection? What did Martin do for her?

She presses on, as I haven't answered.

"You don't have to admit to it." She draws a deep breath, once again sniffing the air between us. "I can smell it on you."

"What do you want?" I wish my voice didn't sound like such a weak whimper. I've never met such a powerful Burner before, but there were whispers behind closed doors. Martin had his own theory about Burners, that we were simply people who were born on this island. It would stand to reason then that the longer we inhabit the island, the more Burners it will produce. Perhaps there are more than I thought.

"I want what your husband has been teasing me. What he promised he, and only he, could obtain." She grips either side of Martin's chair, her fingernails digging into the armrests as she leans forward. "I want the heart of a dragon. You used to work as his Burner. And now you work as mine."

The heart of a dragon? My heart beats furiously, trying to burst out of my chest. Martin would never have promised something so bold! Would he? Even if I still had the dragon's eye, which I don't, I am unable to fulfill her request. I could use the magic sight from the dragon eye to find mythics, sure, but I stood little chance against a dragon once discovering one. What can I possibly burn in defense of such a beast? Maybe if I used the dragon eye and the last of my fairy, I could turn invisible for a time? Sneak up on the dragon? Even the idea of it is ridiculous. Imagining I can do anything against a dragon is laughable. But even more pressing, I can't do anything without the return of my dragon eye. I have to find Darkthorne and take the eye back. Martin always pushed me to my boundaries with the eye, somehow both limiting its use yet always urging me to burn more and more. Had he truly intended for me to use it to find the heart? Had he always intended to give it to her?

"I can't," I confess. "I don't have anything left to burn, and I don't—"

"Oh, you seem an enterprising young woman to me. I'm sure you'll figure it out." She gestures for her men to follow, and she moves to the entryway, pausing to look back in the doorframe.

She really is stunning. And terrifying.

I can't wait for her to leave.

"You have until the end of the new moon to deliver payment, Nyia. Don't make me find you again, or you can be sure I'll bring the boys—hungry."

3

THE PHOENIX FEATHER

The following days are a blur. My mood shifts between sorrow and terror, and Gloriana's threats haunt my dreams. Soon it is the evening of the king's ball, and I still haven't come up with a plan that isn't dangerous. Unfortunately, I don't have a choice. I have to try. The dragon eye is worth the risk. Gloriana is expecting some sort of payment before the new moon and that's only a week away.

Ruben left yesterday, and the house is lonely without him. I find myself startling at every creak, and last night, I swore someone watched me from outside my window. As a result, I didn't sleep well, and I probably look nearly as bad as I feel. In other words, I am woefully unprepared for the ball.

None of that matters. I remind myself just what's at stake. I will get inside the castle and find Darkthorne, no matter what it takes.

We haven't had any fire sprites in nearly a year, and I consider heating water over the stove but decide it isn't worth the bother. The water left in my basin from this morning is clean enough, and I splash it on me with instant regret. It's freezing, and I much would have preferred a hot bath, but I need to hurry if I'm to complete a costume and sneak into the palace before the evening ends. I wrap a towel around myself and dunk my hair into the basin in an effort to tame the riotous curls. I can't help but release a cathartic gasp as the cold water hits my scalp. I finger-comb my long tresses with perla oil, twisting the dark locks into a curl pattern and sending out a silent plea for the hair to dry without frizzing.

I frown at my discarded pile of clothing on the floor. I've searched my entire inventory of meager dresses and found none suitable for the tastes of high society. I try them each on anyway and settle on a simple gown of deep midnight. My satchel is draped over a sturdy three-legged stool that serves as a catchall, and the top lies open, its contents beckoning between the folds of my discarded dresses.

I wish I didn't have to burn the last of the fairy for something so trivial as a dress but can see no other way for it. I experimented with a strand of the succubus hair, but aside from a faint tingling of the skin, I felt no different, and my appearance remained the same. I need more time to practice reading its magic before I can burn it properly. Time I don't have. At least I know how to use the fairy glamour. The only other magic of significance is in the possession of a single feather from a phoenix, and that is already spoken for. This plan will work. It has to.

I stare at the remainder of the fairy. The corpse is mostly intact, only missing the wings, and though it's started to decay, I can still make out the tiny features.

"They look nothing like us," I whisper the lie, but that doesn't make the words true.

I close my eyes and pull the fairy's sparkling essence toward mine.

I'm a Burner. A skill that's become increasingly public and all the more rare. If the king knew I was a Burner, I'd have an invitation to the ball. I'd have my own apartment here in the city and a position in his court. But then, if the king knew I was a Burner, I would belong to him.

Never tell anyone who you really are. Martin's warning rings in my ears. It was our mantra. But was that for my protection or for his gain? He kept so many secrets from me that I now question everything about our past.

No, don't think of Martin. Focus on the burning. Just do it.

When I open my eyes, there is little left of the fairy. The burning has reduced the magic to little more than bones and ash, but I carefully place the remains in a small apothecary jar I keep on my shelf. They will come in handy later. I slip the jar into my pocket.

Now, I see myself in the mirror and the vision is me, only different. The dress is more stunning than anything I've ever worn. It is the color of molten lava and softer than anything I've ever felt in my life. The silky fabric clings to my curves, and I feel beautiful in a way I have not been able to capture for a while. Across my eyes is a delicate mask of gold filigree and rubies. The precious stones and metal sparkle in the dim light. My hair is spilled ink; the curls cascade artfully down my back and over my shoulders. My skin glows like polished copper.

The fairy's magic won't last for long, but at least now I have my way into the ball.

I use the last of my coin to hire a carriage to take me to the castle. It is an extravagance I can't afford, but I have little choice. I can't very well walk in off the street. My pockets are filled with the jar holding the last of the fairy, a small dagger, Sienna's hair, and a single phoenix feather. As far as plans go, this is far from foolproof, but it will work if I stay in control.

I allow the hired footman to help me from the carriage and shake my head when the driver asks if he should wait for my departure. There is only one way I'm leaving here. I pay them and then ascend the steps to the great house. I step behind an older woman with a gaggle of young ladies beside her. No doubt with hopes of catching the eye of the bachelor prince. I'm able to get a good look at the invitation clutched in the matron's hand, and I dip my hand into my pocket, fingers curling around the vial of the last of the fairy's remains. When I pull out my hand, I'm holding a perfect replica of the invitation and am quickly waved inside.

It is too easy to become anonymous, yet another masked figure in a ball gown. The dais roped off for the royal family is empty, and a quick glance around confirms they haven't arrived yet. I wonder if this means Darkthorne has yet to arrive as well. I'm glad for it and lean into conversations, hoping to catch his name among the idle gossip.

King Ernesto has spared no expense. Acrobats fall from the ceiling on soft swinging silk, jugglers throw fire, and a singer accompanies a lively group of musicians. Silver serving trays dot the room, and I take an offered flute to blend in, though I have no intention of indulging. Tonight, I need my wits about me. I take a careful tour of the ballroom, noting all the exits and doing my best to melt into the crowd.

I'm there for nearly an hour, and I've danced more than my shoes allowed before I finally glean any useful information. Darkthorne is a royal guest of the ball. He was given rooms here in the castle, he is likely in them now, and he will be obligated to make an appearance before the royal family. If I can find his room, I can grab him while the rest of the masquerade is occupied with the arrival of the royal family. It is the *perfect* distraction. I wish I hadn't foolishly wasted the last of the fairy on my invitation; the extra magic would have come in handy now. I reach for the phoenix feather in my pocket, the action almost without conscious thought. I just want to be sure it's there. One feather. It's all I need.

It's easy—too easy—to peel away from the guests and venture down the hall of the main keep to the separate apartments within the castle. I've never explored this much of the castle before, though Father and I went over his sketches of its blueprints several times. Father arrived on the island as young man and had found work finishing the construction of the castle. He had boasted that one day he would take Mama and I to see the splendor of his stonework in person. What would Father think, if he knew what I was doing now? I push the thought away. Darkthorne is likely in the upper west wing, sectioned off with semi-private apartments often appointed to visiting dignitaries. Not that many visited these days. Years ago, it was easier to travel to the island, but that was before the gate to the veil corrupted. Now, the gate opens sporadically and never in the same place. Father loved this island and considered his and Mother's migration here his greatest adventure. Mythics and their magic were a wondrous new world for him. I loved listening to his theories before bed.

Pull it together, Nyia. I rarely think of my parents these days, and I'm on too important a mission to get distracted. I blink away the unshed tears and adjust the mask over my eyes.

"Help me." The whispered plea comes from just down the hall and I cock my head, leaning toward the sound. Not a prisoner, surely. The reported dungeon is in the opposite wing and allegedly several stories down.

Perhaps a servant then, injured while attending to their duties. I should go for help, call for the castle steward, but instead my feet pull me ever closer to the sound.

"Please." The voice is weak, a mere whisper, and there is a faint hum in the air that can only mean one thing: magic.

I begin to think better of my actions when I hear the frantic plea again, just on the other side of a heavy oak door.

"Damn it all to hell," I mutter. I push open the door.

The room is small, little more than a storage closet if the low shelves and cleaning supplies are any indicator. And one that hasn't seen much use. The corners of the low ceiling are covered in cobwebs, and dust lines the shelves. Aside from the cleaning supplies and a few random glass jars, there is nothing in the room. I'm mistaken; it's empty.

I sigh, more annoyed than worried. I've wasted precious time following a phantom voice, time I very much need to locate Darkthorne.

I'm about to leave when the tiny voice makes another plea.

"In here. Please, help me!"

It sounds as though they are right beside me, and I whirl around, utterly convinced someone with a foul sense of humor has lured me into this darkened closet and now lurks right behind me. But there is no one there, just the faint, steady vibration of magic in the air. The tiny hairs on my arm prickle at the unpleasant sensation.

Invisible? I rack my brain, struggling to remember what a person must burn to render themselves invisible. Fairy bones can glamour just about anything, but I've never seen them do that.

"Here." The voice repeats itself, followed by a faint glow of blue light.

I blink at the realization. The voice is there, just in front of me; captured in a glass jar is a tiny glowing wisp of light. A will-o-wisp! I peer down into the jar, frowning at my discovery.

It's not that I'm not sure what I'm looking at—I'm certain the glowing bit of material in the jar is actually a will-o-wisp—it's just that I've never seen one before. Hardly anyone has. They are elusive creatures, difficult to find and nearly impossible to catch.

But someone caught one. Captured one, sealed it in a glass jar, and left it here in this closet to rot.

For a wild moment I consider taking it—jar and all—and slipping it into my pocket for later use. I have no idea what happens upon burning a will-o-wisp, but I've heard rumors they can be used to help you find missing objects or light a path when one is lost. That can be extremely useful in helping me recover the stolen dragon eye, in finding Darkthorne and making him pay.

But there is that voice, the miserable plea for help, and I know I could never take the creature from one prison to yet another. I snatch the jar from the shelf and release the cork stopper before I can convince myself otherwise.

There is a cold blast of air, and I shiver against the sudden chill. For a moment, it appears the will-o-wisp has transported itself to freedom, but seconds later, it appears in front of me, hovering just inches from my face.

This close I can make out vague features, the outline of eyes and a mouth, the impression of a face. We stare at one another, and it occurs to me that I might be one of the only humans alive to have ever studied one so closely.

"Thank you." The voice is not quite as weak as before, but it still holds a whisper quality that has me leaning even closer.

"You're welcome. Can you—" I pause, not sure what I'm even trying to ask. "Are you able to find your way home from here?"

There is a light tinkling sound, like bells chiming in the distance, and I realize the sound is the will-o-wisp's laughter. "I can find my way anywhere."

The will-o-wisp holds no apparent gender, but its voice has a light, feathery lilt that sounds feminine.

"Right, of course." I reach for the handle of the door, intending not to waste any more time in my search of the castle.

"Human, I owe you a life debt."

"No, you don't. It's fine."

My hand falters, and I turn back to face the glowing light. Was I about to waste this perfect opportunity? I can ask the will-o-wisp to lead me to Darkthorne.

I open my mouth to speak, but the will-o-wisp silences me with a gentle hushing sound.

"I will tell you where to find what you seek, but that will not give you what you need."

I frown at that cryptic response. And how does it know what I am seeking anyway? Can it read my thoughts?

"Umm, thank you?" I'm not quite sure what I'm thanking it for since it hasn't really told me anything. "But if you can just tell me where to find the dragon eye, or Darkthorne—"

"Beyond the door and to the east, where the sound of laughter and seduction fills the room. Be wary of temptation."

"But what . . ." I trail off as I realize the will-o-wisp has already disappeared.

I hurry along the corridor, anxious to get this over with, when the unmistakable sound of approaching guards echoes down the hall. Only soldiers can be so synchronized, so noisy in their clanking armor.

If they catch me here without an escort, I'll be arrested. I can escape with the phoenix feather, but then I will have to come up with another plan to deliver Darkthorne. No, I won't waste the feather on this. I decide to risk it and reach for the next door I see and yank it open. I press my back against it, not daring to breathe until I am certain the footsteps are once again fading down the hall. Success. No one has noticed me. I'm about to leave when the sound of a door opening draws my attention. This room has a separate entry point. I should leave, take my advantage now, and I open the door, prepared to do just that, when a command stops me from leaving.

"Come on now. Get out of the dark."

I turn my head toward the sound, but I don't see anyone in the unlit hall. Against my better judgment I move toward the voice. The hall opens up to a spacious room. A large silk divider stretches taut against thick poles of guadua, and a figure is illuminated by the soft fire beside the tub.

"Come now. Closer."

My step is hesitant, and I'm grateful because someone heeds the command much more quickly than I. My breath catches in my throat. The voice wasn't calling me after all. This is a rendezvous between lovers—nothing more—and I'm intruding. But I make no move to leave.

The male's voice deepens and he softly curses. "By the forgotten gods, you're beautiful."

A part of me aches to see what he sees. Her silhouette is gently lit from the brazier. I see firm breasts and rounded hips, and when he rises from the tub to greet her, I stifle a gasp at the size of his massive erection.

She mumbles something incoherent, and there is a shift of water as he settles back into the tub. I'm hit with the pungent musk of succubus hormones, the same scent of cinnamon and honey, and I wonder for a moment if Sienna is here visiting a client. But no, this woman is far too curvy to be Sienna. The smell alone is enough to make me wet. It smells different for everyone, and I've wondered why, on more than one occasion, sex always makes me want cookies after.

I need to leave, but all I can smell is honey and cinnamon in the air. I can feel it slide down my throat into my lungs. I stifle a moan.

"Get in the tub," he says.

The woman leans on the edge of the tub, the tip of one breast dipping into the water.

"Ahh, the water is too cold," she whines. I can picture the cold water budding her nipple. I'm in too deep now. The succubus musk in my skin, invading my soul.

He reaches for her, and for a moment, they are just a blur of shadow. I wonder if he is wrestling her into the tub.

She moans and it becomes apparent what they are doing. All I can do is watch the slow, sensual dance between shadows. The undulation of her hips as she grinds closer, no doubt seeking the promise of his tongue. My fingers trail down the front of my gown, sliding through the too-soft silk and reaching for my center. So soft. Fucking succubus musk. My lips part as my breath hitches and my fingers slide—

"Enjoying the show, are we?" a deep voice whispers in my ear.

I whirl around, intending to reach for my dagger, but the enormous gown tangles around my legs and I fall to the ground in a heap of fabric. I've been caught, but by who? A guard? Another nosy partygoer? I push myself up to a sitting position so I'm able to view my observer. He's definitely not a guard. Everything about him, from the expensive cut of his suit, the high shine to his leather boots, and the shimmer from his golden mask all scream wealth. This guy is rich. And sexy, I can tell, despite the fact that half his face is covered by a mask. His single visible eye, dark as cacao, flashes like fresh embers in a brazier. I can see the firm cut of his jaw, just below sculpted lips curving into a sensual smile. A knowing smile, I realize as that smile turns into a smirk.

"I—"

He presses his finger to my lips and shakes his head.

I consider biting the finger off, but I allow myself to be pulled from the room and back into the hall.

"If you think what happened in there was any sort of invitation, you're mistaken. If you touch me, I'll kill you," I promise. I'm on the tall side for a woman, but this man still towers over me; my head barely reaches his shoulder. He is young, probably no more than thirty, but the harsh lines of his expression make him appear older and just a bit dangerous.

He stares back at me, his visible eye dark and intense, but he seems unbothered by my hollow threat.

"You're perfect."

"Let me go."

He releases me but makes no move to back up, intent on crowding my personal space.

"People pay a wicked price to watch such exhibition. Especially when royalty is involved," he says, finally stepping away from me to snap the door shut firmly behind us.

"Surely you knew," he continues, once again closing the distance between us, then grabbing my arm. "You spy upon your crown prince, little voyeur. It's quite the scandal." He gives a tiny mock gasp.

"Let me go." I jerk my arm back, but it remains firm in his grasp. If I have to ask again, I'm jabbing my knee up until I make him release me.

"Not until you explain what you were doing in there." His grip, already impossibly tight, strengthens, and I know he is bruising the tender skin above my bicep. The mocking tone has left his voice, and there is just the hint of danger in his line of questioning. "Are you a lovesick stalker or just some bored wife of a noble? Are you dangerous?" He leans even closer, and for a crazed moment, I think he is about to kiss me. "Yeah, you're dangerous." He shakes his head and releases me so abruptly, I stumble back. "You better start talking or—"

"Succubus musk. They're burning succubus musk, and I . . ." I trail off when I realize his shoulders are shaking with mirth.

It is common knowledge the musk of a succubus is a powerful aphrodisiac. The weaker willed are unable to even consent; it is merely one of the reasons it is illegal to sell at the market. Of course, different rules apply to royalty. I scowl up at him as I rub my arm.

"You know, it isn't any of your business what I was doing in there," I say defensively. "I got caught up in the moment and forgot. I would have handled it myself eventually."

"Oh, I have no doubt of that," he says with a muffled shout of laughter. "You seem quite capable in the department of handling it yourself." His eye roves down the length of me, and I shiver despite myself.

He continues to stare, that soft smile playing on his lips, and once again I'm struck with the idea that we are about to kiss. I wonder what it would be like to press my lips against just half of that perfect mouth, the other half against the stiff mask. Would the golden mask be cool or warm to the touch? I should back away. But I don't move.

The sudden burst of fanfare indicates the arrival of the royal family, and I pale with the realization I've missed my chance. Shit. Now I'll need to create my own distraction.

"Shall we?" He offers me his arm, and I take it without thinking.

My mind races with alternative plans. I've missed my opportunity to corner Darkthorne in his rooms, but that doesn't mean the evening is over. Now I just have to learn his identity and score a dance with him, find a way to get him alone, and seize the moment. The phoenix feather will do all the work.

My escort pulls me back down the hall toward the open ballroom. It really is too bad I've wasted so much time already. Succubus musk aside, this man did make me feel something. Something I haven't felt from anyone—not even Martin—in a long time. Something I wouldn't mind exploring . . . if only time allowed. I bite back a wistful sigh as his hand dips to my waist.

"Would you like a drink? Or to dance? I'd love to take you to the terrace."

This guy moves fast. And I want to say yes, take me to the terrace, so badly that I know these emotions can't be my own. He's a handsome distraction, nothing more, and the only reason I'm panting over him is because of the succubus musk. I need to excuse myself and find Darkthorne.

"I'm sorry," I say, even as I allow him to guide us toward the dance floor. "I just need t—"

"Don Darkthorne, a pleasure." A woman with salt-and-pepper curls and a seductive smile under her mask dips into a curtsy. My escort nods back. *Darkthorne!*

If his hand still hadn't rested on the small of my back, I might have fainted. Or turned around and rammed my dagger straight into his black heart regardless of how many are here to bear witness.

I feel sick. I wanted to kiss him. He is still *touching* me. I stiffen, but he doesn't seem to notice as he expertly guides me to the center of the room. The band begins a merry tune, and seconds later, he spins me around the ballroom.

Martin's killer.

"You still haven't told me your name." His breath tickles my ear.

I'm going to vomit. I *should* give him my name. See what he makes of that.

"Ahh." His grin is wicked. Funny how before it seemed sensual rather than sadistic. "A woman who appreciates the anonymity of the masquerade. I can respect that."

I bite the inside of my cheek to keep the scowl from spreading across my face.

"Still, it does once again beg the question of just what you were doing in the prince's chambers. Aside from the obvious, that is." He wriggles his visible eyebrow, and his golden mask sparkles as it catches the light. "An unregistered Burner." He tsks lightly.

Of course. Only a Burner would recognize burning succubus musk. I was so flustered that I revealed myself to him. And *of course* Darkthorne is a Burner himself. It's likely what made him such formidable competition for Martin. I'm the surprise he hadn't counted on. It also explained why he stole the dragon eye. No one would have better use for it than a Burner. Now it takes all my effort to keep my face neutral.

I spent the entire day plotting how to find him, and Darkthorne quite literally snuck up on me.

"And you? Darkthorne? The king's royal Procurer." I laugh, the sound bitter to my ears. "I'm surprised your skills aren't public knowledge."

He stumbles so slightly I barely notice, but I know I've struck a nerve.

"I don't work for the king. I only work with him at times."

"A lofty distinction." I snort.

"Says the Burner."

"What a hypocritical thing to say." I almost spin away and leave him on the dance floor before I remind myself I'm doing almost exactly the opposite of what I intended. I'm supposed to be seducing this guy into a false sense of security, not insulting him.

"You don't know me." Darkthorne stops dancing even though the song hasn't ended, and we are still in the middle of the ballroom where everyone can see. His arms tighten around me, his single eye piercing and seeming to search my soul. We stand toe to toe, chests heaving, staring at one another for a long moment. I ignore the flutter that stirs in my belly.

"You're Darkthorne. I may not know you, but everyone has heard of you. Don Darkthorne. You've procured more dragon parts than anyone else in history, *combined*. You're dangerous."

You killed Martin. You stole the dragon's eye from him. I want to shout those last words but I don't. Instead, I force my lips together into a pout. Instead, I say, "At least, that's what they say about you."

"Come with me." He doesn't wait for a response as he grabs my hand and pulls me off the dance floor.

I have no choice but to follow as he tugs me along behind him.

"Oi, not so fast. I've been looking for you." The familiar voice belongs to the most beautiful man I've ever seen—it's no wonder he didn't dare to cover it with a mask. He is annoyingly handsome with chiseled features and stunning blue eyes, sharp against tan skin. His long, dark hair is mussed with curls around his perfect face.

"Your Highness." Darkthorne inclines his head just slightly, but the prince takes no notice of the insult. "No need for a mask at your own masquerade, I assume."

The prince! The one I was watching earlier. No wonder his curls are so tousled. Heat stains my cheeks and neck as I curtsy. Don't think about him naked. I admonish myself, which, of course, is ridiculous because now it's all I can think about. I drop my gaze to my shoes and note the soft patterned flames in their design. Fairy glamours are nothing if not thorough.

Darkthorne's hand squeezes at my waist, and I snap to attention.

"It was Mother's idea. Masquerades are so boring, are they not?" He turns to me, eyes widening as though noticing me for the first time. "And who is this beauty? A traveler from some foreign land, for I would have noticed the presence of such beauty resting within my own kingdom."

"Your Highness."

"She's a lady of mystery," Darkthorne says.

"Nyia Marre," I answer. I look over at Darkthorne, but if he recognizes my name, he doesn't react. I wonder if he even bothered to learn Martin's name before he slashed his throat and stole the dragon eye.

"Marre . . . Your father just passed? Did he not?" The prince's chiseled features cloud with empathy.

"My husband." The words still don't feel real. Darkthorne's grip on my arm tightens.

"What a terrible loss for the kingdom—and you, of course." The prince's sympathetic smile is stunning, and it makes me want to punch him in his all-too-pretty face.

"My apologies, Your Highness. You will have to excuse us." Darkthorne once again pulls me after him. Once again, I allow it, though I notice the disappointment on the prince's face when we leave. High on succubus musk or not, I need to focus. This is my chance to get control of my life, and I'm not going to lose it.

Darkthorne pulls me out of the ballroom to the terrace. I barely have to pretend to call up the tears. It's easy to cry when I think of all I have at stake. Darkthorne reaches into his jacket and hands me his handkerchief. I take it with trembling fingers. This is my chance. I can't squander this opportunity. Darkthorne has essentially been gifted to me on a royal platter—all I have to do is take him home.

"I'm sorry about—"

"Don't. Don't say it." Because I can't bear to hear it again.

"You're right. It's a foolish thing to say. It doesn't bring your loved one back," he says. His voice is like a quiet blanket in the moonlight. "I know that loss. It is a pain that echoes still."

"I don't want to talk about him," I whisper. Because I don't. Not when my every thought is on seeking vengeance. On reclaiming what belongs to me. The dragon's eye. I plunge my hands into my pocket and twirl my fingers around Sienna's hair. The succubus strands hum with power, and I burn them quickly, drawing the magic into me. I'm a temptress. You want me. You need me. My skin hums with power. It's working.

"Okay, let's talk about your name. Nyia. It's beautiful." He steps closer to me, closing the distance between us. There is a hungry look in his eye, and he licks his full bottom lip. "You're beautiful."

Mental note—succubus hair is just as potent as musk. Thank you, Sienna. My breath quickens as I burn the last of the hair, pulling the succubus essence into myself and willing Darkthorne closer.

Closer. You want to kiss me. I reach for the phoenix feather and grip it between my fingers. Phoenix feathers aren't difficult to acquire if you know who to ask, but I doubt I will have the funds to purchase another anytime soon. Now is my chance. Perhaps my only chance. I'll have to act quickly once we arrive back at home. He'll be a bit dazed from teleporting, and that will give me the upper hand.

Just a bit closer, I coax as the last of the succubus hair burns away. Kiss me.

I burn the phoenix feather and think of home the moment his lips crash into mine.

4

IS IT FOREPLAY OR TORTURE?

I was not expecting this. The kiss quickly consumes me. There is nothing soft or romantic about it, more of a relinquish of power, his arms crushing me against him and his tongue claiming my own. For a moment I allow my body to melt against his, to revel in the press of his firm mouth against mine—the feel of his exploring tongue. Is this because of the succubus hair? Do I care? I moan against his mouth, my fingers tangling in the soft curls at the nape of his neck, and I barely notice the ashes of the feather catch in a sudden breeze.

All too suddenly, I am thrust out of his arms, and his bewildered expression meets mine.

"What have you done?"

I can't answer as the magic sweeps us up and away.

There are no faster means of travel, but phoenix feathers are never ideal. At least this time I am somewhat prepared for the rush of vertigo. The scent of fire and brimstone assails my nostrils, and for a moment, the world is nothing but a rush of darkness and starlight around us.

Just as suddenly, we're falling into my room, crashing to the floor in a mess of tangled limbs. I don't waste any time leaping to my feet and drawing my dagger.

"Sit down in that chair," I command Darkthorne. He's already clambered to his feet and he studies me, his expression wary as he adjusts his mask and straightens his jacket.

"Interesting choice of foreplay." He smiles.

"Shut up and sit down."

He sits in the chair, leaning back and crossing one ankle over the other.

He's still wearing the golden mask that covers the left half of his face, but from what I can see, he appears bored. I bite back a scowl and stride across my room to where I stashed sturdy rope. I tie his arms to the armrests, then force his legs apart and tie them to the chair's legs.

"Hmm, now this is getting fun. Although I see I'll have to teach you how to tie a proper knot."

"Do I need to gag you?" I ask.

He grins. "I don't know, temptress. You tell me. Would you like to gag me?"

I respond by pressing the tip of my dagger into his neck, just above his collarbone, and he sighs. Is he still under the spell of the succubus hair? "I don't think you understand what's happening here. You're going to tell me what you've done with my dragon eye and then I'm going to kill you."

"Y-*your* dragon eye? What makes you believe I've stolen such a thing from you?"

"I make no meager threats." I step forward, straddling his thigh and mimicking a slice of his throat.

"Why do you want to kill me? Don't tell me you haven't been having as much fun as I have." His voice is still light, but at least now his eye drops to my wrist, to the dagger pressed into the hollow of his throat.

I press harder, piercing the tender skin and drawing a prick of blood. He does nothing as tiny droplets of red drip down my blade. I'm so close to him now, I'm practically sitting on his lap.

"The fun hasn't started yet," I whisper in his ear as I drop the dagger to his forearm and drag it against his skin. The tender flesh rips apart, but I haven't cut him deeply enough to hit anything that will kill him. Yet. "I imagine that hurts." I stare down at his arm and the alarming rate of blood seeping from the wound dripping onto the floor. Shit. Maybe I cut him too deep. A wave of bile rushes up my throat and I swallow it. *Stay focused, Nyia.* I level my face with his so he can look into my eyes and see for himself I mean what I say.

"Someone—*you*—killed Martin and stole the dragon eye from him. Tell me where it is."

He slams his head into mine.

By the forgotten gods, it hurts! I stumble backward, dropping the dagger as I press my palms against my face. How could I have been so foolish? Allowing my guard down like that? He's Darkthorne. I can't allow myself to relax for even a second. I stoop to retrieve the fallen dagger and take shallow breaths to clear the last of my blurred vision. A damned headbutt.

"You're going to pay for that," I promise.

He mutters a response I'm unable to make out, so I glare at him.

"If I were you, I would be careful to stay on my good side. It doesn't have to be difficult, you know. Tell me what you've done with the dragon's eye, and I might even let you live."

"What makes you so certain I have it?" He has a tiny cut above his one visible eyebrow from where he headbutt me. Good. I hope it hurts.

"You already know I'm a Burner," I say by way of answer. He says nothing so I continue. "I asked him."

"Banshee tears?" A puzzled expression crosses his features for a moment. "Banshees are difficult to come by."

Try impossible. The last known banshee died in captivity nearly a decade ago. If any are left, they know well enough to remain in hiding.

"Fairy wings," I admit, biting my bottom lip to keep from scowling. "I asked where to find the dragon eye and he gave me a single word. He named you."

"Ah." A slow smile spreads over his face. "So you don't actually know if I'm responsible for your husband's death."

"He named *you*," I say through gritted teeth, not allowing him to bait me. He can say what he wants, but that remains simple fact. "The magic told me you will lead me to the eye."

He whispers something, but now that I'm keeping my distance, I can't hear. He shakes his head with a sound that is something between a grunt and a chuckle. "Why would I have any reason to steal something from *you*?"

I don't answer. I'm not sure how to answer. Why would Martin have mentioned him if he wasn't the person responsible for his murder? Who else wanted him dead? The dress is suddenly stifling, and I cross the room to my wardrobe, pulling out a loose shirt and pair of pants.

Darkthorne watches me with unabashed interest, and I bite back a retort that would likely only make him smile. I have no interest in entertaining him, certainly not with a peep show. I toss the clothing onto my bed and walk back to him so I can pull his chair around so he faces the door with his back to me.

"You haven't got anything I haven't seen before," he says as his chair inches around. The legs shriek as they scrape against my wooden floor. I grunt in response; he is heavier than he looks.

I push him around until I'm satisfied and then make my way back to my bed, pulling the dress off as I do.

"You know, I can still see you if I turn my neck like this."

I ignore him and get dressed in a hurry, though now that I'm looking at him, he doesn't bother to crane his neck back toward me.

"Why did you do it?" I ask.

He sighs and stretches his neck around to look at me.

"I didn't kill your husband." His exposed eye bores into mine. "I swear it."

He sounds sincere. I'm a convincing liar too. "Tell me what you did with the dragon's eye, and I'll let you go."

His expression changes, the exposed side of his face becoming as expressionless as the mask he still wears. I should rip the thing off him, take away the last of his anonymity while he is still vulnerable in my chair.

"Where is the eye?" I ask again. I have ways to make him talk. Through pain. Through magic. But the only other things I have to burn are some toenail shavings from a manticore. It would be ridiculous to burn something so valuable to find the truth. That leaves torture. My stomach roils at the thought.

He deserves this, I remind myself.

I'm interrupted by urgent pounding on the front door. I ignore it at first, trusting Ruben to deal with any unwanted visitors. Then I remember Ruben is gone and it is only me and my captive alone in this house. The knocking doesn't stop, and Darkthorne clears his throat in an exaggerated manner.

"Sounds urgent," he says.

I glare at him.

They'll go away. But . . . what if they don't? What if it's Gloriana and her goons? They would be early, but they also seemed the sort to play by their own rules. What would she do if I ignored her?

I groan but make my way to the hall, pausing for just a moment in my doorway.

"Don't make a sound or I . . ." I trail off because he is already nodding, and I haven't got a threat in mind. I hurry downstairs, anxiety twisting in my gut at the unexpected visitor. Please be someone harmless like Carmen, who I can just send away. Don't be Gloriana. For a wild moment I believe it is the king's guards, here to arrest me for the kidnapping of his royal Procurer, but surely no one saw our departure by phoenix feather. Most likely the only person who would even notice our absence is the prince, and he will likely suspect it was of a sexual nature. No one knows Darkthorne is here. It's a coincidence, nothing more.

The pounding doesn't stop. If anything it grows more desperate, frantic even. I pull open the door and blink in surprise.

No one. There's no one here even though, just seconds ago, someone surely stood here on my stoop, fists pounding. How? How could they have disappeared so completely?

"Hello?" I call out foolishly, my voice echoing in the empty street.

But I am alone on my stoop under the moonlight. I snap the door shut behind me, locking it for good measure. My breathing comes in strangled gulps, my heart hammering. I was pranked. Some kids playing with charmed brownie bones, nothing serious. Why am I so spooked? I take a few deep breaths. Gloriana hasn't come to collect her debt. I am safe—for now.

There's a muffled noise from the hall, and I'm reminded Darkthorne is still tied up in my room. I hurry back and throw open the door, expecting to find Darkthorne just on the other side. Instead, the chair is empty, the ropes I used to bind him cut straight through.

I scan the room, eyes darting to movement by my window. Darkthorne stands by the open window, guiding someone through while another person—a short woman whose face is obscured by purple and silver curls—stands beside him, wringing her hands and bobbing from foot to foot.

"Oh, leaving so soon?" I don't wait for an answer as I rush toward my tool belt on my bed. I can't take on two or more with just my dagger, but with the toenail shavings, I might be able to hold my own.

"Hurry up!" the woman yells. She's climbed out the window and gestures for Darkthorne to follow. "Come on, what are you waiting for?"

"I'm taking her with us," Darkthorne replies. He moves toward me with surprising speed.

"Let me go!" I squeal as his hand clasps around my wrist. I claw at his face with my free hand, ripping the golden mask off and gasping at what's revealed. A horrific scar covers the other half of his face. The jagged cut has healed, but the angry flesh around it indicates the wound is fairly recent. The scar runs from the top of his forehead down across his cheekbone, intersecting the cheek and the eye, which is covered by a dark leather patch. He must be blind there.

"What's the matter, temptress? Not the pretty face you were hoping for?"

5

BEWARE THE JUNGLE ROAD

Despite my efforts to the contrary, Darkthorne shoves me through my open window and into the waiting arms of a tall man with long silver hair. He grunts in disapproval when I kick him in the shin. I pivot on my heel and try to dash away, but Darkthorne catches me again as I sprint past him.

"Let me go!" I demand. Shoving his chest is like trying to push a brick wall. He sighs and picks me up, throwing me over his shoulder. My hair falls over me, obscuring my vision. Not that I can see much with my head pressed against his back like this. At least he smells nice. A bit like burnt chocolate. My stomach rumbles at the thought. I didn't bother with dinner before the masquerade.

Darkthorne and his companions take off in a sprint that leaves me bashing against his backside during the entire bumpy ride.

"How much farther?" he asks.

"Not much. Just around that building there," the woman answers. She sounds amused.

Moments later he sets me down in front of him, and I grunt as my bare feet hit the packed dirt of the road. At least I had the opportunity to change out of that ridiculous ball gown, but I would have much preferred to be kidnapped with shoes.

The high moon casts a paltry light on us all. There are three horses tied to a post. The largest, a black stallion of some sort, whickers in greeting. Darkthorne's hands are around my waist, and I'm once again lifted into the air and onto the horse's saddle.

"You'll have to ride with me."

"Does she though?" asks the silver-haired man.

"We only have three horses," Darkthorne answers, mounting behind me.

"Do we though?" This time I swear I hear the woman snort.

"Cesar." Darkthorne's voice has a distinct warning to it, and the woman gives a shout of laughter. I wish I could see better, but everyone is vague shadows around me except for Darkthorne.

"Where are you taking me?" I want to look over my shoulder and watch as we leave town, but I don't want to look at him again. His presence is all around me though. His chest brushes my back. His legs press against mine.

"You won't get away with this," I tell him. "People will come looking for me." This is a lie, of course. Ruben might have worried, but he's gone now, and I have literally no one else. Not like Darkthorne. I had him for merely an hour before he was rescued by his comrades. I ignore the pang of jealousy at the thought. How had they even found him? "Tell me where you're taking me."

He doesn't answer, and moments later, we are galloping away from the only place I've ever known. We ride for several minutes, but we soon slow, either to allow the horses to rest or because the road is so dark, it is nearly impossible to see—I don't know which.

I still don't know where we are going or why he decided to bring me along, but I feel that if he wanted to kill me, he would have done it by now—much cleaner to do it in town and leave the mess behind.

That's what he did to Martin anyway. He must want something from me, though I can't imagine what.

I'm not afraid, I tell myself, and this time I think I believe the lie. This is everything I want. Darkthorne will lead me back to the dragon's eye. He has to.

As we journey beyond the city and into the borders of the colony, the jungle's inhabitants begin showcasing themselves. I am soon lost in the wild hoots and screeches from the night monkey, the chirps of insects, and the songs of singing frogs. Their sounds accompany the gentle clopping as the horses crash through the underbrush. The sounds are almost relaxing, but I can't let down my guard. The man behind me is dangerous—incredibly sexy—but also dangerous. Fuck me, he's sexy enough that maybe I don't care. Stupid succubus still hasn't worn off.

Darkthorne is pressed up against me, and I wriggle in the saddle, but only partially to gain better seating. I can feel the tension in his arms, the muscles of his thighs, and the bulge between.

"Stop wriggling," he says. His voice is gruff as he leans down to whisper the command in my ear.

Challenge accepted. I shuffle again, smirking as I feel him jerk in response. I lean forward ever so slightly, arching my back as I stretch to stroke the horse's neck.

"And who is this handsome fellow? Surely you can at least tell me that." This time I do turn back to look at him over my shoulder. Darkthorne's stare is smoldering.

"Moco."

At the mention of his name, the horse's ears flick back.

"Booger? What kind of name is that?

"His. Now, stop. Wriggling. *Please.*"

"Where are we going?" I ask again. But I stop wriggling.

He hesitates, his body somehow growing even more rigid behind me. He doesn't want to tell me. "We will stop soon and make camp."

Camp. Because wherever we were going, it's too far away to travel in a single night. We are definitely traveling beyond the border of the colony. I swallow at the thought.

"Are you going to kill me?" My voice doesn't tremble. I'm not afraid of dying. And I don't really believe he wants to kill me anymore. But Martin *named* him. And there are things you can do to a person that are much worse than death.

He sighs.

"You should know I intend to do everything in my power to make your life miserable," I continue, lifting my chin with resolve. "You might as well kill me now."

"No one is dying," he snaps.

"You might," I mutter.

"Perfect." Darkthorne's voice is a deep rasp in my ear. "Just be quiet."

Like hell I will.

"And you two?" I ask his companions. "You're fine with this? Is this something you do often? Steal women and drag them through the jungle in the middle of the night?"

"Well, usually we save this sort of activity for the full moon." The woman's voice is laced with amusement. I lean over to peer around Darkthorne as best I can to catch a glimpse of the speaker, but it's too dark to make out any actual details.

"It's easier to see their pretty faces," she continues. "I'm Marix. Raf didn't tell us he'd be bringing anyone home with him today. Did you two meet at the ball? What's your name?"

"Marix, that's enough," Darkthorne says, but there isn't any threat behind his words.

"Marix, I see you're the only one in the group with any manners. I'm Nyia."

"Nyia. So nice to meet you."

"I wish I could say the same," I mutter under my breath. Given our proximity, I'm sure Darkthorne heard me, but he doesn't respond. Marix doesn't say anything else, and Cesar has remained silent since his initial mumblings at the start of this journey. I can ask Marix where we are heading—it seems likely she will respond if anyone in this trio will, but I find that at this moment, it doesn't really matter. Jokes aside, the fact remains that they kidnapped me, and I am in danger as long as I am with them.

And now that they have me, it seems the group is happy to ignore me.

Good. The less attention they give me, the easier it will be to make my escape. The question is, do I leave now before they reach their destination, or do I stay long enough to learn everything I can about Darkthorne? He claims not to have the dragon eye, but I suspect he's lying. He can't be trusted, no matter how good of a kisser he is. Stupid succubus.

Moco's pace is slow and steady through the dense jungle undergrowth. I've never traveled this far with Martin, not even on one of our hunts. This is mythic territory and isn't safe. Everyone knows better than to travel into the dangers of the jungle beyond the border of the colony. There are hundreds, perhaps thousands, of different mythics out here. Who are these people? All of my senses are suddenly on high alert. Has Darkthorne taken me on a hunt? Is that what this is? I never went with Martin on a hunt if I could help it; I hated that part of the job. I liked finding the magic in something and granting it a new purpose, not stealing the life force from the living. We continue deeper into the rainforest, and it won't be long before I lose any sense of direction. What if we are on a hunt and we are separated in the heart of the jungle? There's no place more dangerous on the island save for the rocky jetties the mermaids favor on the southern coast. I won't survive on my own, even without the threat of various human-eating mythics.

I look out to either side of me, but it seems as though the jungle is swallowing us whole. What do I do? Stay and hope I eventually glean some information from Darkthorne? Or leave now, take my chances in the jungle at night, and return home while I still know the way? It's now. Now with coverage of so many trees and the thick carpet that will make it dangerous for a galloping horse—now is the time for my escape.

"We need to stop," I announce loudly enough for his companions to hear.

"We're almost there." His response is whispered in my ear, and I shiver at the sudden memory of him and me in the prince's quarters. *Nyia, you are stronger than the pull of the succubus.*

"No, we need to stop *now*," I insist. "Unless you want me to relieve myself all over you and Moco."

His sigh is exasperated, but he draws up the reins and slides off the horse in one fluid motion. He raises a hand to help me dismount, and my leg swings around awkwardly before crashing into his shoulder. He grunts as he sets me on the ground beside him. His fingers linger on my waist, and I step out of his grasp before he can lean any closer.

"I'll be right back," I say.

"I'm coming with you," Darkthorne says, and his companions begin to protest.

"I'm not going far. I'm squatting behind that tree." I paste a big smile on my face and widen my eyes in an effort to appear innocent.

"That one. Right there." I start toward the tree in question before he can change his mind and make a big show of squatting beside it.

My feet are bare. That's going to be a problem. I can tear my sleeves and wrap them around my feet, but taking the time to do so will raise suspicion.

"See? Not far at all." I peek behind the trunk and meet Darkthorne's thunderous stare. Okay, I'll have to be quick.

"Can you hear me? Sing a song so you can't hear me pee," I call out behind me.

"I'm not singing," Darkthorne all but growls, though seconds later, a familiar and especially crude tavern song is belted into the night by his female companion, Marix. My mouth quirks up in a smile. In another time, she and I would have gotten along just swell.

I squint into the darkness behind us. I can barely see a thing aside from the vague outlines of dense foliage. Still, I know the way home.

I tense, preparing my body to run.

"Hurry up, Nyia," Darkthorne orders.

His words spur me into action. I sprint into the darkness. I don't dare look behind me, don't stop as twigs and stones sink into my bare feet. *Run through the pain,* I command myself. Escape.

I run until my lungs might explode, and I hear them in the distance giving chase. How long will they look for me? I draw a deep, ragged breath, willing myself to be quiet instead of the strangled gasp for air my body craves. I lean against a tree trunk. Be quiet. Catch your breath. And run again. It's impossibly silent now, the animals and mythics likely scared away by my sudden flight through the jungle. I swear I can hear my own heartbeat. Just a few more moments to catch my breath and then I will run again. I'll run all the way home.

"Nyia!" Darkthorne's voice is desperate as he calls my name. He almost sounds worried.

My feet feel as though I've run through daggers; the pain is excruciating. They're bleeding, I'm sure, and the idea of another wild sprint on them sounds torturous. But I have to keep moving if I want to escape.

A raindrop, fat and warm, splatters on my shoulder. Then another. Warm, so warm it's almost burning. And that smell . . .

The odor assails my nostrils and it's all I can smell. A putrid, gaseous funk that is more foul than human excrement. I gag, clawing at my throat as I gasp for breath. That's when I look up.

Not rain. A hideous creature stares back at me. Its dry skin is naked of fur and pale as moonlight. Yellow eyes glow, and paper-thin lips are almost a smile over a vicious maw of sharp, bloodied teeth.

It's drool, I realize. It pounces before I can run. I hit the ground hard, sprawling on my stomach and smacking my forehead into something sharp. I moan, pressing my palms into the ground in an effort to push myself up. Vicious claws rake down the length of my back and tops of my thighs, and I shriek. The pain is excruciating, burning hot and wet. Wet from my blood or the creature's drool, I don't know.

I'm rolled over onto my back, and I can barely see as tears pour down my face. I scream, unnatural, high-pitched, and feral in a way I never imagined I could sound. I feel the skin, *my* skin, as it is torn from my bones. I feel those jagged teeth as the creature shreds the meat from my thigh. The pain is unimaginable. I try to scream again, but I choke on my vomit. The pain can't possibly be any worse. And then the creature moves to my stomach.

My gut is ripped open, and my insides spill out. The pain is maddening. Unbearable.

There is a gurgling sound and then finally, *finally* I don't feel anything else.

6

NOT DEAD YET

I'm not dead. I refuse to believe dead people feel this much pain. Everything hurts.

I'm in a bed of sorts, perhaps a pallet on the ground. Not my bed. Not my home. I try to sit up, and it feels as though I'm being ripped in half. Everything comes back to me. But there's no monster here. No sign of any immediate danger at all. I'm safe. I'm alive. I repeat the words to myself until my breathing returns to normal. Once again, I try to sit up and this time manage to shuffle my elbows to brace myself enough to have a proper look around. I'm in a tiny room, little bigger than the mound of blankets and furs that surround me. The walls and ceiling are canvas, and they ripple slightly in the night breeze. Is it still night? How long have I been asleep? And how did I get into this tent? Darkthorne?

I shudder, willing myself not to think of my last memory, though the bandages around my waist and elsewhere indicate I remember the events well enough. How did he manage to rescue me before that creature devoured me entirely?

The flap of extra fabric that serves as a door pulls back, and Darkthorne ducks into the tent. The result is instantly suffocating. He is so big, he eats up the remaining space.

"You're awake." He strides forward, closing what little distance there is between us, looming over me. "I wasn't certain you would m—I'm glad you're up." He clears his throat. "How do you feel?"

"Like I've been ripped apart by a flesh-eating monster." I grimace as he helps me adjust to a full sitting position. His touch is gentle, but I stiffen all the same. He repositions the blankets under me to help support my back and gives me a careful once-over.

"I'm fine," I insist, if only to break away from his piercing gaze and regain some personal space. I wave my hand in a vaguely dismissive gesture, but I'm so weak it just flops by my side.

"How is the pain? I can mix you a tea."

I *am* thirsty. "Yes, tea, please. I can't believe I'm being fussed over by Darkthorne."

"Rafael," he says. "Please, call me Rafael."

The corners of my lips twitch upward at that, but I don't give him the pleasure of seeing me smile. Instead, I squeeze my eyes shut and focus inward, taking careful stock of my injuries. By all accounts, I should be dead. I can't think of anyone who has seen their own intestines and lived to talk about it.

"What did you use to heal me?" My throat burns, sore from all the screaming and bile. I rub it absently. Fairy blood would have been the most effective, but he would need nearly a gallon of it to repair the severity of my wounds. Did he have that much fairy blood? And if he did, would he have wasted it on me? Maybe he had a phoenix heart? Although that was just as unlikely.

"Unicorn horn. Here, drink this." Rafael thrusts a mug at my face, and I grab it, more so in an effort to prevent it from spilling everywhere.

Unicorn horn? That is impossible. Unicorns are more myth than actuality. There are stories of the creatures, tales that whisper of their powers. There were hundreds on the island at one time, but they were hunted to extinction. The last was seen decades before I was born. How did Darkthorne end up with one? Family heirloom? Or is he more skilled of a hunter than he lets on?

"It's not poisoned," Rafael says, interrupting my thoughts and snapping me back to the present. "In fact, it's barely magicked. Just something to help with the pain. A bit of dried leaves and local berries. It's mostly calmweed."

He's being intentionally vague, but the promise of dulled senses has me deciding I don't care. I drink the mug in a few swallows, despite the fact that it was far too hot to do so. There is a lingering flavor of mint and something earthy I can't quite place.

"Where are we?" I clutch the now-empty mug to my chest. It is warm against my bandages.

"Not far from your little run. But we've made it past the border at least. I sent the others ahead, and you and I made camp. You were too injured to move, and besides, we need to talk."

"About you abducting me and feeding me to a monster?"

"Well to be fair, you abducted me first, and you fed yourself to the monster."

I narrow my eyes at him, but I'm too tired to care for long.

"Okay. I guess I can't go anywhere for the moment. Talk."

The tea makes me feel quite warm, and true to his word, whatever it is spiked with serves its purpose. I no longer feel any pain. If anything, I am beginning to feel slightly tipsy. A tiny tingle buzzes down my spine, and a delicious warmth spreads throughout my chest and gut. He seems closer now, as though he's leaned in to confide a secret. So close, I can reach out and touch him. His face is clean, though. I don't know where he found the time to both bathe and shave. His dark hair is pulled back from his face, his leather eye patch gleaming in the soft moonlight. He leans even closer, and my gaze dips to the outline of his jaw, lingering at his lips.

"You have freckles."

"I—what?" I blink at him, startled out of my reverie. And thank the forgotten gods, if I spent any longer examining his lips, I was going to kiss him again.

"I hadn't noticed them before."

I resist the urge to bring a hand to my face to cover the blemishes. He probably didn't notice them before because of the fairy glamour—and the succubus hair. Hell, I still seem affected by the succubus. My eyes keep going back to his lips. I wonder if the kiss was really that good or if the magic of the succubus is simply that strong.

"I like them," he mumbles, and my eyes snap back to meet his singular stare. "First, I want to apologize. I think we've gotten off to a terrible start. But it's not too late to fix this. I'm unharmed, you're mending nicely, and I think we can help each other. Once you're back on your feet, of course. Which shouldn't be long. Unicorn healing is the fastest in the world."

Okay, I can handle this. He's offering a conversation, finally an explanation for everything. And we're starting small, discussing the lore of mythics. Easy. *If he wanted to hurt you, he would have*, I reason. And now, if he's willing to talk, I can find out what he knows about the dragon eye. Why Martin named him.

"How long have I been asleep?" I'm dreading the answer. Perhaps I've lost days in recovery.

"Three hours."

I blink at him. Surely I heard him wrong. Three hours? Is unicorn horn truly that powerful? But I already know the answer. It seems Rafael is way more powerful a Burner than he let on. How did he manage to heal me so completely? I didn't even have to relieve myself.

That in itself is a wonder considering I haven't gone since before I faked it behind that tree. A sudden vision of the monster and its teeth have my fingers pulling back the sheets. Suddenly I'm desperate to see my skin.

"How bad is the damage?"

"Don't." He reaches out to stop me from pulling down my bandages, but I brush his fingers away and frown at my exposed stomach. Thick scars—pale and wrinkled against my tanned skin—crisscross over my belly and down my thighs. Scars in three hours. No wonder the early Burners hunted unicorns to extinction. Magic this powerful would have been priceless. And not only did Darkthorne have it in his possession, he used it on me.

"Why?" I'm not even sure what I'm asking. Why did he bring me here? Why did he save me? Why did Martin name him?

"I told you—no one is dying tonight. Look, I know you want answers, and I want to give them to you. I want to help you, for us to help each other. You'll just have to trust that I'm not your enemy. Can you do that?" He's staring pointedly at our makeshift roof, and it takes me a moment to realize he's doing so to give me my modesty. That makes me smile. Assuming he's the one who bandaged me, it isn't anything he hasn't seen already.

"It's cold in here," I note aloud.

Rafael picks up a fur I kicked down to my ankles and wraps it around my shoulders. "I have a shirt you can wear for now. And I'll start a fire in a moment. Tomorrow, we'll find you an appropriate change of clothes."

"Tomorrow?" I interrupt. "How long do you plan on keeping me? Am I to remain your prisoner?"

"Well, that depends. Do you still want to kill me?"

"I haven't decided yet."

The corners of his mouth quirk up in a smile. "By all means, take your time. I said tomorrow because it will be dawn in a few hours, and I need some sleep before we finish our trek through the jungle. After that, how about we just take it one day at a time?"

"Where are you taking me?" I reposition the fur he draped around my shoulders. It is incredibly warm, almost stifling, and I'm not cold anymore.

"Okay this is good. I'll answer a question and then you answer a question."

"What, like an interrogation?" I cross my arms over my chest, but the movement pulls at my bandages so I allow them to fall back to my sides.

"No, like a conversation." He snorts. "Tomorrow, I'm taking you into the heart of the jungle."

"I'm hardly in any condition to go on a hunt." While true, if the unicorn horn continues to heal me at this rate, I should be fine by morning. The truth is, I don't want to go on a hunt—not again, not ever.

"No hunt. But I do have a proposition for you."

I stiffen. I knew something was coming. He dragged me into the jungle for a reason after all, but as much as I searched for one, I couldn't think of why he might need me.

"What kind of proposition?"

He takes a seat beside me, carefully readjusting the fur from where I let it fall off my shoulder until my arms and chest are once again fully covered. Okay, so not a sexual proposition then. "First, tell me about your husband."

What? This was the absolute last thing in the world I thought he'd ask about. "Why?"

"He's the catalyst of all this, right? The reason you want me dead?"

"He named you." I wrap that knowledge tightly around me.

"One could argue he sent you to me, knowing I could help. What else is it that you're looking for?"

My head spins at the possibility. If that is true, then I am no closer to Martin's killer and no closer to recovering the dragon's eye.

"And assuming I didn't kill him—and I assure you I did not—then someone else in court did. But why? What reason would someone have to murder him?"

"His dragon eye. It's priceless." My perception of the word has been somewhat altered since encountering someone who possesses a unicorn horn, but the fact remains that no one has seen a dragon in years. No one except Martin and Darkthorne. I study him, and there is nothing but open interest in his expression. If Darkthorne is right and someone else possesses the dragon eye, then I'm running out of time. Assuming the person hasn't already destroyed it by selling off pieces to Burners.

"No one should have known he had it. We were very careful," I say, more so to affirm the words to myself. But Gloriana knew, didn't she? "Martin never admitted to sharing that knowledge with anyone, and we told each other everything."

But that wasn't entirely true either. *Yes, keep lying to yourself, Nyia.* Martin kept many things from me: his dalliances with others, his gambling addiction, and our growing debt. Doña Gloriana bade me to follow in his footsteps and acquire a dragon's heart for her. I had never even heard of her before the other night. And Martin promised her a dragon's heart. So many secrets. It is yet another reason why I have to recover the dragon's eye before anyone else. It's more than just financial freedom and a means of escape for me now; it's the only thing that prevents Gloriana from killing me.

"Stay with me."

His words surprise me, as does the intensity of his stare.

"What?"

"I said stay here and work with me. That's what I'm proposing. You need help finding your missing dragon eye, and I need a Burner. We're perfect for each other."

My head tilts as I study him and his earnest expression. What is he up to? What magic exists that can possibly call for the work of two Burners? It has to be something epic. Perhaps another dragon? *But why me?*

I voice the last question aloud.

"Something tells me you're the only person capable of helping me finish this job. You're perfect. I'll help you find Martin's murderer in ex—"

"And help me recover the stolen dragon eye," I interject. This isn't just revenge for me. I need that eye to escape; it's my only chance at a life of my own. "But I agree to your terms. If you help me, I'll stand in as your second Burner." I thrust my hand toward him so we can seal our agreement.

He hesitates for only a moment before he shakes my hand.

7

Partners for Now

He must have spiked my tea. It's the only explanation for the giddy feeling I have when he encloses my fingers within his. Maybe succubus hair is far more potent than musk. Maybe its effects still linger. That has to be it. Darkthorne . . . Rafael . . . is not to be trusted.

Rafael. I whisper the name to myself, tasting it on my lips. It's difficult to imagine him as Rafael—such a normal name—and I wonder if he will always be Darkthorne to me.

"You're shivering," he says, and I keep my gaze focused on my lap, noting the absence of his fingers against mine as he lumbers to his feet. "I'm going to check on that fire. You should cover up and try to get more sleep. We have a long day of travel tomorrow."

He's left the tent before I can utter a reply, which is just as well because my mind is still reeling with what I just agreed to. In fact, *what* had I just agreed to? Darkthorne said he needed a Burner, nothing more. Why would he need a Burner when he is one?

And really, why had Martin named him? Martin said *Darkthorne*. I asked about locating the dragon eye, and he said Darkthorne. He was clear. If Darkthorne—no, Rafael—isn't to blame, then who killed Martin? My only other suspect is Gloriana, but if she killed Martin and stole the dragon eye, then what did she need me for? Gloriana is desperate for a dragon heart—is that Rafael's goal too? But why would he want my help when he is Darkthorne? Is that why he needs a second Burner? I need answers.

I pull Rafael's shirt over my head, surprising myself by how easy the movement is. Between the healing effects of the unicorn horn and Rafael's tea, I barely notice any discomfort. The shirt falls well past my knees and over my fingertips, and I'm pleased by the amount of coverage it provides. I still wrap a long blanket about my shoulders like a cape and tiptoe out of the tent.

Rafael has somehow managed to ignite a tiny bonfire by the tent clearing, and I move toward it, eager for its warmth.

"Are you hungry?" he asks. He doesn't bother waiting for my answer before moving to Moco and digging through his saddlebag. "It's not much, just travel rations."

I take the offered provision of dried meat and look around the makeshift campsite. We are in a small clearing. Moco and the other horses are posted behind the tent, a simple thing strung up between two trees. The ground is covered in soft moss, and beyond the halo of firelight, the jungle is alive with sound. I shudder at the memory of the monster and hope the fire is enough to keep any danger away.

"Do you want more tea? Are y—"

"Why are you being so nice to me?" The question bursts from my lips.

"Why shouldn't I be nice to you?" He squats by the fire and gestures to a tree stump beside him, indicating I should do the same.

I sit on the stump, gathering the blanket tight around me. There are plenty of reasons for him not to be nice to me. I lied to him, used magic to kidnap him, tied him up, and tortured him. I think of how nice Martin was when we first met and the monster he eventually revealed himself to be. We have no reason to trust each other, Darkthorne and I, but for the moment I am stuck in his company.

"Where did your friends go?" It dawns on me that I haven't seen any sign of either Marix or Cesar. But the horses are still here so they can't have gone far.

Rafael furrows his brow, but he answers the question. "They've journeyed ahead. You were in no condition to travel."

"But how did they continue without horses?" I press, wanting an explanation while trying to work on one myself. I keep forgetting Rafael is not only a Burner but a Burner with more access than me. He works with the king. He probably has burned more mythic parts than I can even imagine. He had unicorn horn, so it stands to reason he has other means of swift travel. Perhaps he has phoenix feathers? But no, that isn't it. Not unless one of his companions is a Burner too. Damn, what did I get myself into?

"Nyia. Don't. Move."

I stiffen, all accumulated warmth leaving me as my blood runs cold. I've let my guard down and forgotten we were past the border in mythic territory. Anything could be out here.

"What is it?" My heart beats rapidly, and I force myself to take a slow breath.

"There's a spider."

"A what?"

"A spider. Don't move. Don't provoke it." He clambers to his feet and stares at the empty space to my right.

I stand up, too, my breath releasing in a rapid whoosh. "Provoke the spider?" I blink. "A normal spider? Not some giant mythic varietal, just a tiny bug?"

"I said don't move!"

"But you can't be scared of a spider. One so tiny I still don't even see it."

"I may only have one eye, but I have impeccable eyesight. There's a spider." He points beside me, but I still see nothing. "And I'm not scared of it—I just respect its distance."

I bite back a snort. "Why don't you head inside and get what sleep you can. I'll take first watch—guard you from spiders."

"There's no reason to keep watch. Once you're warm enough, we will go into the tent and get some rest. I do not need guarding from spiders."

"But what if the fire goes out?" I hate how tiny my voice sounds, but I don't understand how Rafael can be fine without one of us keeping guard.

"What happened to you—the attack—was a mistake. A terrible mistake that never should have happened. I can promise you something like that will never happen again."

I smile despite the unrealistic promise.

"You seem like a good guy," I tell him.

"I am a good guy."

That's what they all say. But for some reason I want to take him at face value. I want to believe he had nothing to do with Martin's murder. That he will help me find the dragon eye. That with his help, I can finally be free.

"This game you're hunting. What is it? Why do you need two Burners?"

"Can we talk about this inside the tent?"

"Because of the spider?" I roll my eyes but follow him inside. I was silly to worry that I would be cold in the tent. Heat seems to roll off Rafael's body, and he is impossibly close as he hunkers down beside me. He spends a moment fussing over the blankets, and once I am sufficiently covered, he settles down to lie beside me.

"Is this okay? I can sleep outside if you prefer, but I've got to stretch my legs out if we're going to talk."

At his words, one of his long legs brushes my toes. Succubus. It must last forever. I clasp my hands over my chest to keep them from grazing his arm. He's too close. But I don't protest or try to wriggle away.

"This game you're hunting," I say again. I'm determined to get some answers from him. As many as I can, though now that I'm once again nestled in my pile of blankets, I can already feel my muscles relaxing, my eyes growing heavy.

"There's no game. We're not hunting anything. But I do need a Burner."

I frown. Not that I wanted to hunt anything. I always left that business to Martin and others, content to use the remaining parts given to me. Processing an entire mythic is messy, difficult business, and I'm relieved my agreement with Rafael doesn't involve hunting. So, we were burning something for a spell then. Something big. Does Rafael have a dragon heart? Is one already floating around on the goblin market and Gloriana got wind of it?

"What are we burning?" My voice drops to a whisper but not because I'm tired. Every nerve in my body is buzzing. Maybe I had it wrong after all. Maybe Darkthorne isn't a murderer but my salvation? "Is it . . ." I pause, drawing a deep breath. "Is it a dragon?"

"If it was, could you do it? Are the rumors of your skill true?"

I turn my head and find him staring at me, though his expression is unreadable. *Rumors? About me?* We thought we had been so careful.

"I've burned from an eye before." He doesn't react so I press on. "And scales. I haven't worked with all the parts yet, but—"

"You'll be fine. You're . . . perfect."

It doesn't sound like a compliment. "This is the deal, right? I burn whatever you need me to, and in exchange you help me get a dragon eye."

"That's the deal."

"Is it . . . Will this be dangerous?" I don't know why I'm asking. I'll do whatever it takes. Gloriana and Martin made sure I don't have a choice.

"Nothing will happen to you." He inhales sharply, maybe stifles a yawn. "There are still a few more details of the plan I need to work out. I promise to explain everything when I can, but I'm asking you to trust me for now. I need time. Things are . . . complicated."

But how much time does he need? He teases answers and then gives half explanations. He might need time, but I'm quickly running out of it. Gloriana expects payment by the new moon. I don't for one second believe myself to be out of Gloriana's reach. She probably has dozens of contacts in mythic territory. For all I know, Rafael is one of them. They could be working together. Do I really trust him?

"Rafael." I'm not sure exactly what I want to ask him, but it doesn't matter because he cuts me off.

"Can we talk about this more tomorrow? I'm tired."

"Yes." I try to keep the stunned accusation out of my voice. "Of course. You must be as tired as I am. Tomorrow, then. Goodnight."

I close my eyes, but it is a while before I finally drift off to sleep.

8

To the Heart of the Jungle

The man beside me stirs, and at his sudden, uneven intake of breath, I know he has awoken. The blankets shift, and I imagine he has turned to stare at me but I don't move, concentrating on mimicking sleep. I feel him stare at me for several long moments and then, so gently I can't be sure I haven't imagined it, he brushes a loose curl back from my face. I keep perfectly still for several moments. Minutes pass until I am sure he has left our makeshift tent, and I allow myself to sit up. I wince ever so slightly from the movement, but I can tell I am nearly completely healed. Unicorn horn is a wonder. Does Darkthorne have more? Not that I can afford it. His possession of the rarity only confirms the fact that he has more secrets than I suspect, and if he isn't willing to share his secrets, he isn't likely to share more exotic mythic parts.

I tilt my head and strain to place what he must be doing now. The jungle is a cacophony of chirrups and hoots, but nothing sounds menacing, and if it wasn't for the fact that its image is seared into the back of my eyelids, I might have doubted the jungle hosted the existence of so horrid a creature as the one I encountered the night before. Darkthorne begins speaking, his words too quiet to be meant for my ears, and it takes a moment before I realize he is talking to his horse.

"That's a good boy."

The praise is followed by an equine snort, and I roll my eyes. I could make a run for it now. It's daylight and I'm healed. Darkthorne is distracted. It's the perfect opportunity. An opportunity I no longer feel the need to explore. I hate to admit it, but Rafael's need for another Burner intrigues me. And assuming he isn't one of Gloriana's minions, I'm certainly safer here with him than I am back home on my own. And most importantly, he promised to help me find the dragon eye. He is the only lead I have. Would I be doing myself any favors if I tried to run now?

I stare at my bare toes, cleaner than they should be considering my sprint through the mud and underbrush. Did he wash my feet?

I leave the tent and catch sight of Rafael wiping snot bubbles off the horse's snout. Well, that's one mystery solved. I smile about to call out a greeting but instead moan in delight when I see the kettle left near the fading fire to keep warm. I squat beside the fire just as Darkthorne hands me a thin metal mug.

"Good morning," he says.

I ignore his greeting and take the mug from him, a brief sweep of his body indicating he looks just as good in his rumpled clothing as he did last night. Damn. Surely the succubus isn't still in my system. Which can only mean one thing: I'm actually attracted to the guy. My thoughts go back to our kiss, the passion that ignited in me like liquid fire. I've blamed the pull of the succubus lust, the rush of the phoenix magic. I have no excuses now. I set my face into a scowl as I pour the steaming liquid into my cup and take a healthy sip.

"This isn't pixie powder."

"No, it's better." He straightens beside me.

I take another sip, appreciating the complex, slightly bitter taste. It certainly isn't near as sweet as the pixie powder I am accustomed to drinking in the morning, but it is still comforting and pleasant. I'm hoping it gives me the same buzz I usually get, but I'm not about to complain. That doesn't mean I have to thank him either, so I stare into the mug in an effort to ignore him.

"We should leave shortly."

"To the heart of the jungle?" I can't keep the sarcasm from my voice. And that was about ten seconds of ignoring him. *Good job, Nyia.*

"We ride to my home. If we make good pace, we can arrive before the sun sets." He waits for a beat, and when I still don't look at him, he grunts and walks away.

I take another careful sip of my mystery brew, the flavor growing on me. Pixie powder sparkles like stars on a midnight ocean, but this liquid is so dark, it resembles melted chocolate. Maybe there is even a hint of chocolate in it?

"As soon as you've finished and made ready, we can leave."

I look at Darkthorne adjusting the saddle and pack around Moco. He's already disassembled our tent, though I have no idea how he managed to do so this quickly.

I take my time with my morning beverage, savoring each sip until the drink is gone, and I can practically feel Rafael's annoyance rolling off him. I raise my arms above my head and straighten to my tiptoes, aware of Rafael's shirt pulling tight against my skin and riding up my thighs as I stretch.

He stares at me for a long moment before he spins around and mounts Moco.

"We'll get you some more clothing when we get back to my house," he says.

I try to restrain the smile from spreading across my lips.

"Can you mount on your own or do you need a leg up? The red mare shouldn't give you any trouble. Patience belongs to Marix."

My smile falters just slightly, and damn it, why should I care that I'm not riding with him and Moco anymore? There is a surplus of extra horses now after Marix and Cesar's departure, and it wouldn't make sense to ride double.

"I can manage on my own." Although for being such a tiny person, Marix has an astonishingly large horse, and I grunt with exertion as I heave myself up and over. True to her name, Patience the mare stands quietly until I gain my seat and loosen my death grip on her reins. "That's a good girl," I mumble to her, stroking the side of her neck.

"She's steady on her feet and quick as they come, but not as fast as Moco. I'd rather not exhaust the horses. Do you think you can behave?"

I glare at him.

"Nyia." He sighs. "I'll stand by the agreement if you will. I need to hear you say it."

"I won't try to run." *For now.*

He stares at me for a moment before he clucks softly to Moco, and the stallion starts forward. Patience and the other horse laden with our supplies fall into step behind them, and I am soon staring at the wide expanse of Rafael's shoulders.

"How far away is it?"

"My home? A few hours' ride." He shrugs, looking from side to side and then back at me. "At this pace? Longer."

I bite my bottom lip to stop a smile and tap at Patience with the inside of my leg so she speeds up. We aren't on a road exactly, but it's obvious the trail has had enough traffic to make the ride comfortable. And yes, it is odd that a random trail beginning in the jungle of mythic territory leads to his home.

"Why do you live out here?" I ask.

"Why do I live at my home?"

"Yes, your home in the heart of the jungle in the middle of mythic territory. Is it . . . ancestral?" Back when the pirate king laid claim to the island, the best lands were parceled out to those in power. Most of the places in mythic territories were abandoned, but some still remained, particularly if the holding was fortified enough. If rumors of Darkthorne's favor with the king are true, then such fortification would be all too easy for a man with his influence.

"You could say that," he answers.

Neither of us are ever going to get anywhere with the other if we refuse to open up, but something in his tone makes me want to let this particular line of questioning stop. Time to switch gears then.

"When did you learn you were a Burner?" I ask him.

"I-I'm n—"

"Not the time you learned what it meant," I interrupt. Learning you were different and then understanding what those differences meant were completely different things. "I mean, when was the first time you realized who—*what*—you are?"

"When did you?" He turns the question neatly around on me, but I don't mind.

"I was thirteen." My voice drops to a reverent whisper as the memory washes over me. Back then the entire world seemed to be within my reach. The island full of possibilities rather than the prison it has become. "I knew about mythics, and of course we had access to some of their charmed products, but I had never seen one alive before. But then there was a festival and there was a mermaid."

I can see the beauty of the creature now, the display of magic she used while making the water take shape and dance. Real magic—not some bottled product made by pixies or some enchanted tool—but actual magic emanated from her in waves. I was mesmerized. I felt every molecule of my body come alive that day. "I made my own water bubble. It shouldn't have been possible, but Father knew it then. Looking back I suppose he met another like me at some time. My fingers must have grazed one of her pearls or something without me realizing." I shake my head, coming back to the present. "Anyway, that was the day I knew I was something *more*. I'd never felt anything like that. It was the happiest day of my life."

"And Martin?"

I stiffen at the sudden mention of my husband. "What about Martin?"

"Well, was meeting him the second greatest day of your life?"

I think back to Martin's proposal. The eager smile he wore while his sweaty hand clutched mine. My mother's tears.

"No," I answer honestly. "It wasn't."

Conversation grows stilted after that and eventually turns to heavy sighs and warnings over dangerous terrain as the jungle grows impossibly thick around us. All evidence of any trail has vanished, and Patience tosses her head and lifts her hooves against the creeping vines. I know Darkthorne intended for us to be at his home before nightfall, but I doubt that will be possible now as there doesn't seem to be any trace of civilization ahead. Maybe I shouldn't have lingered so much over my delicious mud water, yet even now the memory makes me itch for another cup. Or some pixie powder. It's weird that Darkthorne doesn't prefer the morning drink. I thought everyone did. It's especially good with fresh honeyed bread. My stomach growls at the thought, protesting its empty contents, and Darkthorne stiffens, drawing Moco to a halt at the sound.

"Shh. I heard something. Be . . ." He trails off as my stomach growls again, louder. "Was that you?"

"It wasn't the spider behind you."

He whips around so fast, he is nearly unseated from Moco, and I can't help but giggle as his thunderous gaze meets mine.

"That isn't funny."

I smirk. Oh, but it was.

"I need you to focus because this last bit of the trip is hard." He gives me an appraising look. "Aside from starving, how are you feeling?"

"I'm fine," I answer without thinking. I take a quick evaluation of my body. My legs and lower back are sore from riding, but otherwise, I feel okay.

"Good." He dismounts, nodding for me to do the same. He scratches behind Moco's ear and tells him to go home. The obedient horse trots away, Patience and Cesar's horse following.

"Wait! Where are they going?"

"Home. Well, to my stables. Teo will look after them."

I don't bother to ask who Teo is because the more pressing question is why he would send the horses ahead and leave us abandoned in the heart of the jungle.

"But I thought . . ." I look around, the setting sun slowly transforming the jungle greenery into darkness. Does he expect us to travel the rest of the way on foot?

"Can you swim?" His voice is appraising, his eyebrows raised in challenge.

I can, though that hardly seems relevant as there is no visible water.

"I can swim." What is he getting at? And why did he send the horses away?

"Follow me." He walks in the opposite direction of the horses, and I have no choice but to follow. "It's not far," he says over his shoulder. His pace is confident, though he stops often to wave a branch to clear his passage. Probably for spiderwebs. I suppress a smile. "How are you doing back there?" he calls as he slows to a halt. "We're almost there, but we can take a break if you need. How are your feet feeling?"

"I'm fine." Was I wrong about him? His reputation as Darkthorne doesn't seem to match the likable man in front of me. Unless it's all a lie.

After several minutes, we come to another stop. I open my mouth to ask him where we are, but the words die on my lips as I stare in wonder. We are at the base of a mountain, its rugged, rocky face rising sharply and towering above the trees. The base is covered in a lush tapestry of greenery with tiny yellow and purple flowers dotting its vines and a scattering of colorful mushrooms in thick moss. More vines and moss cling to its surface, covering the wall as it reaches into the sky. Between me and the sheer mountain is a trio of boulders, also covered in moss and purple flowers.

"You'll jump there." He indicates the trio of boulders.

I'll jump where? He's gone mad. I take a hesitant step forward and notice the gaping hole between the boulders. A tiny canyon in the carpet of the jungle that fades into a black abyss.

"I'm not jumping in there," I say, crossing my arms over my chest for good measure.

"Would you prefer to climb to the top? Because that's the only other way." He grins. "Unless you'd rather dine in the stables with the horses."

My stomach growls again in protest. I stare at the gaping hole and then at the sheer mountain climbing to dizzying heights. There is no way I am scaling that. Rafael must see the indecision on my face.

"It's a bit of a drop, but the water is plenty deep. It's safe, I promise."

I nod and take another tiny step toward the boulders. This is a bad idea. I know this is a bad idea, so why am I about to do this extremely bad idea? This man has yet to earn my trust, and now I'm about to jump into a dark pit for him? Does he truly live at the top of this mountain? That would explain how he kept his holdings safe from mythic attacks. Assuming this creepy hole actually does lead to his home and not a torture dungeon. I am an idiot for even considering this.

"Hey." He places his hand at my elbow and gives it a slight squeeze. "You've got this. I promise I won't let anything bad happen to you." His voice is husky by my ear but he releases his hold before I can lean into his touch. *Focus, Nyia.*

I take another step, then another until I am standing on the edge. Such an idiot. I take a deep breath.

"Swim to the surface and follow the lanterns to the end of the tunnel. Someone will be waiting for you there."

"Wait, you're not coming with me?" I turn to face him and catch a wicked gleam in his eye just before he shoves me forward.

"I'll see you soon!" he calls after me—or at least that's what I think he says—but I can barely hear him over the sound of my screams as I fall into the darkness.

9

DARKTHORNE'S DOMAIN

The water is piercing cold, and I struggle to remain calm as I plunge into its icy depths. I kick furiously, gasping for air when I break the surface.

What the hell just happened? I am going to murder him. I reach the edge of the pool and sling my arm over a rocky edge to haul myself up. I lie on my back and do nothing but focus on drawing long, steady breaths for several moments.

It takes another minute or so for my eyes to adjust to the dim lighting. The only light source comes from the opposite side of the cenote where lanterns are suspended from the cave ceiling. I sigh and make my way toward the light. I have to get back into the water, but this time I am ready for the freezing temperature, and by the time I swim across, my muscles have warmed up.

The brief respite is short-lived as I enter the smooth limestone tunnel. The shredded remains of my clothing stick to my clammy skin, and I am suddenly unbearably cold. I pull a torch from its sconce, but it does little to warm me. At least I can take the light with me. I walk toward the distant light of the next lantern and note the slight incline. So far, everything he said about this experience is true. Which means someone will be waiting for me at the end of the tunnel. Will it be Darkthorne? I can't see how he could scale the mountain faster than this, even if it is a more direct route. I hadn't noticed any ropes or anything that would assist his ascension.

There must be another way up the mountain, but I didn't see one. Perhaps he has a griffon feather, and this was just his way of unsettling me.

Greedy Burner, couldn't even share. Although my experience with burning for two was a first for me. I've never traveled with anyone before, though I practiced once with a straw doll, and that had mostly worked. The fire was easy to put out at least. Assuming he did have a feather or some other means of travel, maybe he wasn't as confident with his burning skills and didn't want to risk hurting one of us.

He asked for my help after all—had practically begged for it. Perhaps he's not as successful a Burner as the king believes. Perhaps I am even better than him. A smile tugs at my lips at the thought. My anonymity is the only thing saving me from the king's reach. But it is also what made Martin so successful.

What if the king knew about me? Would I become the royal Burner then?

I don't want that. Even if working for the king comes with the sort of perks Darkthorne enjoys, it isn't worth it. I won't pay with my freedom.

The tunnel narrows and grows warmer as I ascend to the top, and soon I am sweating, steam curling from my body when I arrive at the final lantern.

I'm at a dead end. I blink at the smooth surface of the rock. No seams. No door. No one waiting for me. No way out.

"Hello?" I call out as loudly as I can. "Can anyone hear me?" I pound at the rock wall with my fists, panic creeping in. Even if I went back to the pool, I could never scale my way back to the surface. This is the only way out. I let out a stream of curses, calling Darkthorne every vile name I can think of. Sure, I maybe started things with my attempted kidnapping at the masquerade ball, but since then, he has put me through a lot. Now I'm stuck in his cave, in his too-big shirt that is still soaking wet, dirty, and hungry and so angry it feels like my blood is boiling. Why did I try to trust him?

I pound on the wall and scream for help until my throat is raw before finally sinking to the floor in defeat. Maybe I deserve this. I was happy my husband died. I tried to kidnap a man under the guise of vengeance when really it was for my own selfish motives. I was just trying to survive. Trying to get out from under Gloriana's thumb and leave this island and all its mythics behind. At least she won't be able to find me down here. No one can.

"Human." The familiar voice is a lilting whisper that seems to echo all around me. A soft light appears beside me, glowing brightly when it senses my recognition.

"What are you doing here?" I ask the tiny will-o-wisp. Did it follow me down here? Has it been following me this entire time?

"Are you lost?" the wisp asks me. It hovers in front of my face, growing to nearly triple its size and affording me another rare glimpse at the details of its tiny form before shrinking back down to a pinprick of light.

"I can't get out," I say, nodding toward the rock wall.

There is the sound of ringing bells as the wisp laughs. "Follow me. I will help you find your way." The light grows brighter until it is as blinding as the sun, and the ground rumbles beneath me. I rub at my eyes and lift my head as the last of the light fades.

"We will meet again, human," the wisp promises, its voice both nowhere and everywhere all at once.

I am alone in the tunnel, but the rock wall magically swings open, revealing a grand hallway beyond.

"I'm out," I mutter as I practically leap over the threshold before I find myself once again locked in the cave.

The thick carpet in the hallway is lush beneath my feet. The walls are covered in embroidered tapestries, floor-to-ceiling illustrations of battles and scenery and many depictions of mythics. There are griffons, harpies, fairies, and unicorns. And more than anything else—dragons.

Well, Darkthorne is the most notorious dragon hunter of all time. It only makes sense for his obsession to carry over into his home. I am examining a gaudy statue of a dragon made entirely of solid gold at the end of the hall when one of Rafael's companions nearly stumbles into me.

She stops short and raises her eyes to mine in a stunned expression, and all I can do is stare back. She is stunning. She is short, her head barely reaching my shoulders, and has a thick mane of purple and silver hair. Her dark skin glows with a subtle sheen against the silver in her hair, and the intricate patterns etched across her face and arms are difficult to look away from. Silver patches dance across her cheeks, a cosmos of glowing freckles. The same silvered skin, almost pale lavender in places, swirls in colored contrast against the dark canvas of the rest of her skin. The effect is startling yet harmonious, and she is easily one of the most beautiful women I've ever seen.

"How did you get out?" She looks behind me to the end of the hall where the stone wall remains open to the tunnel and cenote beyond. "Not that you shouldn't be out," she hurries to explain as my eyes darken at the implication. "I was just coming to get you."

I realize I'm still staring and meet her dark-gray eyes that now twinkle above her freckles. Rafael likes freckles. I wonder if there is anything going on between them.

"I'm sorry you had to . . . somehow find a way out for yourself." She once again frowns at the tunnel behind me. "Anyway, I'm sorry. I'm Marix, remember? We met last night. I'm Rafael's right-hand man."

"He pushed me into that pit. Where is he?"

"Raf? He's, uhh, just cleaning up before dinner. I'm sure you'd like to do the same."

"How did you get up here?" I frown at her. "Did you go through the tunnel, or did you scale the mountain?" I don't give her a chance to answer before throwing my final question at her. "Or did you fly?" It's the only explanation. They are all Burners. Darkthorne's minions, eager to assist him with all of King Ernesto's burning needs.

Marix doesn't answer, but from the way her eyes widen just slightly, I can tell I've hit my mark.

"I want to see him."

"Would you rather go to your room first? We can get you into a bath and some fresh clothing?"

Both of those ideas are enough to nearly make me moan with pleasure, but I stand my ground. "I'd rather speak to him first."

For a moment it seems neither of us are going to give any ground but then Marix sighs, shoulders sagging in defeat. "Okay then, follow me."

We turn down another hallway and up a flight of stairs before traversing a final grand hall that comes to a stop before a behemoth set of doors that are so high, I have to crane my neck to see the top. From what I've seen so far, the king has more than compensated Darkthorne for his services. His house is best described as a castle, and the ceilings are the highest I've ever seen. All this on top of a mountain?

"Wait here," Marix warns as she pushes open the massive double doors.

Like hell I will. I push past her and into his room.

"Where are you, asshole?" I call into the open room. "Thanks, Marix. I've got it from here."

She narrows her eyes at me. "I'm not leaving you alone with him. I don't trust you."

"Good. The feeling is mutual." A large bed dominates one side. The decorations are sparse, but the dark, polished woods and burnished gold accents give the room a bit of life. There's no mistaking the bed is meant to be the star of the room. It is the largest I've ever seen, large enough to easily hold a family of ten.

"Where are you?" I call again, tearing my eyes from the bed.

Rafael emerges from behind a tinted screen in the opposite corner of his room. A towel is wrapped low around his waist, leaving all the muscles of his abdomen on full display. Tiny droplets of water still dance along his chest as they drip down toward his navel. His dark hair curls around his shoulders, and aside from his eye patch and that tiny towel, he is naked.

"Nyia." He smiles at me.

"You pushed me into a pit and trapped me in a cave." I glare at him. "Whatever sick game you're playing, I'm done. Tell me what you want from me and let me go."

His smile falters. "You're not a prisoner here."

"It certainly seems that way. You left me underground."

"It was the only way for you to get inside the house."

I hold up a hand to silence further protest. "Clearly it isn't. Or am I to believe you scaled an entire mountain and had spare time to take a bath? Just save it. I know you flew up here. What did you use?

Griffon feather? Phoenix? Whatever, it doesn't matter. Tomorrow, you're taking me back home."

I try to ignore how sexy he looks when he clenches his jaw. And I definitely don't look at the sharp vee his muscles make just above the towel draped at his hips.

"You said you would give me a chance to explain," he says softly. He looks beyond me to Marix, who quietly nods before leaving the room.

"What is there to explain?" I ask. "You're the king's Burner. I'm sure you believe you have a valid excuse for all your actions. But you don't understand how—"

"I do understand. I promise you, I do. And I know it's hard to trust someone when they're keeping things from you, but I promise you I have a good reason. And I'm sorry I pushed you into the cenote. I should have let you jump in on your own."

I only provide a terse nod, refusing to give him anything.

He eyes me warily. "Do you think you can still trust me enough to hold to our bargain?"

I haven't responded to him, lost in my thoughts, so I can only blink in confusion as he crosses the length of the room between us and opens a chest at the foot of his bed. He pulls out a large leather pouch, scooping fistfuls of golden coins into it until it is near to bursting. I've never seen so much gold in my life. Probably no one has, save the king and royal family. I gawk at his outstretched hand.

"If I offered you this? All this, and a phoenix feather to take you anywhere you want, would you take it? Or would you rather stay and work with me and find your dragon eye?"

I consider this. There is more than enough gold to secure passage off the island, and once I was gone, I could disappear into the vast lands beyond. Gloriana would never find me. I could have everything I ever wanted. But could I actually leave the island without her knowing?

If she was Martin's handler, then Gloriana likely has her hand in everything that happens on this island. Most likely she would know the second I planned my escape and have me back in her clutches the moment I dared to book passage on a ship. Even if I somehow made it onto the ship I wouldn't be able to hide from Gloriana for long. Some of the ships circled the island for years before they found themselves near the gate to the veil at the correct time. A sudden, more pressing question comes over me. If Rafael has all this wealth at his fingertips, what stops him from leaving the island? From making himself even richer by leaning into the king's commands? What does Rafael want?

"Why isn't it enough for you?" I ask instead. "Why don't you leave?"

"This island is my home. I remember when it . . ." He trails off, shakes his head, and moves to sit on the edge of his bed. "You're right. There are things I'm keeping from you. Things I've witnessed from my time with the king, dangerous things involving mythics."

I draw a sharp breath at this new information, but I shouldn't be surprised.

"You have your own desires for acquiring the eye of a dragon and the king has his, but isn't it a damning coincidence that suddenly the most powerful people on this island want the same thing?"

I shake off the compliment even though a part of me squeals at Darkthorne calling me powerful. "You think we want the dragon eye for the same reason."

"Exactly."

My stomach lurches with what I'm about to do, but this is the most forthcoming Rafael has been with me and it's time.

"I do want the dragon eye," I confess. "More than anything. I have to find it, or I'm going to die."

10

An Invitation to Dinner

Rafael reels back as if I've slapped him. "No, that's . . . I don't understand. Dragon parts don't have healing magic. They—"

"I don't need to be healed. I'm not sick. And Martin wasn't either. Someone killed him for the eye. And I'm starting to wonder if it's not the same person who asked me to get it. The same person who threatened my life if I don't deliver." I don't mention the dragon heart, not yet. One dragon part at a time.

"Who?" Rafael is back at my side in an instant, his fingers feather-light on my arm. "Who is threatening you?"

"Her name is Gloriana. She's a parts dealer, I think. Martin was one of her contacts and she . . . she knows what I am. She told me I was her Burner now, and she told me—" I slap my hand over my mouth and bury my face in my hands.

"Told you what?"

"She told me she will kill me if I don't find the eye."

"Nyia, I'll die myself before I let that happen."

I don't know why I believe him, but I do. He's so close to me; if I stretched out my hand, my finger would rest against the rippled muscles of his abdomen. I swallow as my gaze drifts down to the towel still draped around his waist. There is a growing heat between us, and a familiar humming vibration tingles my skin. Magic. Is he burning something?

"Nyia." My name is a murmured caress.

"Hmm?" I drag my eyes back up to meet his stare.

"I don't know if you're still as hungry as I am, but dinner is waiting for us downstairs. Take the Gold Room—it's the door just to the right. Marix will have left some clothes for you there." His stare slides down the length of my body, and his lips curve into a smirk. "Although if you're going to continue looking at me like that, I have to assume you'd rather stay here in my room."

Fuck me, how I hate his beautiful mouth.

A part of me does very much want that. A stupid, idiotic part of me that must be suppressed. I must be attention-starved and desperate for anything. I have to be if I am seriously considering Darkthorne's offer. I don't bother to respond with words. My body says enough when I abruptly leave the room, the door snapping firmly shut between us.

The Gold Room is aptly named as it's swathed in floor-to-ceiling gold. It's not gaudy, exactly, but it is a bit much. Who has a golden toilet? This guy, apparently.

There is a small pile of clothing folded neatly on the gold brocade comforter. I pick up the first item, frowning at the simple yet impeccably made gown. In a house this nice, we are probably expected to dress for dinner. I hold the dress up against my frame and realize it must have belonged to Marix because while the proportions are there, the dress is several inches too short. The next dress is even more beautiful than the first, but it must belong to someone with a chest at least three times the size of mine. No thanks. The next option is better. Soft leather pants that are almost a perfect fit, if a little too tight on my ass. That doesn't matter, though, because the loose tunic I pull on next falls almost to my knees. I roll up the sleeves and tuck the shirt into my pants.

Last my eyes fall on a pair of boots. They are slightly snug, but they will do. The possession of the shoes alone already makes me feel better. At least if I have to run again, I won't have to do so on bare feet. I frown at the expensive carpet and boots, which, while well-made and cared for, were worn recently and still have mud caked on the bottom. I should probably keep them off for now.

I fold the clothing and place the small pile on the chest, leaving the boots beside them. If I put them on, I can leave now. I can't help the thought that I *should* leave now. I definitely don't want to involve myself in the king's business. I already have my hands full with Gloriana. But I've gone this far. Doesn't it just make sense to continue working with Darkthorne? At least for now? There is another insistent rumble from my belly, and I'm reminded of just how hungry I am.

First, dinner. Then I can figure out the rest. I leave my room and peer down the empty hallway. Rafael has left his door open, and a quick peek confirms he has already gone downstairs for dinner. It doesn't even occur to me to scorn his hospitality of a shared meal. I'm too hungry to care. I follow the faint noises of utensils scraping and glasses clinking until I find the dining room. It is a long, formal hall with sliding panel doors, tall, though not as large as the ones leading into Rafael's room. These doors are slid open in welcome, and I try to ignore the fact that conversation halts when everyone notices me.

Despite the grand scope of the hall, a small table sits at its center. The dining hall is clearly designed to host a table large enough to seat fifty, yet Rafael and his friends are neatly tucked around a table for six.

"Nyia! Come, sit, have a drink." Marix waves me over. I take the empty seat between her and Rafael. Cesar's long silver hair falls like a river of moonlight down his back and draws attention to his tight muscles and sculpted features. He sits directly across from me, frowning when our eyes meet. How can someone so lovely wear such a permanent scowl?

Beside Cesar is a short teen with spiky brown hair, his hawklike features wearing an easy smile. A dagger twirls between the fingers of his left hand in an absentminded dance, and he raises a pierced eyebrow in greeting.

"Here." Marix hands me a golden goblet filled with spiced wine. I sniff the liquid and take a hesitant sip. It's delicious, with none of the usual burn expected from alcohol, which only makes me more suspicious.

I place the goblet down and push it to the side, wondering if I should be worried about poison. The table is laden with food, various dishes piled high with offerings. There are platters of steamed fish, wild rice and mushrooms, various legumes, and fresh greens. Alongside the platters are boards of smoked meat and exotic cheeses, mixed tree nuts, and fried bananas.

The only unfortunate addition to the table is a smoked pig that has been so overcooked its charred remains are scarcely recognizable. I scoop some rice, fish, and fresh fruit onto my plate, nearly groaning in pleasure at the first bite. I haven't had a proper meal since Martin died—I just haven't had an appetite—but I eat with gusto now.

"Have some more." Marix refills my empty goblet from a pitcher at the center of the table. I regard the drink with renewed suspicion. But everyone else is drinking from the same pitcher, so I probably shouldn't let my paranoia get to me.

I look over at Raf, who is slouched in his chair, exhaustion etched across his features. He picks at the charred pig on his plate, nodding at something the youth with the dagger says. Their conversation is spoken in hushed whispers, not meant for the rest of the table. I look across the table at Cesar, but he stabs at the salad on his plate and keeps his eyes downcast.

When I once again meet Marix's eyes, she smiles. "So, I heard you two met at the king's ball? Was it romantic?"

I choke on my rice and swallow some more spiced wine to clear my throat. Marix presses on like she hasn't noticed.

"Raf looks good in a suit, but I'm worried about his dancing." She jerks her shoulders in an awkward motion.

"Hey, Raf, she's doing your moves." The youth points at Marix with his dagger.

Rafael scowls in our direction. "I do not dance like that."

"Keep telling yourself that." The youth shoots him a cocky grin before his dark eyes pin mine. "So, you're the Burner. I'll want my boots back."

"Teo, be nice," Marix admonishes.

"They're my second-best pair!" he shoots back indignantly. "And I don't know why we need some lousy Burner anyway. We still—"

"That's enough." Rafael's voice cracks like distant thunder on a starry night. The youth—Teo—falls back against his seat, once again spinning the dagger between his fingers.

"Nyia is a guest in this home. You will all treat her as such." Rafael looks at everyone seated around the table before nodding at me as though the matter is closed.

I swallow the last of my guava, my appetite gone. What was he going to say before Rafael cut him off? I thought they were all Burners—aren't they? Why would they show such animosity toward our powers? Rafael stressed I wasn't a prisoner, but he brought me here against my will and seemed desperate for me to stay. I still can't trust him. I shouldn't trust any of them.

My eyes touch the unused dinner knife beside my plate. It makes for a pitiful weapon, but it is better than nothing. I look around. Rafael and Teo are once again in whispered conversation, and Marix leans across the table in an attempt to poke a smile out of Cesar. *Good luck with that.* I slip the knife up my sleeve and breathe a sigh of relief once I feel the cool steel against my warm flesh. I feel better already. If only I could find something to burn.

My eyes dart across the room, but I don't notice any mythic parts on the shelves. But just because I keep my parts in the open doesn't mean these Burners will. In fact, it's more likely any mythic parts are safe in their pockets. Just to be certain, I take another careful look at everyone. No one here is hiding anything so large as a dragon eye, that's for certain. There is nothing here. Nothing but food on the table except—what is *that*? Just in front of Teo, one would think it might be a loose strand of his spiky hair, but it is too thick for that... It looks suspiciously like a chupacabra quill.

My fingers itch to stretch across the table and grab it. Would anyone notice? I can always play it off like I was reaching for the fruit bowl. I slide my chair closer to the table and reposition the knife under my sleeve before extending my hand.

"I told you, you're not a prisoner here," Rafael says, catching my wrist. He pushes back my sleeve and removes the knife pressed against my skin.

My eyes widen. Grab the quill—do it now! My brain screams at me to lunge into action, but my body remains frozen and helpless as I wait for Rafael's next move.

He moves impossibly fast, his hand darting out to pluck the spinning dagger from between Teo's nimble fingers. He hands the dagger to me, the jeweled hilt pressing into my limp hand.

"Go on, take it. You're not a prisoner here. And I'll give you any weapon you need to feel safe."

11

QUILL & DAGGER

My fingers wrap around the dagger, and I bring it toward me, wondering if my expression is as wild as my emotions. Instead of getting angry that I stole his dinner knife, he's giving me a dagger.

"Can he do that? You all saw that, right?" Teo waves his arms at everyone. "First, she gets my boots, and now he gives her my dagger. Yeah, super fun new addition to the group."

"Teo, she just wants to feel safe." Marix smiles at me, her eyes warm with sympathy.

"And I want that quill." The words are bubbling out before I can stop them. "I don't know where you found a chupacabra quill, but you said I could have any weapon I wanted."

Rafael's eye widens.

"No way. You can burn this?" Teo snatches up the quill in question and holds it up, drawing it close to his face. He frowns at it but looks at me and raises his eyebrows.

Am I to believe he can't? Why else would he have it in his possession? And why is he so surprised I can burn the quill? Theoretically, a Burner can burn the magic from anything. Why would he question me unless . . . Amateurs. They're all amateurs. No wonder Rafael needs me. They're all still learning how to harness their power. I know firsthand just how difficult it is to teach yourself the skill of burning. There are no schools or academies. There are few even willing to acknowledge the presence of such powers among humans. Is this the reason behind their hostility? Are Cesar and Teo jealous?

I suddenly realize everyone is staring at me, waiting for my answer. I wonder what details Rafael has disclosed to them. Do they suspect I'm a fraud?

"I can," I say, if only to break the awkward silence.

"Do it," Teo says. "Burn it now."

I reach for it, but Teo leans back until it is just out of reach.

"No, demonstration first and then we'll see about letting you keep it."

I almost roll my eyes. They're worse off than I thought.

"I can't."

"Can't what?" Teo narrows his eyes.

"I can't burn it if you don't give it to me." He only stares back at me in response and I sigh. "Really, I can't. Possession plays a big part in the magic. If I don't have possession of the mythic part, I can't burn it. And if I haven't burned from it before, I can't even register its magic. But this isn't the first time I've seen a chupacabra quill." I don't tell them Martin once brought home nearly half a dozen of the quills as well as the bloodied nub of one of the creature's fingers.

I expect Teo to have some follow-up questions, but instead his expression slowly fades from curiosity to disgust.

"Here." He doesn't hand it to me though. He simply allows it to slip between his fingertips to the table. "I don't think I want a demonstration anyway." He slumps back into his seat, poking at something red smeared all over his plate.

I take the quill, pleased by its immediate hum of magic, and place it beside my new dagger. Rafael watches me but doesn't say anything.

"Yes, let's all have some more wine." Marix hands me my refilled goblet. She opens her mouth like she is about to ask a question but then she shakes her head and gives me a brilliant smile. "Tell me what you wore to the ball."

The wine continues to flow and conversations with it, the group allowing me to be a silent observer. Topics are light, mostly weather, jokes, and childhood tales exchanged in what I gather is an effort to keep things simple. Safe.

We laugh. Drink. I feel deliciously warm. Tipsy. I welcome the feeling. We drink some more.

Cesar moves to sit beside Rafael and the two fall into a private conversation with fervent whispers. Marix begs Teo to play a tune from a six-stringed instrument he seemed to produce out of thin air.

I stifle a yawn and rise from the table before thanking Marix and Rafael for the meal. The room spins slightly, and I grab the back of my seat until the room blinks back into focus. Neither of them seems to pay any attention, so I pocket my newly acquired quill and dagger and head back upstairs.

I'm exhausted. And drunk. Why did I allow Marix to drown me in that spiced wine? As soon as I lie down, I'm going to fall asleep. I should go straight to my room and do just that. Only I don't. I haven't been able to stop thinking about the chest filled with gold in Rafael's room. Technically it isn't stealing because Rafael offered me the gold. Sort of. Mostly, he did. And he said I can have whatever I want to feel safe. A phoenix feather and a bag of gold will make me feel safe.

I enter his room and go to the chest at the foot of his massive bed. The lid is heavier than I imagined, and I grunt with the effort of lifting it. I can't help but gasp as the treasure within is revealed. By the forgotten gods, why does he have so much?

Part of me wants to begin shoveling as much as I can into my pockets, but instead I snatch up the pouch Rafael offered to me earlier. I'm startled by its weight and have to fight back a manic smile. I have gold. I have something to burn. And Gloriana has no idea where I've gone. I'm safe.

This time I do nothing to stifle the yawn erupting from me. I need to find my room and crawl into bed and sleep for half a century. Rafael's massive bed stretches out in front of me. The cushions and thick blankets look so inviting, and my feet move forward entirely on their own until I'm close enough to stroke the soft bedding. It's softer than I imagined it would be.

I can climb into this bed and sleep until he arrives. Then I can tell him I'm leaving. I wonder what that wine was that Marix kept giving me. It was so good. Does Rafael have any more in his room? I eye the nightstand, but it holds a carafe of water, not wine. When was the last time I drank water? I stumble toward it. Is there a carafe of water in my room too? Where is my room? I look back down at Rafael's bed and groan. Too much wine. I want to climb into these sheets and wait for the obnoxious man. *No, Nyia, you do not need to loiter in Darkthorne's room.* You need to leave immediately, find your own room, and go to sleep. I nod to myself, decision made. Find bed, then sleep.

I spin on my heel, intending to do just that, and slam into Rafael as he enters the doorway. I grab his arms for support, knocking the glass from his hand as I do so. It shatters at our feet.

"Oh! I'm sorry." I squat down with the intention of picking up the broken glass but am suddenly swept into the air as Rafael scoops me into his arms and cradles me against his chest.

"What are you doing?" I squeal.

"You're barefoot. Again." He glares at my feet, and I wriggle the offending toes in question.

"The boots were muddy."

"You'll get glass in your feet." He carries me to the bed and tosses me onto it. "I told you I would have the guest room made up for you." He scowls as he kneels and picks up the bits of broken glass. "You seem intent on injuring yourself while under my care."

He can call for a servant. But he doesn't. He leaves the room, returns with a damp towel, and wipes at the floor, collecting any lingering glass bits.

Under his care. I harrumph. More like under his imprisonment.

"There," he says, more to himself than to me as he gives the floor one last careful study. He turns back toward me, a pained expression on his face. "That was the last of that vintage." He gives one last sorrowful look to the dark stain on his floor and then meets my eyes. "I'm sorry. You must be exhausted. I'll take you to your room now."

I must still be tipsy because instead of rising to follow him, I lean back, stretching against his pillows.

"I thought you said I was welcome to share yours." I've never been so bold in my life, but something about being here with him, something about *him*, strips away my inhibitions.

His stare turns smoldering, and in seconds, he crosses the room and stands beside the bed. He places a hand on either shoulder and wrenches me up on my knees so we are chest to chest.

My breath catches in my throat. He really is terrifying. And sexy. I take several deep breaths to still my racing heart, but his hands slide up from my shoulders and around my neck to cup my chin.

Slowly, so damn slowly, he lifts my chin until my eyes meet his.

"Don't start something you don't want to finish, my little temptress." His single eye searches my face. His expression is hard to read, but there is no mistaking the growing bulge between us.

"Who said anything about not finishing?" The words come out seconds before his mouth claims mine.

If I thought our first kiss was electrifying, then this kiss is something else entirely. *His tongue, fuck me, his tongue!* His mouth is coaxing and sucks at my bottom lip, at my tongue, my name a soft growl in his throat. His arms encircle me, pulling me closer, and I wrap my arms around his neck, tilting my head to give him better access.

I need to be closer still, so I wrap my legs around his waist and cling to him as tightly as I can. He leans forward, and we allow gravity to take over, falling back onto the bed with him on top of me.

Yes, this! The pressure of him on top of me is glorious but still, I need more. The kiss deepens, and I can't help but moan, grinding my hips against him in an effort to find release.

Rafael tears his lips from me, leaving mine bruised and lonely. He kisses my neck, teeth skimming over the delicate skin. He dips his tongue into the hollow of my neck, and I whimper as he begins to suck.

He pulls away before he can stain the skin, and his fingers lightly trace the line of my jaw, fumbling for the buttons of my borrowed shirt. I rip the offending garment off, tearing it over my head so I can pull his lips back to my throat.

"There's only one part of you I wish to mark as mine." His eye lowers, and I feel the heat of his gaze all the way to my core. His head dips to my breast, and I moan as his tongue lightly skims over my nipple. It buds against his touch. He tugs it lightly between his teeth, and I am on fire. Invisible sparks dance on my skin as the heat between us grows. Once again, I'm struck with the familiar buzzing of magic in the air, and I wonder absently if Rafael is somehow burning succubus musk—but no, these feelings are entirely my own.

"This is your last chance. You can leave now, but if you choose to stay in this bed, you are mine." Rafael's deep voice vibrates over me as his mouth dances along my exposed skin. "And I intend to taste every part of you, starting with that delicious little pussy of yours."

In response, my fingers move to the waistband of my pants. He grunts with approval, once again dipping his head toward mine for a lingering kiss.

The kiss distracts me from removing my pants, but I don't care. I could kiss him forever. I thread my fingers through his hair, pulling him closer, when there is a sudden clearing of someone's throat.

The not-so-subtle cough gets louder as it's ignored. Someone is trying to get our attention from the doorway. We hadn't even bothered to close the door, and yet I can't find it in myself to feel embarrassed.

"Go away," Rafael growls.

"Raf, it's important." Cesar's voice is sharp and annoyed.

He tears himself away from me, and I blink at the doorway where not just one, but three people stand. Marix gives me an apologetic wave as she meets my gaze.

"What's happened?" Rafael asks Cesar, but the color has already drained from his face as though he knows the answer.

Teo shakes his head as he hands Rafael a tattered envelope.

"It's Renee. She's dead," Cesar says, and there is so much hatred in his voice, I can barely understand the words. Can barely register the accusation before it's thrust at me along with an angry finger in my direction. "They're dead, and it's all her fault."

Sheesh, what did I ever do to this guy? Obviously, I didn't have anything to do with this Renee's death—I didn't even know her. But if I was somehow involved, if Martin's murder is linked . . . What is going on?

"Who is Renee?" I can't help but ask aloud. I don't bother dignifying the accusation of her death having anything to do with me.

"Stay here." Rafael ignores my question. "I'll be back as soon as I can. Marix?"

"I've got her." Marix comes to stand beside Rafael.

"But wait. Where are you going? And who is Renee?" I turn to Marix. "And no offense, but I've got myself."

She grins and hands me my discarded shirt in response. I pull the shirt over my head and stumble after Rafael.

"I know you need answers." He plants a kiss on my forehead. "Stay here. Marix will keep you safe. I'll explain everything when I get back."

He turns and leaves, his dismissal of me infuriating. How dare he. He was almost inside of me, and he thinks he can kiss me on the head like I'm a child and leave without further explanation? Like hell! I start to head after them, but Marix stops me by grabbing my arm and pulling me back toward her.

"Let me go!" I jerk my arm out of her grip, but it isn't easy. How is she so strong?

She throws both of her hands upward, palms out as if to ward off an attack. "Hey, don't take it out on me. I'm just following orders."

"Stupid orders."

"Raf means well." She snorts. "But you're right. He doesn't always make the smartest decisions. Bringing you here, for instance."

"Another dumb decision?" I suppose that is something we have in common then. Making dumb decisions.

"No dumber than stealing from the person trying to help you." She hands me the small bag of riches from where it fell at my feet.

"He said I can have that." I cross my arms over my chest, suddenly self-aware. I was topless just moments before. My hair is still a disheveled mess, my lips bruised. Why did I allow myself to behave that way? Wantonly throwing myself at him like some spellbound fool.

"He thinks you're the only way."

"The only way for what? Why does he need another Burner?"

Marix shakes her head. "It's not my place to say, and he'll never forgive me for speaking out of turn. He's stubborn. There's no changing his mind once it's made. In any case, I can show you to your room now. That is, if you still want one of your own?"

I ignore the smirk and nod, shoving past her into the great hall.

"And there's no need to be rude with me," she continues, gesturing for me to follow. "I had hoped we could be friends. It's nice to have another woman in the house. I always feel outnumbered with Renee gone for such long stretches. She—she . . ." Marix trails off, words faltering as a wave of grief hits her, tears beginning to flow in earnest.

"I'm sorry." I pull her against me, and her arms are fierce around me as we hug. Once again, I marvel at her strength. She's incredibly strong for one so tiny.

"I'm sorry," I say again, but I don't think she can hear me over the sound of her own sobs. "Renee—it's obvious you were all close . . . Tell me about her."

Marix sniffs, dragging a hand across her cheeks. "Renee was a bitch." At her words, her hand flutters up to cover her mouth as if she surprised herself with the admission.

She blinks at me for a few stunned seconds and then we both burst into laughter.

"Even now, she makes me laugh." Marix wipes at her eyes. "That's the thing about her—she could always make me laugh. She's a talker too. She can—could . . ." She trails off, clearing her throat.

"The Gold Room is just next door." Marix wipes away the last of her tears and forces a smile, and I can tell she's done discussing Renee for now. "Yes, it's nice and *close*, so Raf can keep an eye on you."

I ignore the bait and nod, falling into step behind her.

"The hall is larger than I would have guessed," I say. "Darkthorne must do a considerable amount more for the king than any let on."

"What are you trying to ask?" Marix stops in front of the large oak door with a delicate knob in burnished gold. She opens the door with a flourish, gesturing for me to enter.

"Just that I had no idea the king could be so rewarding."

"The king has rewarded Raf with nothing but pain."

"And yet he still works for him." The words snap out before I have time to think them over or process what she's said.

"Do you know why they call him Darkthorne? That's not his surname. He's gained that reputation by being a literal thorn in the king's side. He does whatever he wants, whenever he wants, and the royal family would have killed him a decade ago if it weren't for the fact that he alone supplies this kingdom with more dragon parts than anyone else combined. Besides, you're one to talk. You're a *Burner*. Why did you kidnap Rafael, anyway?" Marix crosses her arms over her chest, studying me between narrow eyes.

"I—he has something of mine. I need it back."

Marix advances toward me and I stumble back, having no choice but to enter the room.

"Raf is a lot of things, but he's not a thief. If anything, *you're* the thief."

Why am I starting to believe that? "I know that!" Don't I? She stares at me intently so I drop my eyes back down to study the intricate golden brocade of the bedside rug. "I know that *now*. But at the time, I was convinced he'd stolen something of mine."

"What did you think he stole?" Marix crosses the length of the room and hops on the bed like it's her own. She pats the space beside her, but I hesitate, sensing a trap.

"A dragon eye. We—my husband, that is—had a dragon eye, and he convinced me Darkthorne stole it."

Marix's mouth drops open. "You're married?"

"Was. He's . . . he's just died. I'm a widow." It feels strange to say the words aloud. "I thought Rafael was responsible for my husband's missing dragon eye, and I need it back." Desperately, if I'm ever going to find a dragon's heart for Gloriana.

In response, Marix does the strangest thing. She laughs. It starts as a giggle, but soon she is lying on the bed, clutching her stomach as she howls with laughter.

I'm not sure what part made her laugh: the stolen dragon eye, the dead husband, or the fact that I've somehow tangled Rafael and his friends into my mess even though they have nothing to do with it.

"Rafael agreed to help you get your dragon eye," Marix says. It isn't a question. "And so you've agreed to be his Burner." She nods, once again turning thoughtful as the lingering mirth fades from her expression. "Well, there's just one more thing I have to know. Do you want to go to sleep, or should we have another glass of wine?"

Marix and I chat on my bed until another yawn comes over me, and she insists I get some sleep. I don't argue and sleep without any dreams. I awaken, feeling refreshed despite the fact that I should have a massive hangover from the night before. I pour the remains of the bedside water into a glass and finish it off just as I hear a quiet knock at the door.

"Come in." I resist the urge to smooth my hair, knowing it's a helpless mess of curls after my quick morning wash.

"Hi." Marix greets me with her easy grin. "Rafael has asked everyone to meet him in the library, but you have time for some breakfast first if you would like."

"No, I'm fine." Although I wouldn't say no to some pixie powder or Rafael's magic morning brew.

Marix gives me some fresh clothing to change into—more of Teo's borrowed pants—and I take the time to clean and lace up his boots. I tuck the dagger into my boot and the chupacabra quill in my pocket beside my pouch of gold and phoenix feather. Then I follow Marix down the hall.

Rafael is already seated by the time I follow everyone into the large room that is clearly utilized as the library. Books line the walls on floor-to-ceiling shelves, and if the moment wasn't so wrong for it, I would take the time to explore all the titles. Instead, I take the empty seat beside Marix. There are exactly enough seats for all of us. After a moment, I realize I must be inhabiting Renee's chair. I swallow at the bitter thought and sharpen my focus on Rafael when he addresses me.

"Nyia. You're here. I told Marix not to disturb you. You should be resting. Your body is still healing from your ordeal with cuero seco."

I stiffen. I was unfamiliar with the mythic that attacked me, but of course Rafael knows what it was. Marix and Rafael are both insistent that they can be trusted, and my inclusion in this meeting seems a significant step forward. I assumed Rafael sent Marix to bring me to the meeting. Apparently, she did that on her own. So much for being part of the group. "My body has healed perfectly fine, as you well know after your thorough examination of it earlier." I push from the chair. "But I'm intruding. I'll go." I ignore Teo's affirming mumblings and meet Rafael's stare, daring him to allow me to leave. Everyone else remains silent.

"No. No, it's fine. I'm sorry." Rafael sighs, dragging a hand down his face. His fingers catch on the leather strap of his eye patch, and he adjusts it awkwardly around the fresh scar. "You've been dragged into our mess. You may as well stay and hear the whole of it. Renee was our contact with Iara."

The name, though naggingly familiar, means nothing to me, but Marix supplies the answer before I can even ask.

"La cantaora. The siren queen."

I'm stunned into silence. The siren queen is the greatest enemy of the kingdom. Sirens, mermaids, kraken, hippocampus, and other creatures I've never seen roam the sea bordering the entire island coast. There are dozens more, probably hundreds, of unknown creatures among not only the saltwater mythics but also the mythics who made their homes among cenotes and wild rivers on the island. And the siren queen rules them all. Or so I've heard. Water mythics and the sheer scope of powers afforded from the sea remain mostly elusive to Burners. I burned mermaid tears once, and the high lasted for days. The sea is too dangerous for most humans to survive, especially with all the terrible creatures within determined to keep what is theirs.

If Rafael and his friends made an enemy of the siren queen, I can only imagine the terrors that await them. They each hold their own death sentence. Is that what happened to Renee?

"How much time do we have?" Marix asks, her voice quiet and somber.

Everyone around the table exchanges glances, and I'm excruciatingly aware of the silent conversation happening around me. There is obviously more to the story than I'm privy to, and no one seems inclined to share any more.

"Weeks, if we're lucky," Rafael answers.

"And we're never lucky," Cesar intones with a low groan.

"But she is," Teo says.

Three heads swivel toward me, and I wish I could shrink into the high leather back of my chair.

"I wouldn't say that I'm lucky." I mean, I did survive a monster attack, but only because we happened to be so close to Rafael's manor—and the fact that he happened to have spare unicorn horn lying around. If anyone is lucky here, he is. But I don't bother arguing that point.

"Why was Renee meeting the siren queen?" I don't dare to call her by her given name as Rafael did, though I have no intention of forgetting his cavalier attitude about the monarchy. A chill traces the length of my spine when a thought occurs to me. Have I immersed myself in a group of spies? And if so, who do they work for? My kingdom? Or the queendom of our enemy?

"Renee had special skills that made her well adapted to work as an ambassador," Rafael says.

"I wasn't aware the kingdom appointed such a position." I search my brain, wishing I paid more attention to politics.

"More of an unofficial position," Marix offers.

Yup, spies. All of them. I draw a shaky breath.

"And they had her killed?" I force the question out, mind racing as I struggle to understand the implications, to retrace every bit of knowledge I have on the siren queen. I am woefully ignorant. I don't even know how long she has ruled over her subjects. Longer than I have been alive, that is certain. But just how long do sirens live? She could be immortal for all I know. And what is the value of a human life to an immortal? I swallow, noting the sharp pressure in my palms as my fingers bite into the flesh.

"That's what we're trying to figure out." Rafael doesn't look up at me, instead raking a hand through his hair.

"So, what are we going to do now?" Teo has pulled out another blade—I'm not sure from where—and he twirls it with deft fingers. *Show-off.* "If the siren queen won't assist us with our problem, that means we . . ." He trails off, frowning in my direction.

Once again, I'm reminded of all the things this group refuses to speak about in front of me, but they haven't forced me to leave yet, so I don't plan to miss out on this riveting conversation.

"We carry forward with our backup plan," Rafael says. His single eye regards me. His expression is guarded and almost . . . regretful?

"What's the backup plan?" I ask, dreading the answer.

"You."

12

DRAGON BONES

"Me?" I don't want this kind of pressure. I can't handle this kind of pressure. All I want to do is find the stolen dragon eye, somehow find a dragon heart, give it to Gloriana, and get off this blasted island. Preferably somewhere far away, a place where I can forget about my dead husband. Forget about the fact that I am a Burner, an outcast, and alone in this world.

I wish I never urged them to explain what happened to Renee. I wish I was never so foolish as to try and capture Darkthorne.

What can I do to help them? Rafael is clearly more knowledgeable than I, if not as powerful a Burner. And isn't he just as powerful? Didn't he heal me with the unicorn horn? The pain of my previous attack is already overshadowed by the terrifying memory.

They're mad, all of them. And spies. And dangerous. And I'm stuck.

"I still don't like it," Cesar says. Small surprise there. He doesn't seem to like much of anything, especially in matters concerning me.

"Nyia and I have already come to an agreement," Rafael says as if the matter is already closed. And I suppose it is. He is clearly the leader of the group because he makes this statement with an air of finality no one dares to contradict. And yes, we had come to an agreement of sorts, though I still have no idea what he plans to ask of me.

"You all have your individual tasks." Rafael regards each person in turn. "You know what's at stake. Cesar, spend the day gathering your forces. We'll need every ally we can find after the . . . upheaval."

Rafael frowns, jerking his head to the large picture window on the east side of the room. "It's past noon. Everyone, get to work."

How anyone can gauge the time through the thick heavy curtains is a wonder to me. It could be midday or the pitch darkness of a moonless night from what I can tell.

I wonder what sort of time constraint this group is under—if perhaps they are experiencing the same pressure I am. How far does Gloriana's reach extend? And what do Rafael and his group of friends have to worry about? They clearly have sufficient funds for anything they desire. Rafael has the acceptance of the king—what more could he want? It doesn't add up. Nothing does.

"What should I do?" I catch Rafael's eye as the other members of the group disperse.

"First, you need to tell me everything you know about Gloriana."

I nod. "I'll go over everything again, but I've already told you everything I know. What are you hoping to learn?"

"I want to find out if she's the king's private dealer for parts. I want to find out what she and the king are planning. And you're the person who's going to help me do that."

***

Rafael has me pen a letter to Gloriana asking her to meet and discuss new terms to our agreement. Teo is given the task of delivering the letter. I doubted his abilities as a Burner, but he is back with a reply in under an hour. Gloriana will meet me at dusk. Now Rafael is dead on his feet, the sharp lines of his face deeper than usual as he leads me and Marix to our rendezvous with Gloriana. He has to be more exhausted than he's letting on. But Gloriana's timeline is fast approaching, and I won't be any good as a backup plan if I'm dead. Besides, this time away with just Marix and Rafael is almost . . . nice. I can almost pretend to be on an afternoon stroll with friends if I don't include the looming death threats from Gloriana. At least the two of them seem to enjoy my company. Especially so in the case of Rafael, if our earlier dalliance is any indication, but he's a hard one to read. The attraction is there—for both of us—and I know we've both felt it from our first encounter. I wonder if we should talk about it, this growing tension between us. Is he thinking about me the same way I'm thinking about him?

I follow him and Marix around the perimeter of his estate and back toward the jungle. The growth is immensely thick, large fronds and creeping vines covering everything, even any indication of a trail if there ever was one. I walk between them, Rafael gripping my elbow any time the terrain grows especially tricky. Every time he touches me, a pulse of energy shoots through me. I wonder if he feels it too. This all-consuming connection that drives me closer to him, that compels me to touch him.

I want to press myself closer, lean into the solid warmth of his embrace. I can feel the heat emanating from him, and for just a moment, I allow myself to remember those stolen moments. The passion of our embrace that happened mere hours ago, but now seems a lifetime ago.

His grip tightens on my elbow, and for a single second, I think he is going to pull me closer for another kiss. But he is only pointing out a decidedly sharp rock I was about to trip over.

"What is this place?" Between the underground pool and secret tunnel to the outer garden topiary maze at the top of the cliff, I wouldn't have been surprised if a waterfall marked yet another hidden entrance. But the beautiful building we're approaching is massive, as though it is meant to be a warehouse or perhaps a very large barn. The fact that I'm no longer surprised by random architecture in the middle of the jungle does not go unnoticed by me.

Rafael leads me to the entrance of the building, but Marix stays behind, gesturing for us to go on without her after I give her a questioning look. I follow Rafael to the mysterious building, and as soon as I'm able to look around the large inner chamber, I have to choke back the startled gasp of surprise at my surroundings. The building is certainly large enough to house stables, but there isn't any livestock in sight. Well, none living, in any case. Rafael stands just inside the massive gate that serves as a doorway, not quite blocking my way, but his lack of movement causes me to linger all the same.

"I won't have you meet Gloriana again armed with nothing but Teo's discards," he says softly. "Please, take whatever you need."

It takes me less than a second to understand his meaning. No, it isn't the stables or a warehouse, but an arsenal of magical weapons. A mythic graveyard.

And at its very center is a massive dragon. Or what's left of him, in any case. The bones are old, bleached nearly white, and while the skull is mostly intact, it is missing all of its teeth. Dragon teeth can burn powerful magic, so it's no wonder they have all been harvested. I move toward the bones, drawn to the faint rumbling of magic that seems to hum in the air. I have never seen an entire dragon before. While I had some inkling of their massive size from the heavy eye I once carried, it is nothing to prepare me for this. The skull alone is large enough for me to crawl inside, though I have no desire to test the theory out. There is something off about the moment, perhaps made all the more potent from the fact that Rafael refuses to meet my eyes.

How has he come to own these remains? The dragon bones alone are worth a fortune, yet he keeps them hidden away. I suppose he isn't in need of money, but still, the sight of all this fortune is staggering. The rumors are true then—Rafael felled a dragon, one of the remaining Great Ones if the sheer size of the bones is any indication. No wonder he's renowned. His reputation is more than deserved.

I come to a stop in front of the dragon's feet, staring down at the brittle remains of claws. A single talon is more than enough weaponry for any defensive spell I can burn. Neither Rafael nor Marix make any move to assist me, so I press my boots against the ground for leverage and use both hands to wrench a talon free. The single claw is cracked in places but mostly intact, running in length from my elbow to just beyond the tips of my fingers and twice as wide as a great sword. It is surprisingly light despite its size, and I have no problem hefting the thing against my side and returning to Rafael who remains frozen by the entrance.

"Aren't you getting anything?" I ask when he begins to slide the gate shut behind me. The claw is more than large enough for both of us, but most Burners prefer to have their own weapon as only the person holding the object can burn from it.

"Rafael?" I ask when he doesn't answer. I search his expression and find that he's a million miles away.

"Raf?" I ask again, reaching out to touch his arm. He flinches but finally faces me, his expression grim.

"Are you two ready?" Marix calls. She hovers just outside the entrance. Her hands cling together, and her fingers twist in nervous circles.

"Ready," I respond for both of us. I reach out to touch Rafael, but he moves away from me, stomping through the jungle and not bothering to look back to see if we follow.

"What's his deal?" I ask Marix, hoping to gain some insight on how he'd gone from hot to cold so suddenly.

"It's . . ." Her lips purse before she settles on the right word. "Complicated."

Right. Just like everything else about him.

"Are you wondering if you're up for this?" Marix asks.

I note the way she grabs my elbow to steady me, careful not to allow any part of herself to accidentally touch the dragon claw I'm still gripping. It's so wide, I can scarcely wrap my hand around it.

"I'm fine," I tell her. I clutch the claw closer to my chest. I've never burned one before but know they are primarily used for added strength and speed. If one is a fighter, their personal skill will be multiplied tenfold. I'm not a fighter—not really—but I know enough to hold my own in a pub fight, even if my go-to move is to knee my opponent in the groin.

Marix tightens her grip on my elbow and turns to me with an expression that only makes me sigh.

"What is it?" I ask.

"You and Raf—"

"What about us?" I cross my arms, not caring that the gesture makes me appear defensive.

"I just wonder what your intentions are."

I arch an eyebrow. "My intentions? What? Are you his mother?" I stare at her too-pretty face with her sparkling freckles. "Or are you jealous?"

"What? No, I'm his friend." Now it's her turn to be defensive. Marix frowns at me. "I just wonder what your endgame is, that's all.

He helps you find this dragon eye and you, what? Go back to your house in the village? Continue working for the king?"

I narrow my eyes and uncross my arms, stooping to pick up the dragon claw from where I let it fall to the soft carpet of grass. I need to feel it in my arms, to know I have a weapon should the need arise. I feel like I'm stronger than Marix, and I tower over her, but something about the way she stares at me has my senses on high alert.

"First of all, I never said I worked for the king. And if that was a problem, I would think you would take this complaint to your boss. You know, the brooding man over there who has a reputation for supplying the kingdom with more dragon bones than anyone else? Ever?" I bite the inside of my cheek before allowing myself to say anything else.

"I'm not trying to fight you," Marix says. She sounds like she means it, but I'm not backing down.

"Yeah? Then leave the matter alone. I don't have an endgame, okay? All I want is to retrieve the dragon eye, to take back what's mine and then I'll leave you alone—all of you. In fact, I do not care if I never see you again."

"Why do you care about the eye so much? Why is it so important to you?" Marix asks.

"I'll tell you if you tell me what your boss wants with another Burner. What can I possibly bring to the table?"

Marix seems to consider this for a moment, but we are interrupted by a sudden chill in the air. A cold mountain wind caresses our skin and wipes away the sweet summer heat. We exchange glances, and I rub my hands over my arms to smooth the agitated hair. The skin on the back of my neck tingles, and I am overcome with the sudden and certain realization that we are not alone.

"Human. We meet again."

13

SMITE & GASH

The change to the air around me is instant. Magic. It is thick and cloying like honey, and I can almost imagine I smell it in a way Gloriana does.

"Human," a familiar voice coos in my ear. I turn around to face my will-o-wisp, but aside from the cold air, there is no indication that anyone is actually there. Can they really make themselves invisible? Or perhaps just so tiny no visible eye can see them?

"Hello, wisp," I respond to the empty space beside me. Marix cocks her eyebrow. I resist the urge to stick my tongue out at her.

"Human, what is it you desire?"

I frown at the opportunity. How did we stumble upon the wisp? Has it been following me, perhaps waiting for another opportunity to talk with me? But why would it want to talk to *me*? If I have only a single boon, I don't wish to waste it. I know what I have to ask.

The location of the dragon eye is still the most important information I can gain. The dragon heart, of course, but Rafael seems to have no issues finding the great beasts, so perhaps he knows of a lair somewhere. Even if he doesn't, that's the point of the dragon eye—burning it allows me to see through any glamour, to reveal the truth behind any magic. If there is a dragon left on this island, I will find it. And if this is my one chance to truly know where to find the eye, I can't squander the opportunity.

"The eye of the dragon, where is it?"

Marix narrows her eye at me, likely in response to my one-sided conversation with my imaginary friend. I get some perverse satisfaction in knowing the will-o-wisp has chosen to share itself with me alone.

In response, the wisp appears just above my nose, smaller than before, and I hear that same chiming of bells that signifies laughter.

"The dragon eye you seek? To find it, don't be meek. I'll tell you both the same. What you seek is from where you came."

A riddle? I didn't expect that. Especially after it spoke so plainly at the castle.

"Speak plainly. Why did you show yourself to me if to only hide the truth?" I clench my hands into a fist, annoyed I'm allowing my frustration to show. Is this nothing but a game to it?

"The debt is paid, human. Seek no further for what you wish to gain."

I scowl at the empty air beside me, though I'm sure the wisp has gone already and likely doesn't see my displeasure.

"Well," Marix says. The word hangs in the air, waiting for me to dignify it with a response, but I'm not sure what to say. Instead, I replay the words the will-o-wisp said to me. What I seek is from where I came? Is the dragon eye still at my house? Did Martin hide it somewhere? Perhaps in a secret chest or hidden floorboard? And what did it mean when it said it would tell us both? Did it mean Marix and me? Or Rafael?

I eye Rafael from across the field, frowning at the realization that he appears to be in his own one-sided conversation. Is he talking to a will-o-wisp too? More like arguing, if his wild gesticulations are anything to go by. I begin to walk toward him, intent on getting answers, when he glances up and notices me. He waves his arm in a gesture clearly meant for me to go away, and I grit my teeth against the indignation. I'm not some pesky fly he can shoo. Besides, I want to know if he's talking to the same will-o-wisp I spoke with. Not that I have any ownership over the mythic, but I don't want him to get more information on the dragon eye before I can locate it. For some reason, I still don't trust him to tell the truth when it comes to the eye. I'm not sure if my reason has anything to do with the recent discovery of dragon bones in his possession, but it certainly didn't help. My grip tightens around the dragon claw despite the fact that I have no intention of using it against Rafael . . . yet.

After another moment, Rafael jogs over to join us. Marix straightens at his approach like a soldier awaiting orders.

"I don't think this is a good idea." Rafael stares at me, his jaw working. "We should head back to the house and wait for the others."

Marix nods curtly and turns on her heel.

"What? No! You had me reach out to Gloriana. You . . . we—we have a plan."

Marix stops at my words, but when she speaks, she addresses Rafael.

"What did the wisps say to you?" She studies him.

"That she's here. Waiting for us." At his words, Rafael and Marix turn to look at the thick expanse of trees that separate us from the cliff's edge.

"That's good, isn't it? This is what we wanted." I reposition the dragon claw in my arms. "I'm ready," I lie. Maybe the wisp also spoke of Gloriana's arrival. My previous encounter was what started all this mess. Isn't that also back from where I came, just like the wisp said? But then, that's the problem with riddles. You can make the words mean anything if you believe in them enough. I bite the inside of my cheek, my grip tightening on the dragon claw.

"I'm going." I start toward the line of trees, and neither Rafael nor Marix stops me.

Our plan will work. I repeat the words to myself, though I'm not sure I believe them. I didn't even want to believe Gloriana would allow herself to be summoned, but the wisps confirmed it—she's here. It isn't a long walk through the thick copse of jungle trees, but the dense, tangled vegetation makes the journey slow going, and I am alone with my thoughts for longer than I like. What if Gloriana doesn't even bother to talk to me before she kills me? What if, even if Rafael and Marix try to jump in to stop her, she manages to kill me anyway? What if she kills them? I've never fought against another Burner before, and the thought of it has my stomach doing somersaults.

Soon enough I break through the fronds and into a wide clearing. I've made it to the summit. A wild wind whips my hair around my shoulders. It is a balmy wind, but that doesn't stop the chill from reaching through my skin to my bones. Why did I agree to this plan?

Gloriana assured me if I didn't have the heart by the time we met again, she would feed me to her goons. And I am not anywhere close to recovering the missing dragon eye, much less discovering the heart of one.

Nothing will happen to you. I won't let her touch you. I swear it.

Rafael's last words echo in my ears. The plan will work. The plan will work because it has to. I will not die today.

The sun has just begun to disappear on the horizon when I feel a gentle buzzing sensation on my skin followed by the scent of roses.

One moment I am alone in the clearing, and an instant later, I'm not. Gloriana simply appears beside me, stepping out of rippling air. Her eyes meet mine, and a brilliant smile slides into place against her dazzling features. She is dressed in a low-cut evening dress, chest on full display under a bed of sparkling jewels. Seconds later, her two goons appear beside her, their eyes falling on me with manic glee.

"Nyia." Her voice drips honey. "People never surprise me." She folds her arms across her chest, one long tapered fingernail tapping her forearm. "But you do. You are an intriguing creature. I do hope this isn't a waste of my time." Her eyes rove over my body, studying my clothing and too-small boots, frowning at the dragon talon clutched between my hands. I am stripped bare under her stare, and I know she sees everything.

"You've come heavily armed." She lifts a shoulder in a delicate shrug. "I can't say I blame you as I'm sure you knew I would bring along the boys. They do enjoy these outings." She stares at one, then the other, her expression that of someone regarding their favorite pet. "Now let's see, enhanced strength and agility—that would give you a fighting chance if Smite and Gash were human. Boys?"

At her words the two goons drop forward, falling on their knees as their bodies transform from giant men into massive canines. They are monstrous in size, towering over me and Gloriana. The dog-like creatures have coarse gray fur and glowing yellow eyes. Shadows shift and twist about them, and the scent of brimstone fills the air. They snarl at me, drool dripping from their giant maws, and it takes everything in me not to panic and run away. They would probably catch me anyway.

"You're right." I focus my gaze on her face and not the two terrifying mythics beside her. "We've both come prepared. That means we respect one another."

She sniffs at the air between us. "Hmm. Chupacabra too," she murmurs.

I stiffen. Can she seriously smell the chupacabra quill in my pocket? I'm not even burning it. I can't think of anything she can burn that would be powerful enough to enhance one's sense of smell to that degree. Unless... she isn't burning anything at all. And then, suddenly everything makes sense.

Gloriana isn't burning anything because she isn't a Burner. She's a mythic. Just like her goons. She's one of them and so much more dangerous than I ever imagined.

"I don't have the dragon heart," I tell her.

She chuckles. "That much is obvious." Her eyes once again take a quick scan of my body. "Although I have to applaud the audacity you have in choosing this location for our meeting spot." She sniffs the air again, her eyes going to the tree line where Rafael and Marix wait, watching. I have no doubt she can see them, though I can only make out the trees and jungle vines and nothing more.

"If you planned to ask for an extension to your debt collection, then you've wasted our time. My plans are already in motion."

"And what are your plans? Why do you want the heart of a dragon?"

"He doesn't know, does he? I thought he had figured out our plans. How lovely. Nyia, my poor dear, what a mess you've found yourself in. You poor little Burner, you really should leave the heavy magic to the professionals. I'll let you know when it's your turn." Her smile widens as she closes the distance between us. "I don't know what you think you're planning, but rest assured, you will fail." She snaps her fingers, and it feels as though a metal rod has been shoved down my spine. I can't move, my entire body in stiff salute. The dragon claw falls to the ground, useless at my feet.

A soft chuckle leaves her lips, and her eyes lock onto mine. I want to turn away from her stare. I want to snatch up the dragon claw and burn it to ash and rip her apart, but I can't move. My body is not my own. Suddenly, my left hand lifts in a jerking motion. My fingers plunge into my pocket and grasp the sharp chupacabra quill. I bring the quill up to my face, holding it against my eye.

Tears form, but I can't even blink them away. I can do nothing, locked in the grip of Gloriana's magic. I struggle to squirm, to force my body to move. There is nothing, except maybe a faint glimmer from the dragon bone laying at my feet. I send everything I have toward it, begging it to burn with every fiber of my being. Please. A frenzied buzzing echoes in my ears. I think of Rafael and Marix, hoping they remain hidden. My magic is still here, somewhere. That frenzied buzzing grows louder. A familiar tingling sensation raises the tiny hairs on the back of my neck. *Burn, Nyia.* The chupacabra quill bursts into flame. I'm finally free, but I can only stare at her, breathing hard.

Gloriana lifts a hand and holds out her palm, gesturing at the two growling beasts beside her before giving me an appraising look. "Interesting. She's still off-limits for now, boys. Nyia, do hurry up before you find yourself dead." She blows me a kiss and then disappears.

14

SHE'S ONE OF THEM

I sink to the soft earth beneath me, not caring the ground is damp and seeping through my pants. I bury my face in my hands and sob. Because it's not fair. Martin shouldn't have left me with this mess. I am not strong enough to fight a mad mythic hell-bent on creating chaos and feeding me to her goons. The new moon is less than a week away. I have mere days to find the dragon eye, use it to find a dragon, and slay the beast and bring Gloriana its heart. It doesn't matter how many Burners I get to help me, I can't do it. She is right, I am going to fail.

"Nyia. Here. Let me help you." Rafael's grip is firm as he cups my elbow, lifts me up from the ground, and pulls me against his chest.

"That's it. You're okay. You're so brave. So brave." He kisses the crown of my head, and I cling to him, still releasing the sobs I have held back for so long.

"I can't do it," I confess to him. "I can't. She's not a Burner. Rafael, she isn't. She isn't human, she's one of them. She's a mythic." I shudder against him and ache for him to pull me closer, but he doesn't.

A part of me suspected her humanity. Her control of the giant goons, her magic sense of smell and otherworldly beauty. She is mythic—of course she is. But what does that mean for me? And what does a mythic want with the heart of a dragon? All I know for certain is I'm involved in something more terrifying than I can comprehend. And still, Rafael says nothing at my proclamation that Gloriana is a mythic.

"You knew, didn't you?" I push away from him and swipe at my face in a halfhearted attempt to wipe away the tears. "You knew Gloriana was mythic—you've always known. You . . . do you know what she's planning?"

"I have my suspicions." Rafael sighs. "Nyia, you have to know, I'm just as much in the dark as you are. I don't know—"

"Stop it! Stop lying."

"Nyia it's . . ."

"If you say it's complicated, I'm going to scream."

"But it is. You wouldn't understand."

"How can you say that when you won't even give me a chance?" I throw my hands up and let loose a frustrated groan. "Just forget it. I'm going back home. I can find the dragon eye on my own."

"Nyia, wait! You can't leave." He reaches for my arm, but I pull away.

"Why not?"

"Because it will be dark soon. It isn't safe."

"Safe?" I laugh, the sound wild in my ears. "Safe? I haven't been safe since I met you!"

"Nyia, what I'm trying to accomplish is bigger than you or me. It's bigger than all of us."

"Oh really? And what is this big thing you're trying to do, huh? Enlighten me, please. What are you planning?

"I'm going to permanently close the veil between humans and mythics."

My mouth slams shut, the words dying on my lips. How can he possibly hope to accomplish this? He's just a single man. He—oh no. He couldn't possibly think he and *I* would be strong enough to accomplish such a thing? We're just two Burners. The scope of that level of magic is unbelievable. He can't be serious.

"You can't," I manage to squeak out, finally finding the words. Because no one can. The veil has existed for over a hundred years. Maybe longer. It is how the humans first found the island. We had a difficult enough time even tracking its location as it jumped around the island without the added element of figuring out how to open and close it. What would it mean for the island to have the veil permanently closed? Why would he even want to risk finding out?

"You're mad," I whisper. "Stark, raving mad. It will never work."

"I have to try."

"Why? Tell me why. Help me understand. Explain."

"It's . . ." I can see his mind reeling, struggling to describe the situation he has insisted on calling complicated and leaving me in the dark. What can be so complicated as all that? I understand what it means to be a Burner and what it means to forge a relationship with a mythic. There were times with the succubus I almost felt as though I could drink her magic, it flowed from her so freely. I believe mythics like Sienna are rare, but there have to be more of them out there. Sienna noted my power as a Burner but was she only able to do that because of her powers as a succubus? Did her own magic call out to mine or did she sense something on me? Smelling me like Gloriana? Sienna was able to transition from succubus to her human form as easily as breathing but I had thought it a trick unique to her kind. Was Gloriana a succubus too? Or something else entirely?

"Why does Gloriana need the heart of a dragon, Rafael?" The answers are there, hovering between us. I just need him to admit the truth. "Tell me."

He inhales sharply. "The eye . . . the heart. They need the eye to show them the gate between worlds. They need the heart to keep it open. King Ernesto and Gloriana won't stop. I have to protect them. If I don't close the veil, they'll never stop being hunted. No mythic will be safe."

Protect who? I want to ask. My thoughts are scattered pieces of a puzzle, but I'm so close to the truth I can almost taste it. I catch my bottom lip between my teeth, thinking. Rafael somehow has access to a treasure trove of mythic parts. I assumed it was because of his connection to the king, but what if it isn't? What if Rafael isn't shocked by the revelation of Gloriana being mythic because he has suspected it all along.? Why was Teo so eager to witness the chupacabra quill being burned, yet so resentful of the act itself? Why did he have the chupacabra quill at all? The quill that suspiciously resembled his hair . . .

"Teo." Understanding slams into me, and I take a physical step back as if to prepare to run from the realization. No wonder Rafael is so concerned about the mythics. We are probably surrounded by them. "Teo is one of them, isn't he?"

15

A Burner for the Gate

Rafael blinks at me.

"I don't know what you mean," he whispers.

"I think you do. I think you've been covering for him this entire time. And I bet Cesar is too. That's why he hates me so much, why he can't stand that I'm a Burner. What sort of deal did you make with them? Did you offer them sanctuary in exchange for a small body part? Tell them they can stay in the safety of your mansion in exchange for their trimmed toenail clippings? Is—is Marix a succubus?"

My hand flutters to my throat, fingers stretching around the expanse of my neck, scarcely registering the erratic beat of my pulse.

"Is that why she—why you and I?"

"No. No, Marix is not a succubus. I've never used magic against you. Never." Rafael's voice is stern, his eye pleading. He reaches for me again, but I take several steps back.

"Don't touch me!" My voice is shrill, sounding foreign to my ears. "Don't touch me," I repeat. "I need to think."

I can't calm my racing thoughts as I replay every interaction I've had with Cesar and Teo and Marix too . . . By the forgotten gods, they can't all be mythics, can they? The thought is too impossible to comprehend, but what further proof do I need? For them to shift into their mythic forms right before my eyes?

I take a deep breath through my nose, releasing it slowly through clenched teeth, willing my racing heart to calm before I have a full-out panic attack. A thought occurs to me, and I can't control the frantic shudder that takes over my body.

"You said you healed me with unicorn horn." I swallow. My hands fall to my stomach, my thighs, where there is only the faintest remnant of the vicious scars I had just days before. The unicorn's healing magic is still in my blood, coursing through my veins and healing me even now. "Tell me how you healed me. Tell me about the unicorn horn. Tell me Marix isn't a fucking unicorn!"

"She's not . . . Cesar is." Rafael sighs loudly, shoulders sagging in defeat. "You're right. Cesar is a mythic, a unicorn. He's the last of his kind."

"And Marix? Teo? You—you kept this from me! Why didn't you tell me?"

"It isn't my secret to tell!" A shadow crosses his face and he sighs again. "I wanted to tell you—was going to tell you. Eventually."

"When?"

"Nyia—"

"When?" I repeat through gritted teeth. "When were you going to tell me? Before or after you had me agree to this insane plan of yours? Did you plan to tell me after we closed the veil? What will that even mean for a mythic? For humans? The veil has always existed, it—"

"It hasn't!" Raf's hand slices through the air as he reaffirms his negative statement with a vehement shake of his head. "The veil has not always existed. There was a time before the veil tore open. Before humans even knew mythics existed."

My mind spins at the implication. If that's true, then perhaps the veil truly can be closed again. I think about Sienna, my beautiful succubus, and how she was forced to become a Huntress, leading humans to her own kind, whoring herself out to avoid being turned over to King Ernesto and his men. I catch my bottom lip between my teeth, sucking thoughtfully. Is Rafael's plan truly so crazy? Hadn't Sienna and I talked about this very thing? About a world where we can live in freedom, far away from dangerous men like Martin?

"Okay. Say I believe you... that closing the veil is possible. You truly think it can be done by two Burners?"

"I think it can be done by one," Raf responds with quiet conviction. "I know you can do it, Nyia. I just need you to trust me."

"Everything okay?" Marix's voice is soft, but I startle all the same, jerking back from Rafael and stumbling out of his grasp.

"I'm sorry. I tried to wait as long as possible, but we should be heading back," Marix says. I get the sense she's apologizing to Rafael as well as me.

"You're right," Rafael agrees. "We need to get back so I can tell the others. Gloriana is more dangerous than we anticipated. She's not just any mythic. She's one of the Ancients."

16

You Know What I Want

We arrive back at an empty house. Cesar and Teo have yet to return from whatever task Rafael sent them on, and as always, there is suspiciously no sign of servants. A house this size has to have servants. There must be a network of secret passages that allow them to move about from room to room.

Raf was quiet most of the way home, deflecting any questions Marix or I posed about his thoughts on Gloriana or his discussion with the will-o-wisp. I suppose that's just as well since I'm still trying to sort through the day's revelations myself. It's hard to believe how much my life has changed in only a week. I am riven, watching the pieces of myself fight to once again make sense of my life. My thoughts are a mindless jumble, and I feign exhaustion and excuse myself. I'm still clutching the dragon claw, and Rafael doesn't ask for its return, so I assume it's mine and take it back to my room with me.

Once in the privacy of the Gold Room, I discover that I do, in fact, have a bath, and I shimmy in a delighted little dance to find it is also charmed to keep the water hot and sparkling clean. Literally. I suppose the water must be charmed by either unicorn or pixie because what else would leave such a radiant glow? Does Cesar know how to charm objects? Is that what's happening all around us? I suppose there is no need for servants when one can just surround themselves with charmed objects. I allow my thoughts to tumble over themselves, falling into fits of worry over the missing dragon eye and Gloriana's threats and then shoving the thoughts away when I discover a hidden drawer of scented soaps. After a luxuriously long bath, I slip on the fluffy robe left on the bed and curl into a deep, mindless sleep.

I awaken to a steady tapping on my door. I expect it's Marix, likely telling me it's time for dinner, but Rafael stands on the other side.

"I just wanted to check on you and tell you dinner will . . ." He trails off at my sour expression.

"We still need to talk about why you've been lying to me. Why didn't you just tell me about your plan for the veil at the very beginning?"

The corner of his mouth twitches. "At the king's ball, when I caught you touching yourself? Or maybe after you tied me to a chair in your bedroom? You used to play so kinky."

I bite the inside of my cheek and pray to all the forgotten gods he can't see me blush.

"Don't. I need answers, Rafael."

He crosses the length of the room and kneels beside the bed. If he wanted to, he could reach out and touch me.

"I never wanted to keep anything from you. I was going to tell you—I planned to tell you everything, when the time was right. I'm trying to keep everyone safe."

"Safe," I repeat. Sure, I suppose he tried to keep me safe as much as he had placed me in danger. Is there really any excuse for his lies? His eye stares up at me, the intensity of his gaze searing my skin and rattling my bones.

"I mean it, Nyia. You're important to me."

I hate the way my heart leaps in response to his words.

16

YOU KNOW WHAT I WANT

We arrive back at an empty house. Cesar and Teo have yet to return from whatever task Rafael sent them on, and as always, there is suspiciously no sign of servants. A house this size has to have servants. There must be a network of secret passages that allow them to move about from room to room.

Raf was quiet most of the way home, deflecting any questions Marix or I posed about his thoughts on Gloriana or his discussion with the will-o-wisp. I suppose that's just as well since I'm still trying to sort through the day's revelations myself. It's hard to believe how much my life has changed in only a week. I am riven, watching the pieces of myself fight to once again make sense of my life. My thoughts are a mindless jumble, and I feign exhaustion and excuse myself. I'm still clutching the dragon claw, and Rafael doesn't ask for its return, so I assume it's mine and take it back to my room with me.

Once in the privacy of the Gold Room, I discover that I do, in fact, have a bath, and I shimmy in a delighted little dance to find it is also charmed to keep the water hot and sparkling clean. Literally. I suppose the water must be charmed by either unicorn or pixie because what else would leave such a radiant glow? Does Cesar know how to charm objects? Is that what's happening all around us? I suppose there is no need for servants when one can just surround themselves with charmed objects. I allow my thoughts to tumble over themselves, falling into fits of worry over the missing dragon eye and Gloriana's threats and then shoving the thoughts away when I discover a hidden drawer of scented soaps. After a luxuriously long bath, I slip on the fluffy robe left on the bed and curl into a deep, mindless sleep.

I awaken to a steady tapping on my door. I expect it's Marix, likely telling me it's time for dinner, but Rafael stands on the other side.

"I just wanted to check on you and tell you dinner will . . ." He trails off at my sour expression.

"We still need to talk about why you've been lying to me. Why didn't you just tell me about your plan for the veil at the very beginning?"

The corner of his mouth twitches. "At the king's ball, when I caught you touching yourself? Or maybe after you tied me to a chair in your bedroom? You used to play so kinky."

I bite the inside of my cheek and pray to all the forgotten gods he can't see me blush.

"Don't. I need answers, Rafael."

He crosses the length of the room and kneels beside the bed. If he wanted to, he could reach out and touch me.

"I never wanted to keep anything from you. I was going to tell you—I planned to tell you everything, when the time was right. I'm trying to keep everyone safe."

"Safe," I repeat. Sure, I suppose he tried to keep me safe as much as he had placed me in danger. Is there really any excuse for his lies? His eye stares up at me, the intensity of his gaze searing my skin and rattling my bones.

"I mean it, Nyia. You're important to me."

I hate the way my heart leaps in response to his words.

"And the bones? You basically have the rotting corpse of an entire dragon. How do you explain that? And how does a Burner come to have so many mythics he calls friends? A chupacabra and a unicorn? How long have you known about Gloriana? And when did you get this plan for the veil? How can you say you don't want to keep things from me when that's all you've done? Am I along for the ride simply because I'm the only other Burner you can find?"

"Nyia, it's not like that—"

"No," I interrupt him because I'm on a roll. "No, I've been nothing but honest with you and yet you continuously lie to me!" I shove the last of the sheets away from my ankles in an effort to get out of the bed, out of this room, and away from him.

"Please, Nyia. Please, don't go. Not yet."

His hand catches my own, and I freeze in place. The sudden contact has my skin buzzing, and I sense the faint, familiar hum of magic in the air. Is he burning something? I turn to him, voice pleading.

"Just stop hiding things from me, please. Tell me right now, right here in this moment, what do you want from me?"

He swallows, his jaw working before he captures my face in his hands. "I think you know what I want from you," he murmurs, bringing his lips to mine.

Whereas before his mouth was desperate, insistent, this time the kiss is a soft exploration of my body. His touch is feather-light as he presses his lips against mine, and I hear the soft intake of breath when his tongue dips into my mouth. He angles his head, drawing me closer, tongue teasing and coaxing mine.

He pulls away for just a moment, eye searching. "Is this okay?"

I blink, wondering what he's asking. No, we still have so much to discuss, so many secrets between us and yet, yes. *Yes*, this is more than okay. This is everything I want.

"Nyia, talk to me, baby. I need to hear you say you want this too." He dips his head to my neck, kissing and sucking from the hollow of my throat to the curve of my earlobe.

"I want this," I say. I want this more than anything I've ever wanted in my life. I grab his face, fingers tangling in the length of his hair as I bring his lips back to mine.

He moans against my mouth, hands sliding from my face, to my shoulders, down my spine. He pulls me closer, angling my body so I'm pressed against the length of him, his body hard against my own. The kiss deepens, and I can't get enough of him. My fingers move through his hair, to the back of his neck, tugging him closer.

He pulls on the robe, sliding the material off my shoulders so it pools at my waist. His fingers are rough and calloused, so warm, so hot despite the sudden chill against my exposed skin. He pulls away from my mouth, kissing a trail down my neck to my shoulders, breath hot on my nipples, and they harden in anticipation.

"You're so beautiful," he whispers before dipping his head to my breast, catching my nipple in his mouth and sucking gently.

I moan, and my head rolls as I arch my back to give him full access. He moves from one nipple to the other, hands exploring every inch of my skin.

I don't remember falling back against the bed, but I am suddenly staring up at the gold mosaic of the ceiling, and Rafael has moved to the floor, kneeling in front of me.

"Can I?"

I nod, barely aware of what I'm consenting to. I just know that I need more. More of him, his skin against mine, his wet, hot tongue on my body. His hands slide down my thighs, behind my knees, before he pulls me close to him so I'm flat against the bed, legs up and ass barely hanging on the edge.

Then his mouth is on me again. Licking the length of my folds before flicking his tongue against my clit. I buck against him, wanting—no, *needing*—more, and he latches on, hands reaching up to clutch my ass and hold me tighter, pinning me in place against his mouth.

"I've dreamed about this, about tasting you," he says.

I grab his head and hold it against me, riding his face and taking this pleasure, this moment for my own. It feels so good, so perfect, I don't want him to stop. And he doesn't, even as my body seizes under his, convulsing with my orgasm.

"You're perfect. So deliciously perfect," he says, licking the length of me, devouring my cum with his tongue.

"More," I mumble, scarcely aware of what I'm saying, just knowing I don't want this feeling to ever stop. I arch my back, gasping at the feel of his wet tongue sliding against me.

"I've wanted this since I first saw you in Sabastian's room. When I saw these beautiful fingers of yours playing with yourself. Show me what you would have done if I hadn't interrupted you." His tongue plunges into me again, and I give in to his muffled demands of "show me," stretching my fingers down toward my clit.

"That's my girl," he praises, his voice a near growl before sucking me harder. I thrust my hips up, once again seeking release.

"Rafael." His name is torn from my mouth, and I moan. There are no words, only pure pleasure erupting from me. "I want you, all of you, inside me now." I struggle to rise to a sitting position, dismayed to find him still fully clothed. I need more of him. I need to feel his skin against mine.

I pull at his shirt, practically ripping it from him. He obliges just long enough to pull the garment over his head but then his mouth is on mine again, seizing me in a frenzied kiss.

I give in to the kiss, to the pure ecstasy of feeling his bare skin, deliciously hot against my cool fingers, wanting more, needing to touch him, all of him, and claim him as my own. I reach for the waistband of his pants, tugging at them, delighted to find him erect and straining against the fabric. I pull his pants downward but lose focus on completing the action when I grasp his massive girth.

Oh fuck, I'm going to enjoy this.

He moans against my mouth, shuddering as my fingers struggle to close around him. He's huge, but I'm dripping wet and more than ready for him. I begin to guide his dick toward me, pressing against the tip and moaning at the sheer anticipation of what's to come.

"Nyia, wait." He stiffens just slightly. "I need to—"

"It's fine," I tell him, arching upward with my hips, drawing his length into me. I sigh in pleasure. "I take the monthly tea," I say, gasping at the sensation of him filling me. "You don't have to worry."

For a moment it looks like he will say more, but then he is fully inside me, and I rock my hips beneath him. It's only him and me and this frantic motion between us.

I never knew it could feel like this, that I could feel so utterly filled and complete. He reaches between us, pulling my right leg up and entering deeper, rubbing my clit with his fingers.

"Yes, yes, just like that."

He grunts in response, pumping faster and making me scream my release. Moments later he shudders against me as he finds his own, and we lie intertwined, breathing heavily.

"Nyia, you . . . we—"

"I know." I lean forward to kiss him. It was better than good. In fact, he just created a new standard I doubt anyone will ever match. "I know," I mumble against his lips before falling back on the bed, completely and utterly spent.

We are still naked, lying in one another's embrace. I am on my back, and Rafael is curled around me. His long, tapered fingers trace the thin lines of scars left from cuero seco, now so pale they are barely visible but somehow still sensitive. Or perhaps it is that I am just hyperaware of Raf's touch. By the forgotten gods, I haven't been fucked like that—well, ever—and yet I'm still not sated. I want more of him. I want to take hold of him and wrap my lips around the tip of his dick and feel it grow hard in my mouth.

I bite my bottom lip, considering. He probably needs more time. I sigh and wriggle closer, content to simply be at his side, to feel his hands on my skin as I wait.

"What did you ask the will-o-wisp?" I ask, surprised by the dreamy quality of my voice.

"Hmm?" The sound is muffled, his face buried as he nuzzles my neck.

"Earlier, you were speaking to one, weren't you? Did you ask it to lead you somewhere?"

"I asked it where I could find the prettiest pussy in all the land, and it pointed right at you. No surprise there."

I giggle, despite the fact that I'm well aware he is using flattery to distract me from my question.

"I'm serious," I say, placing my palm on his chest and spreading my fingers over his skin. So hot, his skin is always burning at my touch. There's no need to huddle under a blanket with his warmth. Not that I can even think of sleeping with him so close to me.

"What did you ask your will-o-wisp?" He turns the question around on me.

I frown. How had he known I spoke to one as well? His "discussion" with the wisp had been visible for all to see. Had Marix told him?

"I asked it to tell me where I can find the dragon eye."

He stiffens slightly, then his fingers reach up to my breast, and my nipple buds under his touch. He appears so relaxed, I wonder if I imagined the reaction.

"And did it?" he asks before drawing my nipple into his mouth.

I gasp at the sensation. At the sudden heat of his mouth, then the cool air as he moves his head from one nipple to the other.

"Did it what?"

"Tell you where to find your dragon eye." He nuzzles his face between my tits, and I feel his dick grow hard between us. He needed less time to recuperate than I thought.

"A riddle." I have to force the words out, thoughts flitting away under his expert touch. "Something like seeking it from where I came." I gasp as his fingers dip down to stroke my center, to spread me open and dip further. I'm already so wet for him. "I think it might be at my house. Maybe Martin hid it somewhere."

"Mmm," he says in response. He begins to leave a trail of kisses down my body, and when his head finally dips to claim my clit with his tongue, I moan in pleasure. I could get used to this.

He is ravenous for me, drowning me in sloppy kisses that tug and suck at my folds and clit. In no time at all, he's made me come for him again. He presses his tongue against the length of me, and I shudder under my release.

"I could do this every day for the rest of my life," he whispers against me.

"I would let you," I mumble. I was wrong about not being sleepy with him around. After this latest session, I could definitely use a nap.

"Do you promise?" he whispers so softly I can hardly hear him. Or maybe I'm already drifting to sleep.

I reach for him, intent on returning the favor, but he catches my hands with his and brings them up to his lips.

"Stay here—sleep. You'll feel better when you wake."

"I already feel perfect," I say, but allow my eyes to drift closed.

Before he leaves, Rafael mutters something so quietly I barely hear him over the snap of the door, but it sounds like he says:

"That's because you are."

17

THE DRAGON EYE

When I wake up, the house is still and quiet, and I am sure it is the middle of the night. I've likely slept through dinner if my ravenous appetite is anything to go by. I sit up slowly, stretching my arms above my head and arching my back, surprising myself when another small moan escapes. I've made more noises of pleasure in this bed than I have in my entire life. Martin tried, or at times it certainly seemed he did, but he never came close to making my body respond the way Rafael did. Not even Sienna and our handful of encounters gave me such pleasure, though I know that is due in some part to the fact that she held back her succubus powers out of respect for our friendship. I wonder what she would think of my latest adventures. I think she would be proud, and the thought pushes a small smile to my lips.

I toss my legs over the bed, wincing at the slight pain between them, though the pain is not entirely unpleasant. It only serves as yet another reminder of Rafael and what we did together. I walk over to the window and pull back the heavy drapes, shocked to find pale morning light on the other side. I slept through the entire night! I eye the tousled bed and frown. Why didn't Rafael wake me for dinner? Did he try to come back at all? Or did he crave a night in his own bed? I consider taking another bath, the empty porcelain tub already beginning to fill with steaming water at the mere thought, but a low rumble from my belly confirms the need for another simple pleasure. It feels like forever since I've eaten anything, the lost hours blending together. I search for my discarded clothing, pleased to see they have been laundered and folded neatly on the giant chest at the foot of the bed. I wonder if the borrowed clothing was cleaned by a servant or by some other enchantment and make a mental note to ask Rafael.

I dress quickly and once again choose to leave the borrowed boots on the floor where I discarded them earlier. Though we are close enough in size, there is no denying Teo's feet are just smaller than mine so as to make them not quite comfortable, and I see no reason to squish my toes. Not when I'm already feeling so gloriously relaxed.

I open the door to my room and peer down the empty hallway before leaving in search of food, my bare feet silent against the thick carpets. Rafael's room is open, and I take a moment to peek inside the familiar room, but it's also empty. Steam still floats above his bathing pool, and his scent lingers in the air, fresh pine and burnt chocolate. I resist the urge to snoop around his belongings and leave, snapping the door shut behind me. I don't think Raf would mind exactly, but I don't want to spoil things between us by snooping after our shared intimacy.

I could do this every day for the rest of my life. His words echo in my thoughts, and this time I can't help the tiny squeal that escapes my lips. How did I get so lucky? I quite literally forced my way into Rafael's life. I planned on taking back what was rightfully mine, and instead I found so much more. A true partner—someone who swore to protect me, someone who wants, *needs* my help as much as I need his. I'm not sure how, but I know we will accomplish everything he promised. Together we will close the veil. He alone will help me locate the missing dragon eye.

At that thought, a small pinprick of worry nags at me. I should have told Rafael about Gloriana from the very beginning. Just like he should have told me about his suspicions. From this moment on, we need to be completely honest with one another. No more secrets. Maybe Martin named him for this very reason. Rafael is my only hope for reclaiming the dragon eye. We will do this. Especially with a unicorn and chupacabra helping us. And Marix . . . is she a Burner or some other sort of mythic? Rafael hasn't said, only that it wasn't his business to say.

The thought sobers me a bit, and I frown at the implication. How did he come to ally himself with these mythics? Cesar certainly didn't seem like the loving creature of light I always associated with the mythic unicorn. Although, perhaps he was only warmth and goodness when he was in his unicorn form. Perhaps being human brought out his more sordid qualities. It would certainly make sense. Sienna always warned of the differences her succubus form brought out. That her power was curbed, muted by her human appearance, and I wonder if that is the case for Cesar.

And what of Teo and Marix? Rafael didn't give me a clue as to their true nature, though I figured out Teo's abilities all on my own. Chupacabra are impossibly fast and can even make themselves invisible. I try not to think of what else I know about them, about the fact that they are some of the jungle's most dangerous predators, that they prefer the taste of human blood.

At least the island is still terrorized by dozens of chupacabra. Teo definitely has companions if chupacabra ever long for their own kind. Poor Cesar is the last of his. How lonely Cesar must feel. My heart aches at the thought. No wonder he hates Burners with the ferocity he directs toward me, considering Burners are the cause of the unicorns' near extinction. Rafael and he must have some sort of deeper understanding for Cesar not to feel as darkly toward him.

Rafael and I still have many secrets between us, despite our growing connection. Well, no more. We need to have a serious discussion, one in which we remain clothed long enough to actually learn more about one another, especially if we are going to work out in the long term. I shake my head at the thought. I've only just met the man, and I'm already planning a future together. I need to pull myself together. But then I remember the intensity in his eye when he told me he'd been thinking of us together.

I could do this every day for the rest of my life.

I could definitely get accustomed to that. My belly rumbles, reminding me once again of my baser needs, and I start toward the dining hall and kitchen. Food first and then a long conversation with Rafael. And then more sex. Yes, definitely more sex.

My pace is ambling, my bare feet softly padding against the thick carpet. I hear voices ahead, likely coming from the dining hall. The voices are muted, and I don't hear the clinking of glasses or scraping of utensils on plates, nor do I smell the intoxicating scent of roasted meats and vegetables that was present during my last visit to the dining room. They aren't eating then. Hopefully I will arrive just in time to be served and this is not an indication they already ate.

The large double doors to the dining hall have been drawn shut. They were open during my previous visit so I pause just outside them, frowning at the intense tone of the voice coming from inside. I pull the sliding doors open barely, and when I recognize the stern voice as Cesar's, my shoulders slump in relief. Not to worry there. His voice always sounds that way. I'm about to open the door and make a joke saying as much, but Rafael's voice stops me, his words clear now.

"No, I know. She's probably still sleeping. She was exhausted when I left her room."

"I bet," Marix answers with a barely suppressed chuckle.

I roll my eyes.

"I can't believe you're sleeping with her. A Burner." I reel back, startled by the venom in Cesar's voice. I know he doesn't like me—in particular doesn't like Burners, and not without reason—but I'm still surprised to hear him speak this way. I'm even more surprised by Rafael's response.

"Careful. You know we need her."

"We need a Burner. That could be anyone. But of course you're enjoying the benefits," Cesar retorts.

"Why shouldn't he have a bit of fun on his last days—"

Teo is interrupted by Marix, her voice quivering as she asks, "Are you sure there isn't another way? Perhaps if I go to Iara, I can talk to the siren queen. She'll listen to me."

"No. La cantaora is no longer up for discussion. Neither is Nyia and the relationship we have." Rafael is insistent, and I picture his hand slicing through the air as he shakes his head, perhaps crossing his arms and scowling. I slide the door open just a bit more so I can see. I know I shouldn't be eavesdropping on their private conversation, but I can't help myself—they're talking about me. I shuffle forward until I'm practically pressing against the door and peer through the crack into the room.

Rafael's back is to me and his arms aren't crossed over his chest like I pictured. Instead, one arm is draped over his head, fingers curling through his disheveled hair in the way he does when he's agitated. I smile at the thought. I'm getting to know his idiosyncrasies.

Marix and Teo, bored and flipping his dagger, are seated at the table, but Cesar paces back and forth, appearing more like a caged jungle cat than a mythical horned horse. By the forgotten gods, it must have irked him to heal me.

"I still think we should explore other options," Teo says. He palms the dagger, studying his reflection in the polished steel. "We still have time to find another way . . . one that doesn't involve her."

"I agree with Teo," Marix says.

Ouch. And I thought she liked me.

"We should try everything else, explore every other option," she continues. "Or at the very least try talking to her. Maybe Burners know something we don't. She is very desperate to get the dragon eye. Maybe we use that as leverage."

"No, she's too close to learning everything already, and I won't threaten her anymore." Rafael sighs, his voice heavy. "The wisp told her to seek the dragon eye from where she came. It's only a matter of time before she finds it." He gestures down the length of the table, pointing at the large circular object at the far end of the dining hall.

My body goes rigid, breath catching in my throat. No. No, it can't be. I blink several times, telling myself that I'm seeing things, that I'm not staring in the face of the biggest betrayal of my life. Because there, at the end of the table, glowing with its faint hum of magic, is my dragon eye.

I take several steps back, my hand fluttering up to my face to cover my mouth, to prevent a startled gasp from escaping. I don't know if the action is needed, though, because I can barely breathe. He has the dragon eye. Rafael has my dragon eye, there on his table. He's likely had it this entire time. He's been lying to me, all this time. Even after everything that just happened. He lied. How could he do this to me? I turn on my heel and run down the hall, leaving the voices and buzzing of magic behind me.

18

PART TWO

19

WORST BLOW JOB EVER

RAFAEL

Thoughts of Nyia and the way she looked when I left her have me distracted. She was spent. She was so beautiful, curled on her side, breathing slow and steady with one small hand tucked beneath her cheek and wild curls fanning all around. My little Burner. *Mine.* Flames above, I don't know how I waited so long to take her. My dick strains as I replay all we had just done. Fuck, I haven't been this horny since I was a teenager.

Enjoy these moments while you can, a small voice inside me whispers. They'll be gone all too soon. Like I need the reminder. Aside from Nyia, it's all I think about. I sigh, forcing my attention back to the discussion at hand.

Cesar is right—they all were right—but we don't have time. Not only in our own timeline but in Nyia's, too, and Gloriana is no one to trifle with. I'm still unsure how Nyia got tangled with her. Of all the Burners Gloriana could have approached, why her? No matter how it came about, Nyia needs me, and I will do everything in my power to save her from Gloriana's wrath, to save her from everything.

Cesar's opinion on this subject doesn't matter—nothing matters except Gloriana, her devious plans, and what I will do to stop them. I will do what needs to be done. I will keep them all safe.

"No, she's too close to learning everything already, and I won't threaten her anymore." I sigh, putting an end to whatever new argument my friends are about to launch. "The wisp told her to seek the dragon eye from where she came. It's only a matter of time before she finds it."

We all turn to look at the dragon eye at the opposite end of the dining room table, and I can't help but curl my lip in disgust at its appearance. It is no small object, of course—how can it be—but I still marvel that it could be the source of so much trouble. I need to tell Nyia. It's time I confess the truth about the eye, about everything, consequences be damned, and yet... I can't. How can I look into her beautiful, soulful eyes and break her heart?

There is a small clicking sound from the hallway and I turn, frowning at the slightly ajar door. I walk over to the door and slide it open, half expecting—no, hoping—to find Nyia on the other side. But the hallway is empty and quiet. There would be no easy way out of this. I have to tell Nyia the truth on my own.

"When are you going to tell her?" Marix asks, her wise eyes knowing. She alone always seems to know what I am thinking.

"Today. As soon as possible, really. I'll tell her everything and let her decide if she wants to remain and help."

Cesar snorts, the sound decidedly horse-like. "That's a terrible idea. What makes you think she'll do anything to help us?"

I don't know that she will. But I also know I can't continue lying to her, not after these last twenty-four hours, not anymore.

"You're welcome to venture out on your own. Try your own plan to close the gate." He won't call my bluff. It's not possible. We've exhausted every other option and he knows it. We all do.

"I think what you're doing is brave." Marix smiles encouragingly. "She cares about you—anyone can see that."

I squash the tiny glimmer of hope that threatens to grow inside me. It would be too perfect, too easy, and therefore it is impossible to believe.

"We'll see."

Marix looks like she wants to say more, but I excuse myself and head outside, needing a quick escape to clear my mind before I tackle the problem that looms ahead of me. Before I tell Nyia the truth.

***

It's nearly an hour later when I return. My hair is a windblown mess, my cheeks ruddy, but I've never felt more alive. I try to calm my racing heart, to tell myself this is all for the best as I make my way up to the Gold Room, to Nyia's room, to tell her the truth.

I rap on the door with my knuckles, unsure if she is still sleeping, and I am loath to wake her if that is the case, but the door swings open immediately. Nyia's hair is unruly and rumpled, her cheeks are slightly flushed, and her eyes sparkle above her adorable freckles. Her appearance gives the impression she's just enjoyed one of our bedroom sessions, and damn if my dick doesn't harden at the thought. She's so fucking beautiful.

"Darkthorne."

I lift an eyebrow at the old name. Something has put her in a playful mood.

"Temptress," I answer, pushing the door open myself after she fails to step aside. "I came to check on you since you haven't yet made an appearance this morning. I wanted to let you catch up on sleep though."

"Oh, I'm all caught up." Her lips press together, and there is the faintest hint of danger in her eyes.

"Did you sleep well?" I feel my internal guard go up. Something is off, though I can't say what.

"I did." She cocks her head, studying me in a way that is not altogether unpleasant. "And you? How was your morning?"

"Stressful," I answer honestly. I take a seat on the edge of her bed, beckoning her forward. "I missed you. Come here."

She obliges, coming to a stop between my knees and going so far as to pry them open just slightly. She leans her body into mine, twining her slender fingertips around my neck.

"Why so stressed? New developments with Gloriana or the eye? I hope it was nothing I did." She draws that perfect mouth of hers into a pretty little pout, and for a moment all I can think about is pulling her closer, pressing my mouth to hers, and tasting her sweetness once again.

"Impossible. You're the one thing in this world that only brings me joy." My hands come up to rest on her hips, and I press my fingers into her soft flesh. I want her, I always want her, but I hoped to have a serious conversation with her before claiming her once again. I take a deep breath to still my racing heart, to remind myself of the task at hand.

"Hmm. That's interesting."

Mental alarm bells go off at her strange choice of words. I try to think of what she could possibly be thinking. Maybe I pushed her too hard, too fast. She said she bore no love for her husband, but the shock of his death surely hasn't worn off. Fuck me, I've taken advantage of her, and now she's harboring regrets over what we did.

"I could barely think about anything else while I was away from you." I am unsure how to broach this difficult subject. It isn't that I have trouble with honesty; it's the fact that I've never felt this close to anyone before. And I'm terrified of how Nyia will react once she learns the truth.

She leans forward, brushing my lips softly with her own.

"What were you thinking about? This?" She kisses me again, deeper this time, her tongue slipping into my mouth to gently suck on mine. My dick grows painfully hard, straining against the fabric of my pants. I've never wanted anyone as much as I want her. From the moment we met, she has occupied my every thought, and from the first moment I tasted her, I couldn't wait to do it again. She's so fucking passionate. Her mouth moves expertly over mine, and now all I can think about is once again claiming that sweet pussy as mine.

"Yes." I moan against her lips and tighten my hold on her hips, tugging her closer until she's pressed against the length of me, my dick rubbing against her soft abdomen.

"Tell me what else you were thinking about," she says, sinking to her knees. She stares up at me, wide brown eyes blinking and a soft smirk playing on her lips.

"Nyia, wait." As much as I want her—flames above, as much as I *need* to taste her again, I need to slow down. We have yet to have an honest conversation between us, and I literally just promised myself that changes today. I am determined to confess my truth, to tell her everything. But then her soft hands are in my pants, and I forget how to breathe.

"Nyia," I say again. But it's more a moan of pleasure than an admonishment for her to stop.

Moments later she is pulling me free, her slim fingers closing around my dick, firm and yet somehow still whisper-soft as she brings her mouth down to me.

"Nyia, wait," I try again. "We need to talk."

She pauses for just a moment and looks up at me, eyes serious. "Talk? Is there something you need to tell me, Rafael?"

Tell her! my mind screams at me. Tell her now. I hesitate for another moment, unsure what to do. It can wait. Fuck her first, then tell her after. Tell her everything after.

"Nothing," I answer with a soft groan and then her mouth closes around me, and it's hard to think of anything else except for her mouth, that soft pretty mouth, and how it feels wrapped around my dick. She cups my balls and takes me deeper, deeper still. Sucking and pulling and she is so wet, so smooth and perfect I can't help the small whimper that escapes my throat. I've never made that noise before, and if I hadn't completely succumbed to how fucking good she feels, I might have felt embarrassed.

"Nyia . . . Nyia, that feels so good. You're perfect, so fucking perfect." I reach down, fisting my fingers in her tangle of curls so I can fuck her mouth harder, driving as deep as I can, nearly gagging her. She takes it all, little mews of pleasure sounding from the back of her throat, and I think I might come just from the noise alone.

"Don't stop, baby. Right there." She's incredible. She is—

Sudden piercing pain in my leg causes me to spasm. Her teeth skim down the length of my cock as I jerk back, but that pain is nothing compared to the burning sensation in my thigh.

I look down, my eyes glazed and confused as they struggle to focus on Nyia, on the vicious smile spreading across her lips. Then I see the source of the pain—Teo's bejeweled dagger embedded to the hilt in my thigh.

"What the fuck?" I reach for her. To strangle her, to shake her, to place her pretty mouth back on my cock, I don't know, but she scrambles backward just out of reach.

"You're a liar, Rafael. You're a liar, and I hate you." The Nyia who stares back at me is an impostor. This woman is venom and cold vengeance and bears no resemblance to my sweet, brave Nyia.

I try to stand up but curse when I stumble. The blade is buried so deep in my thigh that my muscles spasm when they try to hold me up. And the blood. Already there's so much blood pooling around the weapon, warm and sticky as it slides down my leg.

"What? What did you do?" Nothing makes sense. My Nyia wouldn't stab me, not like this, not after everything. I don't understand.

Nyia backs away, shaking her head and staring at me with vicious contempt. "Don't touch me. You'll never touch me again."

No. She can't mean that. She doesn't mean that. Doesn't she know how much we need her? How much I need her?

"Nyia, please. Whatever happened, whatever this is, don't let it change us—how you feel about us."

"There is no us." She reaches into her pocket and pulls out a phoenix feather. The last one I had in my arsenal. I don't even know when she took it.

The feather burns bright, illuminating her skin, highlighting the breathtaking features of her face. Her full lips, those adorable fucking freckles. And then in a blur of magic, she is gone.

20

Gloriana's Choice

I need to chase after her. I don't know how she managed to stab me so deeply—she must have been burning dragon bone as well. It's the only thing to account for her superhuman strength. She timed everything perfectly. She has no intention of getting caught. I always knew she'd kill me one day; I just didn't know it would be now.

There is a tentative knock at the door, and I groan out in pain as I fumble to gain my footing.

"Rafael? What's happened?" Marix rushes to my side, eyes wide with horror as she takes in the messy scene. Me, crawling on the golden carpet as my crimson blood pools all around me. The image would make for one hell of a tapestry.

"I'll get Cesar." She spins on her heel and is racing down the hall before I can grind out a response. Cesar, unicorn healing—that is a good start.

Flames above, Nyia must have hit an artery. There's no other reason for this much blood. For me to feel so lightheaded. Why did she do this? I refuse to believe that this was her original plan, that she gave herself to me so freely only to attempt to kill me. She . . . We . . . There was something between us. There still *is* something between us. Something worth fighting for.

FAIRY BONES & A DRAGON'S EYE

Cesar races in, falling to his knees at my side. Marix and Teo hover in the doorway. Marix wrings her hands, silent tears streaming down her face. Why is she crying? It's just one stab wound. Cesar should be able to heal this in his sleep. Cesar places his hands on my leg, and I grit my teeth against the pain.

"This is going to hurt," he warns but doesn't give me a moment to process what he means before wrenching the long dagger from my thigh.

"It was embedded in the bone," Cesar says to no one in particular. "Nicked him pretty good, but I can heal him. You'll be fine," he mutters.

I struggle to focus on the soft silver light emanating from his hands.

"Did Nyia do this?" Teo asks, frowning as the dagger is handed back to him.

I don't answer, biting the inside of my cheek as the muscles in my thigh slowly stitch back together.

"She took us all by surprise. I'm guessing she's a sombra, one of the king's assassins." Marix wipes at her face.

I shake my head at the accusation. No, Nyia is nothing more than what she said. We were the liars.

"The eye," I manage to gasp out. "Where is the eye?"

Teo's face pales, but he turns on his heel to retrieve it.

I can locate her with the eye, of course, but that's not why I asked for it. There's only one reason for Nyia to betray me like she has: because she knows I betrayed her first.

Teo returns minutes later, and by then Marix and Cesar have managed to get me on my feet. The wound is healed for the most part. Just a slight discomfort remains as a reminder. Well, the slight pain and my blood that has forever stained my imported carpets.

"Well, did she?" Everyone knows what I'm asking.

"It's gone." He shakes his head. "And I'm pretty sure she was still wearing my boots." He says the last pitifully, like he was the one to lose something he regarded more precious than anything else.

She knows. Maybe not everything, but she knows I've been lying to her. That we all have. I have to find her. I can't leave her out there waiting for Gloriana's assault. Gloriana is more dangerous than she could ever imagine, and I will die a thousand fiery deaths before I let her harm one hair on Nyia's head.

No one says much during the noon meal, a sparse selection of fruits and cheese that no one touches. What is there to say? Not only are we back to square one—we're worse off than ever before. Now we know the king is not only working with a mythic, but one of the Ancients. We've wasted too much time on this plan with Nyia, and I'm worried we won't have the time to locate another Burner and convince them to help us close the gate. We need Nyia back. *I* need her back.

Teo returns just as my enchanted kitchen sends out dessert. I frown at the chocolate cake. Normally it's a favorite, but the thought of it turns my stomach.

"Did you find her?" Marix demands as soon as he enters the dining room. She stands from the table so quickly her chair topples over.

Cesar gives her a long-suffering look before snapping at the chair to return to its place. Marix and I ignore him. She's only acting out what I would like to do.

Teo shakes his head before plopping in his seat and shoveling some cake onto his plate. I let him eat before pestering him with more questions.

Did he thoroughly search her home? Was there any indication she'd been back there? Was he sure he didn't miss her on the roads as he traveled? But there is no sign of her or the dragon eye. She has disappeared.

Humans don't just disappear, not truly. We have to find her. I should have been truthful with her. If only I had hidden the dragon eye in a better spot—or at all—instead of taking it out to rest on the damned table. If only I'd found another way to close the gate. If only I was strong enough to prevent the gate from ever opening. That last one is ridiculous, I know, but I've never felt so helpless in all my life.

I stare into my lap for long moments after our plates are cleared, trying to gather my thoughts and form a course of action.

The letter blinks into existence in front of me. One moment I am staring at a particularly mesmerizing whorl in the grains of cedar, and the next, the folded parchment is there, the scent of roses in the air.

Rafael Ogardojor. My full name is written in precise lettering, and I swallow against the bitter tang of magic. For a wild moment, I think the letter is from Nyia. That she's changed her mind and is open to speaking to me again after all. But after I devour its contents, I realize I couldn't be further from the truth.

Rafael,

May I call you Rafael? Informal, I know, by any standards, but I have it on good authority that is what your friends call you, and I do hope you'll consider me a friend. It has recently come to my attention that you have lost your pet, and even worse, that she has absconded with the dragon eye. How very interesting. It is only a matter of time before she delivers it to me. Perhaps you would like to save us all the trouble and turn yourself in before then?

Of course, you're welcome to say no and we will stay the course of this long game between us. I am so fond of games, but I rather thought you might be interested in an exchange. You for her safety. Do think about it.

Gloriana

I crumple the missive and consider burning it to a pile of ash. The bitch will go after her regardless of what I do. Nyia is nothing more than a tasty morsel for the Ancient to play with. I draw an unsteady breath, hoping to quell my nerves.

"What is it?" Marix asks, eyeing the note with suspicion. "Have you heard from her?"

I wordlessly hand her the note as I consider my options. I can't give myself over to Gloriana; of course I can't. But I also can't leave Nyia alone and defenseless against her greatest enemy, which means I don't really have a choice at all.

21

THE HELPFUL PRINCE

It isn't much later that Marix and I are dressed and ready to leave the safety of my keep. If only I could hide us all within its enchanted walls, sheltering away from any who would do us harm. But that's the coward's way, and my parents taught me more responsibility than that.

"What's the plan?" Marix stretches forward in a show of loosening her muscles, her tiny frame bending toward her toes.

"We find Nyia before Gloriana finds her."

"And the eye?"

"Burn the eye. I'm not worried about it." I would pluck out my only eye and go blind for the rest of my life if it meant she was safe. "We have to find Nyia. We have to."

"We'll find her," Marix says, placing her small hand on my forearm. "I promise you. And I think we both know where we should start."

I can't help the soft groan of disgust at her words, but Marix is right. We have no leads on Nyia's location, but there is someone who might.

Sabastian is, in a word, annoying. I can think of a few other words to describe the human prince like pompous, arrogant, self-centered . . . He's also my strongest connection to the seedy underbelly of mythic underground trade. Sabastian swears no allegiance to anyone, least of all his father, and though I sometimes wonder whether or not Ernesto would be happier with his son dead, I have never witnessed a public altercation between the two. Of course, that doesn't mean there aren't any number of secrets between them. I know I have plenty of my own.

Sabastian agrees to meet me on the outskirts of Nyia's village. Nyia still hasn't returned to her home, though Teo was able to confirm there was at least evidence to suggest she returned at some point for fresh clothing. Her room was packed up, the doors and windows firmly locked. Not that there was any way to deter someone like Teo from gaining entry. He returned with a triumphant smile as he waved his borrowed boots like a trophy.

The prince, while no friend of mine, has proven himself useful time and time again. Part of that is due to Prince Sabastian's good nature toward anything debaucherous, and the other part is how easy it is for Teo to spy on the princeling. Earlier this morning, Teo intercepted his missive from a source claiming to know of a new acquirement for the palace that might interest a collector such as myself. Yeah, consider my interest piqued. If the king is getting mythic parts from a supplier aside from me, it can only mean one thing: Gloriana. If Gloriana used Nyia to get to me, then I will do the same.

And isn't it just like the princeling to be late? *Fucking royals.* As if the world has nothing better to do than wait for their beck and call. I allow my thoughts to drift to Teo and Cesar, each with their own tasks for the evening. We all know how desperately we need our plan to fall into place. Marix waits in the shadows. The prince has my trust for the most part, but Marix would never dream of allowing me to put myself in any danger without her there as backup, and I'm more than happy to oblige her. It's unwise to get on her bad side.

The prince arrives thirty minutes after the agreed upon meeting time. His small contingent of guards spreads out, performing a careful survey of the perimeter. Sabastian allows them to confirm his safety before dismissing them for our privacy. As always, Marix remains unnoticed throughout the guards' search.

"Princeling."

His lips quirk into a smirk that makes my fingers itch to punch him, not that I want to give him the satisfaction of knowing just how much he bothers me. I know he hates when I call him that, so I'll continue to do so until the day I die. Or he does.

"Darkthorne." His smile widens. He knows I detest the nickname as much as he dislikes being called princeling. It was the prince who gave me the name all these years ago, calling me a dark thorn in his father's side. I don't think either one of us knew it would stick.

"Perhaps, just for today, we skip the niceties and get straight to the point. You have information?"

Sabastian pulls his full lips into a pout. The action makes him appear a decade younger than his thirty-odd years. Petulant child. It remains a wonder to me that half the kingdom throws either themselves or their daughters at him. I suppose they can't see what's so obvious to me: the prince is a hedonist who goes through life searching for one pleasure after the next.

"But I do so love the niceties." Prince Sabastian gives me a tiny mock bow. "Tell me, Darkthorne, how have you been?"

"Busy."

The smug smile returns. "I hope the widow Marre has something to do with that. She's a delicious creature."

This time I can't help my hands flexing and clenching into fists at my side. My fingernails bite into my flesh. I wonder how many times I can punch him before his guards have time to react. If I'm quick enough, I could break that perfect nose of his.

"Prince Sabastian, as we've established, I'm busy. Shall we get on with it?" I ask through clenched teeth.

Sabastian chuckles, no doubt reading my reaction well enough to know my line of thinking. "Apologies. As you've said, you're... busy." He gives me a careful once-over, but what he's looking for, I can't say. "My father intends to acquire a new piece for his collection. Gloriana will deliver it later today." Sabastian studies his perfectly manicured fingernails, giving the impression of boredom. It's a ruse, I know. He clearly enjoys baiting me.

My face tightens at the mention of Gloriana. The prince has never mentioned her name before. Is she getting sloppy, allowing the prince and king to know her true identity because she is so close to making her move? Or has the prince always known about Gloriana? How long has she been toying with me?

"Where?" I ask him, my voice tight and clipped with barely concealed rage.

"I'll tell you on one condition."

My fingers flex. "What condition?"

"That you take me with you. I've never seen a unicorn."

My blood runs cold. No, it can't be. Cesar is safe. Word would reach us if he was ever caught. But if it isn't Cesar, and there truly is a captured unicorn, then that means Cesar is wrong. He isn't the last of his kind. Whatever the case, I have to go there. I have to see for myself. I hope the appearance of the alleged unicorn means Gloriana will be distracted. I hope wherever Nyia is, she stays safely hidden until we can find her.

"A unicorn?" I ask, careful to mask any expression other than casual interest.

"That's the claim. And my source isn't the type to lie, if you know what I mean. Father is delighted by the prospect of one, and I have to admit I can't think of anything better than spiriting it away before he has a chance to claim it. He used to tell me stories about them.

They were hunted to extinction back in my grandfather's time. I can't believe one has been here on this island all this time. And just imagine if it's a mare." Sabastian grins. "I even considered keeping this from you but then there is the matter of our agreement."

Ahh yes. Our agreement. That I would pay triple the asking price of any mythic brought into the palace and ten times that amount for any dragon.

"And your . . . fee . . . for such a mythic?" I've never met a royal who enjoys a barter as much as this one. But perhaps he just likes the thrill of the game. The prince holds a nasty reputation at the village gaming hall and the not-so-reputable Goblin Den. Foolish princeling. He probably doesn't even know the rigged games are run by actual goblins. Whatever his knowledge, he knows enough that I have no doubt the price is about to be exorbitant.

"Well . . ." the prince drawls. He makes a show of looking around before leaning forward with a wink. "It is believed to be the last of its kind."

No, not the last, but damn near close enough. *Because they're not Cesar,* I promise myself. They haven't caught Cesar. My chest tightens, and I dare a quick glance near the trees where Marix remains concealed in shadows. She hasn't made a sound, but I imagine she is livid.

"I'll accept one hundred times the usual rate. This mythic being especially rare, of course."

"Of course." I force out a smile. I have no idea why he asks for the money; he and his father are already the richest men on the island. But then, the cost of greed has no limits.

"Brilliant." Sabastian spreads his arms wide. "If it's all settled, should we be off? You can ride in my carriage."

"I have my own transportation. I'll meet you there." There is no way in hell I'll allow myself to be stuck in a moving carriage with this man. Of course, Sabastian should have noticed there is no carriage of my own around.

The prince's expression darkens for a moment, but he nods in acceptance. "You're an interesting adversary."

"Adversary, am I?" My lips press together.

"Advocate," he says smoothly. "I always get those two words confused."

22

A RESCUE MISSION

Marix waits for all of thirty seconds after the prince's exit before dropping down in front of me, her compact body poised in a crouch, her expression wary.

"It's not Cesar," she says, though it's hard to believe the sincerity of her words when I note the steady tremble in her voice. She runs a shaky hand through her purple and silver curls.

"It's not," I agree. Although I'm tempted to fly home just to make sure. How could Cesar have been wrong? If there truly is another unicorn, how did we miss them? How have they remained hidden all this time, and why haven't they reached out to Cesar? His identity is a secret, true, but there are those who know—another unicorn would know . . . wouldn't they?

"What if it's a trap?" Marix asks.

She voices my concerns. Has Sabastian finally tired of our long-standing agreement? Perhaps he's discovered my desire to close the gate. What if he told his father? Or Ernesto told him his suspicions, and now he's working with his father against me? Even if it is a trap, I have to go, but that doesn't mean I have to put anyone else in danger.

"Oh, no. Don't you dare." Marix places her hands on her hips, glaring up at me.

"Don't dare what?"

"Don't you dare suggest I get back to the keep where 'it's safe.' I can take care of myself, you know. And I'm not letting you near this exchange without someone there to watch your back."

She knows me so well. And she's right. She would never let me face danger alone. It's one of the many things I love about her.

"I would never dream of it." I smile, even though I was about to do just that. "I assume you're ready to go?"

"Whenever you are." She bares her teeth in her semblance of a smile. "Race you there."

She's off before I can stop her, and I'm forced into motion even though I have little hope of catching up to her. She's always been faster than me.

***

Marix is nowhere to be found when I arrive. The docks are nearly empty at this hour, the workers and fishermen likely headed home to their wives or the village taverns. Each of the storage buildings stretching along the docks belongs to King Ernesto but there is little question to which is utilized for mythic transport. The large building dominates the others, and its square appearance reminds me of a hunched giant. Not that I've seen a giant in the last decade.

I beat Sabastian's carriage, but to his credit the prince doesn't seem surprised.

He simply wags his finger at me. "One day you're going to tell me how you do that."

It's a secret I intend to take to the grave. I only shrug in response.

"Gloriana's associates should be here already with the mythic. But unless we've missed him, the king shouldn't be here for another hour. That gives you enough time to procure the creature?" Sabastian waves off his entourage of guards and checks the sword sheathed at his side. I wonder if the decorative blade has ever actually seen bloodshed but don't bother to ask.

"Maybe you should wait outside," I suggest. The last problem I need to add to this mess is a dead princeling.

"And give you the chance to do whatever magic you use and whoosh away before I get a proper look? I think not." He gestures vaguely with his hand and whooshes in imitation of my assumed magic. "I've heard Burners use phoenix feathers to teleport."

"Do they?" I ask, refusing to give him the answer he so desperately craves.

"One of these days," he repeats. But he lets the matter drop and gestures for me to follow him to the side of the building to a smaller one in its shadow.

"We'll enter here from the side. The door will be locked, but there is only one guard stationed on this side. I figure that won't be a problem for someone with your talents?"

"Nope, not a problem." I roll my shoulders and neck, loosening my muscles in anticipation. It would be easier without the prince lurking, watching my every move, but there is no getting rid of him now.

I follow Sabastian around the side of the single-story warehouse. I've never entered this smaller one before. The ceilings aren't exactly low, but certainly short enough to suggest any mythic inside would be of average size. Not that unicorns are known for their bulk. Plus ogres, giants, and trolls know better than to hover around humans.

I pull out a slender dagger, not that I need the thing, but I don't want to give Sabastian more of a show than he deserves.

I crouch low to the ground, and Sabastian follows my lead as we scurry toward the side entrance he indicates. I can handle a single guard in my sleep, but my senses remain on high alert. I still can't shake the idea that this might be a trap, that instead of a single guard around the corner, there will be a dozen armed soldiers lying in wait, prepared to arrest me for all my traitorous acts.

But when we turn the corner of the building, no one is there. I turn to meet Sabastian's stunned expression and, unless he's a far better actor than I give him credit for, he's just as surprised as I am. I trade my dagger into my left hand and adjust my eye patch, still unused to its presence, even after all this time. I stand perfectly still, shushing Sabastian until he presses himself against the wall of the abandoned building. Did the guard abandon his post? Did the prince have the location wrong? I glance around, searching for clues. There. Nearly two dozen paces to my right, propped up against a tree, is the missing guard. At first glance I think he is dead, his neck cocked at an awkward angle that would be uncomfortable for anyone to manage for any length of time, but then I note the steady rise and fall of his chest and realize he's just sleeping . . . no, unconscious. I note the twin trenches leading from the door to our warehouse to the distant tree. He was knocked unconscious and then dragged to the tree, his sturdy guard boots leaving furrows in the dirt.

Marix? But it isn't her style to leave remains. Besides she wouldn't have interfered unless I gave her the signal.

Now I note the door, not quite open, but definitely no longer locked and secure. I turn back to look at Sabastian and see he's drawn the same conclusion.

"Someone got here before us."

Understanding dawns on his face, and I detect the faintest shade of red darkening his tanned cheeks.

"Fuck," he mumbles. "I think I know who."

"Are we compromised?" Why the hell would he have told anyone else about our intended escapade? Had he drunkenly confessed our plans in his local pub? I wouldn't be surprised. "You should wait here," I tell him, not bothering to soften the tone from anything but the gruff command it is.

The prince only bristles slightly at being bossed around by someone he considers his lesser.

"No, let me talk to her. She—"

But then a familiar scent catches on the evening breeze, and my heart stutters in my chest. There is no need for Sabastian to explain who he's told.

Nyia.

23

SHE HAS ME

Fuck. What is she doing here?

I spin on my heel and face Sabastian, shoving him against the building wall.

"What is she doing here?"

The prince doesn't bother to ask who I'm talking about, though I know it bothers him I know of her presence without even seeing her. But how can I explain that her scent is tattooed on my heart, that I would know her anywhere, even if I was blind and not the miserable one-eyed beast that I am?

"I only mentioned it to her in passing. I didn't know she would come here. I never thought—why would she . . ." He trails off as his brain connects the dots, surprising me that he grasps the situation so quickly. "She's a Burner—you both are."

"Stay here."

He moves to follow me, but I shove him back to the wall with so much force his teeth come together with an audible click, biting off any protest he might have made.

"Don't move. I'll call for you if your presence is needed." I shove my forearm against his neck and glare down at him. I may only have him by a single inch, but Sabastian's eyes are wild as they meet mine, and he manages a single nod before I release him.

I open the door of the warehouse and am immediately plunged into darkness. Logic tells me there must be other guards stationed inside, surely several around the unicorn, so I move as stealthily as I can, carefully placing the heel of my boots one in front of the other, watchful of my surroundings.

The warehouse is mostly empty, a few shipping crates and a low table and chairs near the entrance. I creep to the nearest shipping crate and note the spaced holes throughout the top third of the box. My chest tightens when I realize what they're for.

The transport of living mythics. The king has moved on to what I always knew was an inevitability for him. He is no longer content to maintain his personal collection. No longer content to watch his Burners play with discarded parts. He moved on from his warped menagerie and now intends to share his possessions with the rest of the world. He's shipping mythics away from the island, back to the human world where there will be no hope of escape. I have less time than I thought. I need to close the veil now. Which means it is all the more important I find Nyia and win her back to my cause.

I rush along the length of the shipping crate, pleased to see that it, along with the ones near it, are all empty. How much time do I have? Gloriana is obviously providing him with the means to acquire more mythics. Dozens of them if the empty containers are any indication. But where did she find the means to procure them all? After the first reaping, nearly all the mythics shifted into their human forms. It was too dangerous otherwise. Unless . . . the dragon eye. My blood turns to ice. No wonder the dragon eye holds such importance. No wonder Nyia is so desperate to find it. It explains everything. Why Gloriana wants the dragon eye. Why she threatened the Burner who can wield it. I need to find Nyia and get her the fuck out of the city, away from all of this. Find Nyia. Beg her forgiveness. Close the gate to the veil. And pray Marix will be strong enough to lead them on her own. Fuck.

I've nearly crossed the length of the warehouse by the time they finally come into view. *She* comes into view. She is glorious. Nyia is here, teeth bared as she clutches the remains of the dragon talon between her hands. She's burned over half of it, the scent of sulfur in the air as she burns more still.

"Give me the key now, and I'll consider allowing you to live," she says through gritted teeth.

I swallow hard and try to force back the rising panic at seeing her in danger. She is surrounded by four men, not in the familiar red and gold of palace guards, but in dark shades of various leathers. Gloriana's men, then. If only it were just the guards. I'll need to act quickly.

One of the men laughs, the sound shrill and manic.

"Little human like you. We're not afraid."

She narrows her eyes, bracing her feet apart as she burns more of the dragon claw. "You should be."

Why doesn't she have the dragon eye with her? If she burned even a bit of the eye, she would see the men for what they truly are: mythics.

I crouch low, pressing myself against the side of the final crate, willing them not to see me in the shadows. I'm about to sprint forward when Nyia turns, and I finally catch a glimpse of what she's protecting.

Flames above, Cesar was wrong. He's not the last of his kind. The young woman lies on the floor, hair so long it covers most of her exposed body. So young—in her late teens in this human form—but her ageless eyes glare at the men full of hate. Her long hair is a strange combination of pink and gold, her eyes glowing with the same hue. Some ageless instinct must seize her because her eyes drift toward me, staring into my soul even though I'm still hidden. I know in that moment she sees me for what I really am.

One of the mythics, an ugly troll, leaps forward, aiming to snatch the claw from Nyia's hands. But she must have been burning more dragon claw than he thought because she sidesteps his attack, moving so quickly she is just a blur of color. Another of the mythics lunges toward her, but she stops him with a swift knee to his groin. He falls over, moaning loudly. She pivots tightly, swinging the claw in a high arc above her head and connecting it with the skull of her next attacker with a vicious crack. The man drops instantly, but over half of the remaining dragon claw crumbles into ash, covering her arm in silvery soot.

She frowns at the claw, now about the size of a dagger, and doesn't hesitate for another second before plunging it into the chest of the next man.

"Nice tricks. But what will you do now, Burner? You haven't got any more dragon to burn." The mythic sneers at her, helping his companion off the floor.

I make my move, stepping out of the shadows with a sinister grin.

"She has me."

24

Part Three

25

ON THE ROAD HOME

NYIA

I surprised myself with how easy it was to stab Rafael. I was high on the strength of the dragon claw as I plunged the dagger in all the way to the hilt. I still feel nothing but anger. Dark, all-encompassing anger that begins from a rumble in my chest where my heart might have been. Rafael didn't see it coming, but it is little comfort that he is just as blinded by the betrayal as I was by his deceit.

After it happened, I was frozen for a moment or two, blinking at the pain etched into the familiar lines of his face, at the blood, so much blood flowing from his thigh. I told myself I should pull the dagger out. Make him bleed out faster, give myself a weapon as I make my escape. But . . . I couldn't. I needed Cesar to fix him, to heal him. Because as much as I hate this man, I don't want him dead.

I am back in Raf's room where I've stashed the dragon claw. I frown at the remains of the phoenix feather. It isn't much, but gods willing I will be able to burn the last of it to make my escape. There's just one other thing I need. I press myself against the wall behind the doorway as Marix walks by, her steps slow as she moves down the hall, which means she hasn't discovered Raf yet.

Shit. I'm running out of time. I clutch the phoenix feather between my fingertips and will it to transport me to the dining room. It's a frivolous waste considering I haven't got much left and doubt it will even be enough to take me to the clearing outside the keep, but I can't risk Marix spotting me in the halls.

The dining room is blissfully empty and there it is, still resting on the edge of the far end of the table. The dragon eye.

The eye is a perfect orb, a mix of swirling colors against stark white and large enough I need two hands to lift it, though it isn't particularly heavy. There is a sheen to the eye that makes the colors iridescent like stained glass. You would think it would be sticky, but it is smooth and warm to the touch. I scoop it up, hefting it against my chest and grunting under its familiar weight.

The phoenix feather is now woefully depleted, but if the commotion upstairs is anything to go by, I haven't got much time. I need it to get me out of there fast, to take me and the dragon eye out of the keep and anywhere else. Anywhere but here.

It's a terrible thought to have while burning. Magic is always unpredictable, but Burners can have some essence of control with practiced intent. Burning the feather and screaming at it to take me anywhere could have had disastrous results. I could have burned to the bottom of the lake, to Gloriana, back to the glade with the wisps—anywhere.

I am thrown against the hard-packed dirt of a road, and I roll with the impact. I clutch the small fortune of dragon parts tightly to my chest, and though my elbows nearly make me scream in pain as they scrape along the loose gravel, I am able to hang on.

I groan as I struggle to stand without the support of either hand, but I manage to make it to my feet. The phoenix feather is completely gone, of course, and while the dragon eye and claw are emanating heat, they appear to be intact.

I look around, noting the midmorning position of the sun. The road is barely cobbled, and there is no one in sight, but the road seems to be one well-traveled so I walk along the side of it, hoping my surroundings will eventually become familiar. If this is a road that leads into town from the border of the colony, I can follow it all the way back to my house. I swallow. Martin's house. I have nothing now. The widow Marre. I should have inherited his fortune, small that it was, but instead I've inherited nothing but debt and trouble. I've inherited Gloriana.

I square my shoulders and start walking. I walk for perhaps an hour, just long enough for blisters to begin working on my heels from my too-tight boots. If nothing else, I will be grateful to get home and finally change into my own clothing. Although I will miss Rafael's enchanted baths.

There it is again, that familiar sound. A carriage. The steady sound of clipped, synchronized hoofbeats traveling this way both frightens and soothes me.

"Friend or foe?" I wonder aloud, if only to quiet my racing heart. I press back into shadows offered by the creeping edge of the surrounding jungle, away from the road, but the carriage man must have spotted me anyway because the carriage slows to a stop.

I refuse to move, just in case they haven't actually spotted me, but after a moment, the driver hops from his seat to open the door for his passenger.

"Are you in some sort of trouble, señora?" The voice is familiar, though I can't say from where. He peers into the shadows and I don't dare move. "If you need a ride back to the village, I'm happy to escort you. Or I can send guards from the palace if you would prefer."

He's persistent, I'll give him that. I shove the dragon claw behind my back. Under Teo's loose shirt, it tracks the length of my spine, and I tuck the tip into the waistband of my pants. There really isn't much to do with the dragon eye except shove it in my satchel. It doesn't quite fit, the satchel now too stretched to close properly, and if anyone were to look closely, they would notice the soft light emanating from it, but it will have to do.

"I give you my word, no harm will come to you. Let me assist you home. These roads are not safe, especially so close to the jungle. Please, allow—"

"Your Highness?" I blink up at that annoyingly beautiful face that has no business belonging to a man. He really is too pretty for his own good. The too-long eyelashes over his intense blue eyes are ridiculous.

"Guilty." He holds up both hands, palms out as if to stop my advances.

I still haven't joined him on the road, but there isn't any point in holding out now when I've already given myself away by addressing him.

"Yes, please, come into the comfort of the carriage. It's my duty to see all my citizens safely home, of course, but it is a special privilege to escort a beauty such as yourself." His voice oozes hospitality, and I roll my eyes. At least I know he is truly harmless.

"Thank you, Your Highness." I step forward, and he inhales sharply as the dazzling sunlight reveals my identity.

"Señora, we have met before, I believe."

"We have." I press my lips together in a tight smile and dip into the impression of a curtsy, just deep enough so as not to be considered rude. "At your father's masquerade." Was that only a few days ago? It feels as if a lifetime has passed since then.

Confusion spreads over his face for just a moment but then he snaps his fingers as the memory comes to him.

"The widow Marre."

"Nyia, please."

That sensual smile spreads across his lips. "Nyia. It's a pleasure to be reacquainted." He peers behind me as if affirming I am truly alone, and I wonder if he is looking for Rafael.

"You said you can give me a ride back to the village?" I prompt with a slight raise of my eyebrows.

"But of course. Your wish is my command." He gestures wide, and I fall into step beside him, flinching slightly as his hand slides into place at the dip of my back.

He leans his arm forward to assist me into the carriage, but I ignore the proffered hand, clutching the satchel with my contraband tightly to my chest.

"To the Marre property?" he asks before climbing in after me.

"Actually, the Den of the Huntress, please. Do you know it?"

"I know it well." He tilts his head, tsking. "Out for a bit more fun, are we?"

"Something like that." I settle against the plush seat. "I need to visit a friend."

26

THE DEN OF THE HUNTRESS

The pub is lively as ever despite the early hour, and though I tell the prince to leave me, he insists on escorting me inside. The host nearly swoons at the sight of him, and we are welcomed with a flourish. We are directed to a corner booth, and I am surprised to find one empty until I realize it was recently occupied by other patrons who were quickly evicted upon the prince's arrival.

He orders a flagon of wine, and I take small sips from the offered tin goblet as I scan the pub in search of Sienna. The Huntress makes her rounds, a suggestive touch on a shoulder, a delicate whisper in one's ear. It's obvious to anyone searching for telltale clues, but to the average person, it all appears innocent.

She catches me staring and lifts her chin just slightly in acknowledgment. Moments later, she sidles toward our booth, eyes widening at the prince.

"Your Highness." She dips into a low curtsy, flashing the prince a dazzling view of her ample chest. Sienna holds out a hand, her slender fingers begging to be kissed, but I all but leap over Sabastian to grab her hand before he can touch her. I don't know if she planned to use any of her powers on the unsuspecting prince, and I haven't the time to find out.

"Excuse us," I say over my shoulder to Sabastian and pull the startled succubus after me.

"Nyia, that hurts." She pouts, snatching her hand back and rubbing her wrist.

I'm startled to see dark fingerprints mottling her flesh. I must have been burning the dragon claw without realizing it.

I take a deep breath to still my racing heart.

"I need your help," I whisper.

She peers over my shoulder at Sabastian, who is obliviously drinking his wine.

"I'd say you're doing just fine," she drawls. "Your human prince is certainly a step up from Martin."

I ignore the suggestive smirk she gives me and start again, thrusting my dirty satchel toward her.

She frowns but is forced to take it from me to avoid it dropping on the floor or smearing her spotless dress.

"Here. Take this."

"What is it?" She pulls at the leather thongs barely holding it closed, and I slap my hand over hers.

"No! Don't open it. Please, just hide this for me. I'll be back for it later."

Her eyes widen. "There's enough magic buzzing in this bag to power a small army of Burners. What have you gotten yourself into?"

"I'll explain everything later. Just hang on to it for a few hours, okay? I'll be back for it later—tonight."

Sienna looks like she wants to argue, but she nods and leaves for the upper rooms of the brothel, hopefully to stash the bag someplace safe.

I head back to Sabastian, surprised to find him deep in conversation with someone. The newcomer is nearly as short as he is wide with twinkling brown eyes and wild red hair floating about his head. A smile stretches across his face, and his already ruddy cheeks blush to a deep purple before he meets my gaze.

"Ah, just in time." He bows deeply to the prince before turning to me with a flourish. "Her beauty is unmatched," he says, allowing his eyes to roam the length of my body. He reaches out a hand, but for some reason I take a marked step back. The man doesn't seem to take offense. If anything, his smile widens.

"Allow me to present myself. I am——"

I blink. His name is what? I don't have time for this. Now that I have the eye, I need to come up with some sort of plan. I no longer trust Rafael, and I can't face Gloriana alone.

"I need a private moment with His Highness." My voice sounds thick in my ears, and I rub at my arms.

The mysterious man's eyes narrow as his smile slowly fades. "Of course. I'm sure you have much to . . . discuss." He gives me one last leering look before turning back to Prince Sabastian and clearing his throat in exaggerated fashion.

The prince hands him a small purse that jingles, heavy with coin, and once again the man is all smiles.

"Your Highness." He bows again before tipping his head toward me. "Nyia."

I stiffen. How does he know my name? And where did he come from? Wasn't it just me and Sabastian in the booth? I am about to ask him but he is gone, disappearing from sight and leaving only a faint shimmer of magic in the air. I shake my head to clear it.

"A Burner?" I ask, wrinkling my nose. I know Rafael and I aren't the only ones in the kingdom, but as a general rule, we tend to keep our identities secret. It irks me that the man clearly knows who I am and I've never met him before.

"Something like that." Sabastian smiles, but it doesn't quite meet his eyes. "More wine?" He pours the remainder of the flagon into a glass and thrusts it toward me, frowning at the dark liquid as it sloshes over the rim and spills down his fingers.

"I think I've had enough," I say pointedly. I would never presume to tell the prince he should finish as well, but he seems to get the hint.

"Where to next, my beauty? Shall I procure us a room?"

I suspect his grin is meant to be charming, but I notice the drunken slur to his words that are anything but. "I think we should both go home. To our homes. Separately." I stare at him until he seems to get the point. He sighs and reaches into his pocket, leaving another small purse of coins on the table. I eye the money warily. It's more than enough for our wine—enough for wine for the entire pub, likely—but I figure the barmaid has earned it if she had to put up with even one suggestive smile from this one.

"Come on. Can you walk?" I wasn't talking to Sienna for that long. How did he get so drunk? I was under the assumption most royals knew how to hold their spirits, though I suppose Sabastian is the only royal with whom I have a first-name friendship. Did he catch me on his way home after a long night of partying? He didn't seem this drunk before . . . did he?

Sabastian stumbles to his feet, and I loop my arm around his waist to steady him. His stomach is nothing but hard planes of muscle, and he leans far too much of his weight against me. I grunt and half carry, half drag him out of the brothel. The prince is such a lightweight. Or . . . I frown at the sudden realization: he's been drugged.

Something nags at the back of my mind, a memory I just can't reach. We talked to someone besides Sienna . . . didn't we? I remember frizzy red hair and a mischievous smile.

"Who was that man?" I ask aloud. The words are a labored grunt as Sabastian stumbles again and we almost topple over. The point of the dragon claw digs into my skin, and I'm once again reminded of its presence. I burn a bit more so I can hold Sabastian's weight with ease.

"What man?"

"Your . . . the man . . ." I trail off, struggling to remember the name he gave me. It is the oddest thing. The more I try to remember the man, the more the memory of him fades away, dancing on the outskirts of my thoughts.

"Ah." Sabastian gives me an exaggerated wink. "You mean——" Once again, as soon as I hear it, the name fades from my memory. "He has that effect on people." He taps the dainty silver ring on the little finger of his left hand. The only problem is he chose to do so with his right hand, which causes his massive arms to loop tightly around my neck in a gagging chokehold, once again throwing me off balance. I burn a bit more of the dragon claw to stay upright. I need to lose this deadweight before I burn it all on him.

"You need one of these."

"Your ring?" I have no choice but to stare at it since my face is still locked in place, inches from his hand. The ring is a thin silver band with dark-purple engravings etched into the stone in a language I don't recognize. Not that I speak anything other than the native tongue.

Sabastian nods solemnly. "It's the only way to keep him here." He slurs, releasing his hold around my neck to tap his temple for emphasis. "Otherwise, he goes poof." He mimics the effect by squeezing his hand into a fist and then flicking his fingers outward.

"But who is he?" I press, more interested than I want to let on. I haven't heard of a mythic with these abilities. And if he can also mimic a human, what will stop him from confusing every human he encounters? I have a sneaking suspicion I would be in more trouble if I wasn't burning the dragon claw. Sabastian claims the ring protects him from the effects of the mythic, but that doesn't seem to be entirely the case. "How do you know him?"

"He's an associate of the king."

The king—not his father. I blink at the information.

"But he works for me," Sabastian says. He beams down at me, his expression proud. "You're very attractive, did you know that?"

"Thank you." I tug him toward his carriage, grateful for his men who rush forward to help me. They don't seem at all surprised to find their prince intoxicated.

"We should get back to my rooms at the palace. We could have fun together, you and I." He wriggles his eyebrows in a suggestive manner, and I roll my eyes.

"No, thank you. But I would appreciate a ride back to my home." I climb into the carriage after him, shoving him deeper into the box when he refuses to make room for me.

"Why?"

"Why do I wish to go home?"

"No, why don't you want to go home with me?"

I think of Rafael and bite my cheek in annoyance. Rafael should have nothing to do with this conversation. I'm a free woman. If I wanted to bed the prince, I could. I remember the silhouette of his body I glimpsed at the masquerade and feel heat rush to my cheeks at the thought. He is more than ample and willing, and yet . . . Stupid Rafael.

"I prefer not to sleep with men prettier than me," I say, and the prince guffaws in response.

"Take the widow home!" he yells to his driver and slaps the side of the carriage door.

His shout is loud enough to be heard inside the brothel, and I wince at the scene we must be causing. Not that I care a bit about my reputation, but I'd rather not draw unnecessary attention to the current location of the dragon eye.

"You are though. Very beautiful."

"Thank you. You were telling me about . . ." Damn. Once again, the man's name eludes me. What sort of magic is that? "You said he . . . works for you?"

"He's a spy," Sabastian says in a loud stage whisper. He's lucky the carriage is moving at a clipped pace now as His Highness has no concept of being quiet.

"A spy?"

"Yup. That's how I know about the unicorn."

I stiffen, clenching my hands in my lap so they don't cover my mouth in shock. Certainly, he doesn't mean Cesar. He can't. And yet, Cesar is the last of his kind. Rafael told me himself.

Sabastian leans his head back against the cushions and begins to play with my hair. He looks at me through half-lidded eyes.

"Does he tell you you're pretty?"

"Your spy?"

"No. Don Darkthorne." He narrows his eyes. "Because he should. I would tell you you're pretty all the time."

"I think I believe you would."

He beams.

"Tell me about the unicorn." I try to keep my tone casual, but my hands are so tightly clenched that my knuckles have paled.

"Ah, a unicorn. The rarest of the mythics. More so than a dragon. Not even Darkthorne has been able to procure one."

"But that man told you about one. He knows where it is?"

"He's the one who captured it." Sabastian closes his eyes. "It's probably a good idea you're going home. I'm tired." He yawns as if to prove his point.

"No, no, no." I lean forward, clutch his shoulders, and give him a harsh shake.

"Ouch." His eyes fly open, and he rubs the back of his neck. "You're strong, you know that?"

Damn it, I'm burning more dragon claw. I've never burned without realizing it before. I am really off my game. I take a deep breath, inhaling slowly through my nose and exhaling through clenched teeth.

"Sabastian. What did he tell you about the unicorn?"

"Who?"

Curse it all. I can't remember the man's name either. I try another tactic.

"I've never seen a unicorn before." I make my tone wistful and place a hand over his, looking deep into his eyes and batting my lashes. "I wish I knew someone who could show me one, but no one knows where one is."

"Hey, I know where we can find one! My father is receiving one tonight. It will be in his warehouse," Sabastian says. He leans forward, so close our noses are practically touching. "It's on the edge of the east side of the pier. The abandoned building with the gray-and-blue roof. I can take you there after . . ." He trails off, blinking at me. "You're really pretty."

I sigh. It's going to be a long night.

27

Manticore Toenails

The carriage stops abruptly, and I heave the door open with more strength than necessary as I leap out.

"Don't leave yet," I call over my shoulder. "I have something for you." At least I hope I do. What Sabastian needs more than anything is to get home to his bed to sleep it off, but I can't in good conscience leave him this way. The problem is, aside from dragon parts, I don't have anything left to burn. Gloriana saw to the chupacabra quill, not that its magic could help the prince. The increased strength of the dragon claw might help him metabolize the poison better, but no . . . maybe those manticore toenails will work in a pinch if I can shove one down his throat.

I'm fiddling with my front door when Sabastian's nose slams into the back of my neck.

"What are you doing?"

"You told me to follow you."

"No, I said wait for me in the carriage."

"You said not to leave," he corrects.

I make a sound that is very much a growl and gently—well, as gently as I can manage—shove Sabastian back to my curb.

"Just wait here. I'll be right back."

Moments later I literally force-feed him the toenails and tuck him back into his carriage, too eager to watch them drive away.

Finally, I'm back home and I have the dragon eye. I should feel accomplished, but instead I just feel lonely. What am I supposed to do now? I go to my room, frowning at my meager belongings. The chair I used to restrain Rafael is still in the center of my room, the jagged lengths of rope still at the chair's feet. Aside from the chair and my bed, there is only a single chest beside my mirror. The rest of the room is woefully empty. Most of our possessions have been sold to pay for Martin's massive debt, but I have a few personal belongings. Worn leather pants and undergarments and, most importantly, my boots. I take off Teo's and nearly moan with relief. They may be nicer than my scuffed and worn pair, but at least mine fit. I wriggle my toes and pack up the remainder of my things, taking little time to marvel knowing everything I own fits into a single bag. After sharing my supply with Sabastian, I have a single manticore toenail, the dragon claw, and the eye . . . which I left with Sienna.

I wonder if I should go back across town to retrieve it now but eventually decide the time I would spend retrieving it is not time I have to spare. Cesar is counting on me. And yeah, he was a jerk to me literally from the moment we met, but he also saved my life. I owe that unicorn a fighting chance.

I hurry down the stairs, pausing in my doorway for the briefest of moments. If I leave now, there is no turning back. There's a chance Rafael, Marix, and Teo are already on their way to rescue Cesar. Rafael certainly has enough dragon bones in his arsenal to equip himself with everything they need to make the rescue. Do I want to see them again? A small part of me wonders if that's not the reason I'm so willing to fight for Cesar, but another part of me knows this is the right thing to do. What if I'm Cesar's only hope of rescue? If the others don't even know he was taken? Or what if they can't find him in time? I know all too well what the king has planned for his mythic treasures. I sigh. It's up to me to save him.

I take one last lingering look at the place I called home for the last eight years of my life. I once believed I could be happy here, but that belief died long ago, long before I lost my childhood fantasies and longer still since I lost my husband.

Good riddance. And I close the door behind me.

28

ROSADELA

Once again, I've severely overestimated my abilities. I am outnumbered, outmagicked, and in a matter of time, I will be dead. I choke back a strangled cry of sorrow for me and the poor girl in chains behind me.

I don't regret a thing. Sure, the unicorn isn't Cesar, but this girl needs help. She needed a hero, and I will die trying to be one.

I'm not the best fighter, but I give it my all, burning as much of the dragon claw as I can and attacking with a fury I didn't know I had inside me. For a moment, I thought I had a chance of winning, that I could save the girl and get us both out of here alive.

But then the last of the dragon claw burned to ash, and I realize just how foolish I am. I'm outmatched, and now, not only have I failed to save the girl, I've failed to save myself. I'll never be able to retrieve the dragon eye. Never get to leave this village, the island . . . will never see Rafael again.

So stupid. Why do I even care about Rafael? It's not like he cares about me. He's a liar, a thief, and he . . . He is here, walking out of the shadows.

He moves like a man possessed. His body is lithe, fluid like a lost dance, and only he remembers the movements. He sidesteps a punch, moving faster than my eyes can track, ducking low to land a swift punch to the other man's gut, then kicking him in the knee. There is a loud crack and the man crumples, but Rafael doesn't spare him another glance as he moves on to the other man limping toward him.

"I know who you are," the man says, pointing at Rafael. His lip curls up, illustrating his disgust. "You're the d—"

His words are cut off with a sickening crack as Rafael twists his neck so viciously, it's a wonder he doesn't rip it clear from his shoulders.

Afterward he is panting in the center of the felled bodies, now dead, where I left them unconscious but still breathing. I knew he had a reputation for being a good fighter, but that was unlike anything I've ever seen before. I don't know what to make of it.

"Are you okay?" he asks me, chest heaving. His single eye glows brightly, burning into my soul.

"I'm fine." I tear my eyes from him and squat next to the young woman chained to the floor. She stares up at me with wide eyes, but I know she isn't frightened—not of me. "Don't worry, we're going to get you out of here." I frown at the sturdy paddock of the chains. Surely rope would have been enough to suffice.

"Here." Rafael tosses something shiny toward me, and I catch it instinctively, though I don't recognize it for what it is until it's in my hand. The key.

I move quickly, fitting it into the lock and freeing the girl while Rafael continues his search of the dead men's pockets. Once I remove all the chains, I hold my hand down toward her. She blinks at it for a moment before grasping it, and I pull her to her feet.

Her steps are uneasy, a bit like a newborn colt, though I suppose that has something to do with the fact that her long legs have been forced under her for so long.

"Thank you." Her voice is scratchy and hoarse from lack of use or perhaps screaming. There are quite a few bruises in various places on her skin.

"Here."

I turn to see Rafael's outstretched arm, a garment suspended from his fingers.

I blink at him. He's removed his shirt. A gallant gesture, but why does he have to be so damned nice and so muscular at the same time.

The girl's eyes widen even more in shock, something I wouldn't have thought she was capable of just moments before, and she dips into an awkward curtsy, nearly stumbling over her own legs. Raf catches her by the elbow and mutters something under his breath, and I swear he's blushing.

"Please, there's no need . . . Just put this on." He practically forces the shirt on the girl, and she resembles a small doll playing dress-up in the oversized garment.

"There. You're safe now. We'll get you fed and rested, and you can return to your form in no time." Rafael's voice is impossibly gentle, and I'd be lying if I said the sound of it didn't make me weak in the knees just a bit. *Don't be stupid, Nyia.* He can't be trusted. But this girl trusts him—I can see it her eyes. She stares at Rafael like he is a god brought down just for her.

She nods slowly, her eyes solemn.

"Can you tell us your name?" Raf asks, his tone still impossibly soft and gentle.

"Rosadela," she answers. "Thank you both." Her voice is mellifluous, and I find myself leaning forward, hanging on her every word.

"Rosadela, do you feel ready to walk?" I glance around the empty warehouse, my shoulders tense with unease. "We need to get you out of here before reinforcements arrive."

There is a loud bang on the opposite side of the warehouse, and for a moment, my heart sinks. We've run out of time! But the sound is only the heavy door slamming open with the arrival of Sabastian.

He frowns at the scene around us, at the bodies on the floor and the young woman cowering under Rafael's shoulders.

"What's going on in here?" he asks. "Who's that?"

29

YOUR SECRET'S SAFE WITH ME

I'm about to explain who Rosadela is, but Rafael stops me with the smallest shake of his head.

"Is she all right?" Sabastian looks around the room, noting the men on the floor, the chain marks bruising Rosadela's wrists and ankles. A muscle ticks in his jaw. "They got a quicker death than they deserved," he says grimly. "I can't believe they would use the excuse of transporting mythics to cover their human trafficking."

Sabastian looks horrified, and Rafael doesn't bother to correct his assumption. I once assumed a human form was limited to mythics like Sienna, mythics who fed off humans and therefore needed to blend in. But that isn't true at all. I've seen it proven otherwise time and again throughout this last week. Cesar, Teo, Gloriana, and her boys—all mythics masquerading as humans. Can all mythics take human form? And if that is the case, how many hide among us?

"Come, my carriage is outside. We'll get her to an infirmary."

"No!" Rafael and I shout at the same time, and Sabastian startles from our sudden explosion.

"My friend Marix is . . . a healer," Rafael says. "She'll want a woman's touch," he says pointedly and Sabastian nods.

"Marix is here?" I ask Rafael.

"She is. She's been here this entire time, waiting." He answers so softly I am forced to lean closer just so I can hear him.

I nod, biting the inside of my cheek as his familiar scent washes over me. Rosadela is silent, golden eyes darting back and forth at the exchange.

Marix is indeed just outside the warehouse, leaning casually against the wall. Her face lights up when she sees me.

"Nyia! You're here. Are you . . ." She trails off as she catches sight of Rafael, and she rushes forward, ripping off her cloak to drape it around the unicorn's human shoulders. "What have they done to her?"

Rafael shakes his head. "Can you take her to Cesar? He'll know what to do."

Sabastian looks around, confusion etched across his perfect features. "Take her—but where is your carriage?"

"Can you take Nyia home?" Rafael asks him, ignoring his question.

"But how will she . . ." Sabastian blinks at Marix and Rosadela's steady retreat. "Surely they need—"

"They'll be fine," Rafael says. "Nyia?" he asks again, though his gaze is directed at the prince.

I stiffen.

"I'm not your responsibility," I say through gritted teeth. The nerve of this asshole. "And I don't need to go home." I think of the empty hovel and practically shudder. "I'm going to the brothel." To see Sienna, to ask why she never mentioned that all mythics can turn human. To get my dragon eye back. To repay Martin's debt and get off this godforsaken island.

"Of course I can take you, but . . ." Sabastian looks between me and Rafael, and his eyes widen. "Oh, they're gone already."

I don't have to look behind me to know Marix and Rosadela have disappeared. If she's not a mythic, then Marix must be one powerful

Burner because how else could she have disappeared so quickly? Because she is a mythic—they all are. *Don't be foolish, Nyia*. It's the only thing that makes sense.

Rafael reaches for me, capturing my hand in his.

"Can we talk?"

I look down at our joined hands, at my treacherous fingers that have somehow become interlaced with his.

"I don't have anything to say to you." I snatch my hand away. "Are you ready?" I turn to Sabastian.

"Darkthorne, may I offer you a ride since your friend has taken your carriage?"

"No. He's fine on his own," I answer for him. "Let's go." I march toward the waiting carriage, not even caring I've turned my back to a royal.

The two men exchange a few words, but moments later Sabastian jogs to catch up with me.

"Lover's tussle?" he asks.

"No."

"I'm a great listener."

"I have nothing to say about him," I repeat. Perhaps if I say the words often enough, they will become true.

Sabastian gestures for me to climb into the waiting carriage and follows, nodding at his man to shut the door. Moments later we are in motion, and I manage not to look behind me at Rafael, not even once.

I ignore all the prince's efforts of small talk on the short journey back to the brothel. Eventually I'll have to face what Rafael means to me, but not now. I don't want to think about him at all. Instead, I allow my thoughts to trail back to Marix and the rescued unicorn, at what the existence of multiple unicorns masquerading as humans could possibly mean for the island. Rafael wants to close the gate to the veil. It has to be to prevent any more humans from traveling through, to stop the genocide of mythics. Because that's what it is, isn't it? Cesar is right to hate Burners, to despise humans. Wouldn't I hold the same prejudice?

We arrive at the brothel just before dawn. The late hour has done nothing to decrease the number of patrons. If anything they have more than doubled since our last visit, and the atmosphere outside the place is alive with laughter and merriment.

"I wanted to thank you for what you did earlier," Sabastian says as the carriage draws to a stop. "And to let you know I won't tell anyone your secret."

He's referring to the manticore toenails, of course. To me burning the magic that brought him back to his senses after his encounter with . . . damn. Someone.

"No thanks necessary. You would have done the same for me," I mutter, surprising myself to realize how much I mean it.

"I would have. Well, if I had the skill to do so." He looks like he wants to say more on the subject, but he falls silent as one of his men opens the door to the carriage box. "Shall I wait for you?"

My heart softens a bit at the offer. He might be too pretty for his own good, but he truly is a nice guy.

"No, that's not necessary. But thank you. For everything."

"He cares about you, I think."

There's no need to ask who he is talking about. But Sabastian is wrong. Because you don't lie to someone you care about. You don't steal from them and hide every part of your intentions.

"No," I say as I step out of the carriage, "he doesn't."

30

NEVER TRUST A SUCCUBUS

I blink against the dim lighting of the brothel. More people, sure, but the gay lighting from earlier has been replaced with softer, dimmer sconces, likely in an effort to make the setting more romantic. As if a brothel could be romantic.

I scan the room for any sign of Sienna, but after a cursory look, I don't find her and give up. I make my way to the bar to wait her out. She is likely entertaining a patron upstairs. It is a codependent relationship for her. She, more beautiful than any human has any right to be, offering her lovers nights of passion and cleansed memories while she feeds from their desire. The scent of succubus musk is heavy in the air, and I order some wine from the barkeep, taking slow, careful sips.

I don't have anything left to burn, and honestly, now, I'm not sure I want to. I think back to the giant dragon bones in Rafael's arsenal. Did dragons masquerade in human form too? The thought is unsettling and has me regarding each patron with suspicion. I am nearly done with the too-sweet wine when I spot Sienna making her way down the staircase. She has a soft glow about her, indicating she is both sated and fed. She stops to talk to a young woman. Their laughter echoes across the room. I throw a few of Rafael's coins on the bar and make my way toward her. I make it only a few paces before an all-too-familiar scent of pine and burnt chocolate passes by and someone grabs my arm. I spin around, a scowl fixed on my face as I glare up at Rafael.

"Are you following me?"

"I just want to talk."

"So you said. And I said we have nothing to say to one another."

I frown at his hand wrapped around my bicep until he drops it back to his side.

"I told you, Darkthorne. I have nothing to say to you. Leave me alone."

"Please. Just let me explain. I didn't mean to—"

"Steal from me? Lie about it?" I laugh. The cackle rises above the merry folk in the hall, drawing attention. "There's nothing you can say to excuse your actions. I don't need to listen to any more of your lies. I see you for what you are. Now go away."

"Nyia."

"The lady asked you to leave her alone," a burly man says, stepping between me and Rafael. The man towers over Raf, and for a moment, I have the wild thought that he is a giant masquerading as a man. I need to get out of this place. Rafael's expression darkens as he stares up at the man, and the two appear as if they will exchange more than just words. I shake my head and use the opportunity to disappear into the crowd, catching up with Sienna just as she descends the final steps of the staircase.

"Sienna!"

She sees me and her face pales. Her welcoming smile fades away. She turns on her heel to go back up the stairs but is blocked by a couple descending arm in arm.

She turns back to me and forces a fake smile. "Nyia. You're back."

"As I said I would be." I narrow my eyes at her. "Look, I'm eager to get out of here. Just give me back my bag and I'll be gone. For good."

"You're leaving?" She tilts her head. "That's wonderful."

"Yes. I just need my bag."

"I . . . I'll have to look for it. Can you come back tomorrow?"

"No. I can't. Go and get it. Now, please." I cross my arms over my chest. What game is she playing at?

"Nyia, there's something you should know. About the . . ." She trails off, eyes widening when something behind me catches her attention. If I thought she paled when she saw me, it is nothing compared to the panicked look on her face now. What does she see? I turn around and come face to chest with Rafael. Not something she saw—*someone*.

"Fuck," she mumbles as she visibly begins to tremble. "It was yours?"

"Did you look in my bag?" I demand. "Where is it?"

"I don't have it."

She could have said anything. Anything but that.

"What do you mean, you don't have it?" I have the wild urge to shake her. To press my fingernails deep into her shoulders and scream in her face. She doesn't have it?

"What have you done with it?" Rafael asks from beside me and I jump, startled by his presence. I forgot he was there. Not that it matters. Nothing matters anymore because Sienna no longer has the dragon eye. Once again, it is lost to me.

Sienna and I both frown at Rafael, and my fists come up my hips, planting themselves there as I work my jaw.

"How do I know you haven't taken it somewhere?" I ask him. "This isn't a game, you know. This is my life, Sienna," I say, spinning back toward her and stabbing a finger into her chest.

"I'm sorry," Sienna says. Her attention is still captured by Rafael, at the subtle fury she sees on the surface of his features.

Fine, maybe he is as in the dark as I am about its location. Maybe he even needs it as badly as I do, but somehow, I doubt that. My life is tied to it. Without it, I have nothing to bargain with. I have nothing.

"Sorry?" I blink at her. "You're *sorry*? Where is it?"

I shrug off Rafael's touch, not caring he is trying to be sympathetic at a time like this.

"I'm sorry," she repeats, blinking rapidly to hedge actual tears.

A small, distant part of me laments the fact that I have nothing to bottle them up, to store them away for future use. What happens when one burns succubus tears?

"I'm sorry," Sienna says again. "She came for it. Said I had to give it to her. She threatened to hurt me—"

"*I'm* going to hurt you!"

She flinches from my outburst, burying her face in her hands. I see red, the world exploding about me.

"Who?" Rafael asks her. "Who did you give the eye to?"

I should question how he can remain so calm. How he doesn't experience the loss as sharply as I. Probably because no one promises his death should he fail to deliver it. Probably because he is as rich as the king and hasn't a worry except for convincing me to help him close the gate.

I'm so lost in my sea of self-pity, feeling wave after wave of desperation crash over me, I almost don't hear her response. Or perhaps I knew the answer all along.

"Gloriana. Gloriana has the eye."

31

IT'S COMPLICATED

My body falls limp. I might have swooned were it not for the thick man-chest pressed against my back, the steady presence of Rafael's arm wrapping around my waist.

We're outside now, though I don't remember leaving the brothel.

Gloriana has the eye.

She got it herself before Sienna could give it to me, and there isn't any reason for her to keep me alive now. Sienna has signed my death warrant.

"Nyia, look at me, love. You're okay."

I blink up at him, staring in confusion at the light pink stretching across the night sky. Dawn. How has morning come already?

"You're okay," he repeats. "You don't need it."

"You don't understand. It's the only way I can locate a dragon heart. It's the only thing keeping me alive, Rafael."

I watch the muscle in his jaw tick once, twice.

"I'm not going to let anything happen to you."

I want to believe him. I want to press my forehead against his chest and allow his strong arms to wrap around me and squeeze all the worry away. But I can't. Martin promised to always take care of me, but he is the reason I'm in this mess. And if Rafael hadn't lied about the dragon eye, if he hadn't hidden everything from me, maybe I could have bargained with Gloriana. Maybe I would still have a chance.

"I don't believe anything you say anymore," I tell him.

He blinks his eye. Nods once.

"I deserve that. I know I've kept things from you, Nyia. I had my reasons." He clears his throat. "Reasons I thought justified lying to someone I respect very much. But I promise you, I'm going to do everything in my power to keep you safe. I'll get you any dragon part you need."

"You don't know what you're saying. Gloriana has the eye now. How will we find the heart of a dragon without it?"

He's watching me carefully, and a slow, sudden certainty washes over me. I think about the dragon bones on his property. Of Cesar, the hidden unicorn, his circle of tight-knit friends. Suddenly I'm wondering if he and Gloriana want the same thing, if the two are locked in some sort of sick race against one another, and I managed to get caught between them.

"You know where one is, don't you? You've had one all this time."

"I . . . I do know where one is."

"Of course you do." I roll my eyes.

"It's not what you think," he continues. "None of this is what you think. I want to explain. I want to tell you everything when the time is right. I promise to explain everything. Can you wait for that? Give me a chance to explain?"

"That depends, are you going to stop lying to me?"

"Just give me the chance to prove to you I can be trusted. Follow me."

We begin walking down the hard-packed street. I hold my hand above my brow to stop the strain of the sun. How far he plans for us to travel without horses or a carriage, I don't know, but I refuse to bend first. I refuse to let him know I'm tired. We could walk the entire way to the palace as far as I am concerned.

"I know how hard it is to lose someone. Someone who was responsible for your entire world. How losing them can reshape it into something new, something impossible." His tone is casual as though he's talking to himself, but when I look over at him, he studies me with a guarded expression.

"Martin wasn't my entire world. He just ruined it."

He says nothing, perhaps waiting for me to continue.

"I was so young when I married him. He was so worldly. He traveled quite a bit before stumbling upon the island. When we met, he spoke of other islands, of faraway places and new adventures."

"How old were you when you got married?"

"Eighteen." I bark out a bitter laugh. "It feels like a lifetime ago."

"Did your parents make you marry him?"

"No one made me do anything," I retort, and now it's Rafael's turn to laugh.

"I believe that. You have your own opinion about things. Were you in love?"

"I thought I was." I bite the inside of my cheek and blink back tears. "What about you? Who did you lose? Who changed the way you saw this world?"

"My father."

I crane my neck up to look at him, squinting against the early morning sun, but his expression is blank. He's never spoken about his father before, and though I'm loath to admit it, I want to hear everything.

"Were you close? You and your father?"

"For a time. Toward the end it became . . ." He trails off, likely searching for the right word.

"Complicated?" I supply with a wry twist to my mouth. "You say that a lot."

"Do I?" he asks, but I can tell he doesn't expect or want an answer. "We never had much in common. He was very old-fashioned."

I nod, remembering my mother and all the useless lessons on homemaking she drilled into me. In the end, none of it mattered. Martin never wanted a wife in the traditional sense. He wanted me—a Burner.

"How did he die?"

Rafael doesn't answer, and we fall into an uncomfortable silence.

We walk for a bit longer, seconds fading into minutes and even longer before he reaches for my hand.

"Wait here. I think I see Marix up ahead."

I look up the road but don't see anyone, the dusty public street as empty as it's been all morning.

"Why do I need to wait here?" I ask.

He's already jogging forward, but he does take a moment to call over his shoulder, "Please, just a moment."

I sigh loudly so he can hear my annoyance, then stoop down to empty the gravel from my boots and adjust my laces.

The loose gravel on the road jostles for a moment, and I suspect a carriage approaches, but there is none in sight. After a moment I begin walking toward the curve in the road. It's been a long night, and my nerves are getting the best of me.

"Rafael?" I call out. I tilt my head, straining to hear any indication of him and Marix, or a carriage of any sort up ahead, but there is only silence. "Marix?"

Nothing. I continue walking, frowning against the rising sun as I follow the curve of the road.

He wouldn't leave me here, would he? I don't want to believe it's possible for such deceit, but it wouldn't be the first time he's lied to me.

It's too quiet. There is a charged buzzing in the air, the sort that only comes from one thing: magic.

I hesitate for a moment and then break into a jog just as Rafael had, hurrying to catch up with him and Marix. I might not have anything to burn, but I'm not completely helpless, and I refuse to stand and wait.

My feet pound against the loose gravel. I round the bend and come to a stuttering stop.

Rafael is there, standing in the middle of the road, and he isn't alone. But he's not with Marix. Standing next to him is a massive dragon.

I do the only logical thing I can think of. I open my mouth and scream.

The dragon is easily ten times the size of Rafael. It turns toward me and roars, tilting its neck back and blowing a bloom of fire into the early morning sky.

Shit. I have nothing, literally nothing, with which to defend myself.

Rafael spins around and sees me. I see his mouth moving, but I can't hear what he's saying over the roar of the dragon and rushing sound of its fire.

He holds up a hand in the universal signal for me to stop.

My legs couldn't move even if they wanted to. The dragon's indigo scales shimmer in the sun, and it lowers its neck to blink at me. Its head is easily the size of my entire body. The dark-purple scales cover the entire length of its body. Twisted among the dragon's dark scales are shimmering silver ones that swirl and sparkle in an incandescent pattern that seems familiar somehow. Twin horns in deep purple twist above the dragon's head, and small silver spikes run down the length of its neck.

The dragon lifts one clawed foot toward me, and I stare at the claws, all the more menacing now that they're attached to an actual dragon. Was it truly just hours ago I wielded one of these claws as a weapon? That I imagined burning the heart from such a majestic creature?

I always knew Rafael was a powerful Burner, that he somehow has skills that make him more capable than anyone else. There is a reason he collects more dragon parts than anyone else. A reason he holds the entire corpse of one at his home.

"Nyia. I can explain."

Explain what, exactly? Explain that he is more than capable of bringing a dragon heart to him? Explain how the dragon seems to be waiting for some signal from him—how it seems aware of everything, turning from him, then back to me with eyes that hold a wisdom beyond anything I've ever comprehended.

How is this all possible? And just as quickly as the thought enters my brain, another startling realization takes over.

I think I see Marix, he said. He looked out toward the road, but had he? Or had he been looking up at the sky? Cesar is a unicorn. Mythics can take human shapes . . . Is this dragon actually Marix? My friend?

"Marix?" I whisper. My hand stretches toward its snout.

The dragon—Marix—chuffs in response, twin tendrils of smoke rising from her nostrils.

Rafael approaches from my left, his steps slow and steady, though whether that's in an effort not to startle the dragon or me, I don't know.

"Say it," I tell him. My eyes don't leave the dragon as she lightly bunts my hand with the tip of her snout. "Tell me I'm wrong. That this isn't Marix."

"Nyia, I was going to tell you. I wanted to tell you."

"How is this possible? How do you know a dragon and a unicorn and . . ." I lose the words, my thoughts a torrent of stunning realizations. Even now I can still feel the magic buzzing in the air, an invisible current of power all around us. Rafael is the most infamous Burner alive—only he isn't a Burner at all.

It's yours? Sienna asked. She was talking to Rafael. It was always Rafael.

"The dragon eye." The words are barely a whisper, but he hears them all the same.

"It's mine. It's always been mine."

I stare up at his rugged face. At the dark leather patch and vicious scar covering the left side. I remember Martin bragging about the accomplishment, showing me the sword he'd used to flay the dragon's eye from its body. Rafael's body.

"No. No, it can't be." But the words are lost to me. Lost in the wind, lost in the early morning sky that slowly fades to black.

32

THE DRAGON IN ME

When I open my eyes, I see Marix frowning down at me.

"She's awake," Marix says, smoothing loose curls back from my face. "How do you feel?"

"Like I'm being cradled by a dragon." I groan, pushing myself up into a sitting position, blinking at the familiar surroundings.

I'm back in the Gold Room. Rafael is framed by the doorway, his massive form blocking the hallway where I spot Teo and Cesar peeking through.

"How did I get here?" I ask. My eyes widen. "Don't say that you carried me." I level a stern look at Marix.

"I didn't! Umm, Raf did."

Raf did. Of course he did.

"As a dragon?" I ask even though I know the answer. I have to hear him say the words.

"It was the quickest way to bring you here. We couldn't stay out in the open so close to the village. It isn't safe." Rafael begins walking toward me, but something in my expression must give him pause because he stops at the foot of my bed.

Not safe. For the two dragons. Right. He and Marix are dragons. I look from one to the other, struggling for my mind to catch up to this new reality.

"I'm going to check on Rosadela. You two need time to . . . talk." Marix and Rafael exchange a glance, and Cesar snatches Teo's arm, dragging him away from the doorway.

"Thanks for taking care of my boots," Teo calls out from down the hall.

"A dragon, huh? I guess that counts for complicated." I draw my knees up to my chest, hugging my arms around them.

"I was going to tell you. Eventually. May I?" Rafael sighs and takes a seat at the foot of the bed when I say nothing in response.

"What was this to you? Some sort of game? We had a deal. You needed another Burner. You . . ." I trail off, willing the pieces to fit together.

"I do need a Burner," he says softly. "Nyia, what do you know about your gift?"

"Just what anyone knows, I guess. If I hold onto anything mythic, I can sense the core of its magic. I can burn the object and draw its essence into myself."

"Did you ever think about the fact that if you burn a dragon claw, something relatively small compared to the size of a dragon, that it amplifies your own strength to that of a dragon—considerably more than a dragon's if you compare your tiny human size."

I ignore the slight jab as he continues. "Nyia, Burners don't just source magic from mythics, they amplify it. That's why Gloriana doesn't only need the dragon eye—she needs you to wield it. You might not be able to sense the magic pouring out of you, but we can. You're a walking target for mythics everywhere. Believe me when I tell you there isn't a more powerful Burner anywhere on this island."

"So that's it then," I say, struggling to digest the meaning of his words. "I'm a pawn to you all. King Ernesto, the dragons, whatever Gloriana is, you've all been using me." I try to keep the hurt from my voice, but my tone wavers at the end.

Rafael sighs, raking a hand through his disheveled hair. "Nyia, I never wanted to hide things from you, never wanted to use you. I made that deal because it's the only way I can see to save my people."

"Your people," I parrot.

"The other mythics. Everything I said before was true. I need your help to close the gate to the veil. And in exchange for your help, I would have given you the eye. I would have given you everything."

"But you're saying you . . . I mean, how did you let it get this far?"

"I knew the king was working with a mythic, but I didn't know who—not until you came along. And even then, we didn't know who Gloriana was. She's one of the Ancients. One of the original mythics to claim this island as home. And while we don't know what sort of mythic Gloriana is, we want to keep her in her human form for as long as possible. We're not exactly sure the reason behind it, though Marix suspects it has something to do with the way the veil was created. Mythics are beings of magic—you know that—but being in our human form dulls our gifts, mutes our powers somehow."

I nod because I surmised that already with Sienna.

"Once you revealed to us who Gloriana was, the pieces began to snap into place. A Burner can take that spark of magic and wield it as something new. With my eyes I am able to see mythics for what they truly are, even if they're in human form. But a Burner wielding that same eye, they can use it to locate mythics, to find hidden objects of greater power. If a Burner were to wield something as powerful as the heart of a dragon—one of the oldest and most powerful mythics ever created—their power could be limitless. Only a Burner is capable of wielding the necessary power. We need a Burner to wield a dragon heart, to seal the gate closed forever and prevent any more mythics from being hunted."

"If a Burner can close the gate with a heart, why does Gloriana want one? Why does she want to close it?" I don't know much about the magical gate; no one can predict the pattern of its magic. It simply exists.

"For a century now, the gate to the veil opens sporadically and in random locations both on the island and around its coast."

I nod. Though the gate is never open for long, everyone knows to stay clear of the volatile magic unless they are prepared to cross through the veil to the wide open world of humans. I never suspected wielding the eye could reveal the location of the gate to a Burner. Had Martin suspected? Had he somehow been part of all this from the beginning? Does it matter?

"I believe Gloriana wants to force the gate open, permanently. To make it so that humans can cross into the veil whenever they want. Maybe even without gifted sight. She'll use you as the conduit. With the magic of a Burner amplifying her power, she'll be unstoppable." Rafael shakes his head. "It's likely why she captured Rosadela. A unicorn heart would stand a chance of being as powerful as a dragon's. I'm only guessing, of course, but I think that's exactly what Gloriana has planned. I think the human king has tasked her with this. That's why we have to close the gate now. I refuse to allow any more of my people to face such danger."

I bite my bottom lip, allowing the implication to play out in my mind. "But if your plan was always for a Burner to burn a dragon heart to close the gate, then you—" I gasp, my hand flying to my mouth in a weak effort to stifle the sound. "*Your* heart? You planned for me to burn your heart? Rafael, you can't! Surely there's another way, another mythic we could—"

"You would have me sacrifice someone else? No. This is my task, my duty as their king."

Their king. And there it is, the last piece of the puzzle. The pirate king discovered this island and laid claim to it all those years ago. There was a brief negotiation for peace but then the ruling king dispatched his dragon on them. The pirate and his crew survived, felling the dragon and proclaiming himself the new king of the island. The king's dragon. The dragon king. Rafael's father. I think of the collection of dragon bones Rafael has in his arsenal. Not an arsenal—a mausoleum.

Rafael is willing to sacrifice himself for the safety of his people, and who am I to try and stop him? I was always their backup plan. Rafael's *life* is the backup plan. All this time . . . he meant for me to kill him? To carve out his heart and burn it like . . . like he was any other mythic I've burned before. I feel sick. I choke back a rush of bile, willing the room to cease spinning around me.

"I didn't . . . I can't. Rafael, no. No. I won't."

"You will," he says firmly, catching my hands with his. "It's the only way. Don't you think I would find another path, if it were possible? Please, Nyia, I've made my decision. Do this for me, for everyone."

"You can't ask this of me." I rip my hands free and jump off the bed to pace the golden carpet. "There's another way—there has to be. We just have to try harder. There's a secret text somewhere or an ancient relic or something!"

"We're running out of time," he says. He hasn't moved from the bed, but he tracks my movement. "I'm so sorry to ask this of you. I wish there were another way. I wish we had more time together."

"Then fight with me. You can't just accept this. You can't be willing to kill yourself. There has to be another way!"

"Don't you think I've tried everything? Don't you think I would do something else—anything else—if it would allow me to have just a bit more time with you? Nyia, please, I can't allow the mythics to continue being hunted. I'm their only hope. I have to do this. And I hope you'll help me. Help me save them, Nyia."

Hot tears form, and I can't blink them away. They fall down my cheeks in steaming rivulets.

"No," I whisper. I shake my head, denying the truth right in front of me. "No. What if I won't do it? If I refuse?"

"You would sacrifice all these lives for us to have a few moments of happiness?"

I would sacrifice everything! I want to shout the words at him, but I know the admission will only make things harder.

Somehow, I'm sitting back on the bed, though I don't remember when I decided to stop pacing. I'm only aware of Rafael shifting now, of him moving from his seat on the bed to kneel before me.

I cradle his head between my hands. Swallow against the tears.

"Please don't make me do this," I whisper.

"I'm so sorry. I know it's not fair." He brings my hands to his lips, then kisses my palms. "I bet you wish you still wanted to kill me. It made things easier then."

"Is that why you chose me? Raf, I don't want you to die."

"I know, love." He turns my hands over, kissing my fingers. The insides of my wrists. "I know."

"Rafael, I—"

"If you want me to stop, I will. Tell me to leave your room, and I will. But I'm asking for this, for one last day together. Please, let me stay." His mouth leaves a trail of kisses down my arm. His tongue skims the inside of my elbow, and my legs widen so he can move closer. So I can pull his chest against me.

"I don't want you to stop," I say before tilting his head back and claiming his lips with my own.

This kiss, this desperate, all-consuming kiss, is everything he can give me, and I still want more. I moan, teeth crashing against his, and I pull frantically at his clothing, needing more—his touch, his skin against mine.

There is something fleeting in this moment—that this might be our last time—that makes it all the sweeter.

"Nyia, I—"

"Don't talk. Please, just . . . I need you." And I do. By all the forgotten gods, do I need this man. His mouth angles against mine, tongue plunging to dance with my own. He sucks my tongue, drawing it deeper into his mouth. I curl my toes, arching my back to feel more.

His hands slide up my back, pressing me closer. The kiss is a promise of what's to come, a heartache because of all we can never be—but now, in this moment, he is mine, and I am his, and nothing else matters. I pull at him, drawing him toward me until I'm falling backward on the plush mattress, legs widening even more so I can feel his body, strong and solid against my own. His hands reach under my arms, shoving me back onto the bed so he can climb on top of me, covering the length of me. I wrap my legs around his waist, clenching my ankles together so he doesn't escape my embrace.

He tears his lips from me to kiss my cheeks, licking away the tears, sucking at the hollow of my throat. He reaches for my waist, pulling at the loose fabric of my shirt and wrenching it from my body. I lock my fingers around his neck, then pull his mouth back to mine and give in to the sweet release of his teasing tongue once again. I don't want this to end, not ever. I reach for his shirt, whimpering when I can't get it off fast enough. I need to feel his hot, searing skin against my flesh.

And then he is on me, hands everywhere, sliding along my torso, kneading my nipples until they tighten and bud just for him. I buck against his hips. My nails scrape along the length of his spine, digging into the tender flesh of his naked back, and he moans against my mouth.

"Take off your pants," I demand. But he is already reaching between us, pulling my hands down with his so I can feel his dick straining against the fabric.

"Rafael. Fuck, Rafael, I need you." I pull at my pants, wishing for a way to rip them off me and then Raf does, the fabric tearing in his hand. He claims me with his mouth, his tongue against my clit, sucking, pulsing against my hot center. I am undone. Liquid fire burns me from the inside, and I scream with my release, clamping my legs together to hold him in place as I am racked with shudders of pleasure.

He growls, burying his face in my pussy, and my hands find their way to the back of his head, tangling in his hair and pulling him closer, his tongue deeper. He licks the length of my folds, plunging deep inside my hot core, and it's not enough until his fingers are there, too, thrusting deep inside me.

"More," I demand.

"So greedy." He chuckles but obliges, flipping me over and pushing me into a new position so my stomach is flat on the bed, my legs spread and pressed against the mattress. For a moment I am empty, and I look over my shoulder to demand more from him just as his massive cock nudges my pussy, and I arch my back to grant him easier entry.

"Nyia, you're so beautiful," he murmurs as he thrusts so deep I see stars, so deep all I can do is scream against the soft comforter. I hope everyone has left the house because I can't be silenced. Not now.

He thrusts faster, hands on either side of me, fingers digging into my hip bones for leverage. I push against his thrusts with my toes, giving him all of me, giving him everything.

I can't think of anything, nothing except the way he feels, dick slamming in to the hilt, filling me completely.

I clench around him, knees quivering, but he grabs my hips to hold me steady.

"No, not yet." He growls. "I want to see you."

He pushes me farther back on the bed, and I whimper at his brief departure before he climbs on after me, flipping me onto my back. He presses his tongue against my clit, lapping up my juices and growling deep in his throat before he enters me once more.

"You are mine, Nyia. Say it."

"I'm yours." I gasp against the force of his thrusts.

"Then come for me, love. Show me that you're mine."

And I do.

33

Telaraña

Once again, the kitchen has outdone itself, and I'm patting my full belly in contentment. I'm too full to move. I doubt I can even make it back upstairs. I catch Rafael looking at me and squirm as heat floods my core. Okay, so I could probably find my way up there with the right motivation. I'm wondering if it's too soon for us to excuse ourselves for the evening when Teo enters the room.

"We need to make our move. Gloriana and the king have something big planned."

Marix widens her eyes and looks over at me, but Rafael nods.

"She knows. Everything, now."

Marix sighs, face full of relief. "About time! Well, then what are we waiting for? Teo, what's the news?"

"The king has taken a small contingent of soldiers and moves toward the southern coast." The chupacabra assassin spins a familiar dagger between his hands as he talks. "They're moving quickly. They should reach the other end of the island by tomorrow."

"That's la cantaora territory." Rafael's expression is intrigued, a contrast to the stark terror that fills me at the mention of the siren queen.

"That's a good thing, isn't it? They won't stand a chance against the siren queen, right? That should buy us some time to—"

"Not if they've found the gate to the veil. If they've used the eye to locate the gate, we may be out of time."

"But I thought they needed to burn a dragon heart to close it? Are there more of you out there?" I don't know what to do with my hands so I bring them together in my lap.

Rafael and Marix exchange a look.

"We're not exactly sure," Marix admits. "Most everyone went into hiding after the veil was first opened."

"And though we know a dragon's heart is the level of power used before to create the gate, it doesn't guarantee it is the only applicable power source. Maybe there are more unicorns, or perhaps Gloriana has something else in play. We can't risk it."

I swallow. "So that's it then. We make our way to the southern coast. We stop Gloriana."

"And we close the gate once and for all," Rafael finishes.

I don't say anything to that. How can I when he's right? It's the only way to save his people. But how do I admit to him I won't be able to do it when the time comes, that I will fail him?

We meet in the actual armory as opposed to the dragon king's mausoleum. The room is tiny, yet it manages to house hundreds of various weapons. I admit I don't know how to wield anything beyond a dagger, and I haven't the strength for a sword without constantly burning something. Marix insists on strapping me full of daggers, though I suspect if I have a need for them with two dragons on my side, then I'm already dead. *Don't think about that now, Nyia.* One thing at a time. First, we locate Gloriana. Then we kill the bitch. Maybe we can find a way to rid ourselves of both her and the king, and Rafael can live. I ignore the fact that I have no idea how to kill an ancient mythic. That killing the human king will cause riots in the streets, that Sabastian will start a war.

"So how do we get there? Flying?" I don't know if I'm excited or terrified by the prospect. On one hand, Rafael has already carried me as a dragon; I just wasn't conscious for the experience. I've never seen him in his true form, and somehow that makes the idea still an abstract concept—something I know to be true because they've told me, yet somehow not true until I witness it myself. Maybe if I had seen Rafael in his dragon form I would have thought twice about fucking him. But then again, maybe not. The knowledge certainly hadn't prevented me from thoroughly enjoying myself. Marix, on the other hand, I haven't been able to stop picturing as the gigantic, glorious beast I saw on the road, and a small part of me thrills at the thought of riding such a magnificent being.

"No. Too big, too noisy. We lose all advantage if they can spot us coming." Rafael frowns, considering.

"So, phoenix feather? Too bad Teo isn't a phoenix. Do you know any phoenix?" I look at each of their faces.

"Unfortunately, no. And someone stole the one I stashed away for emergency." I ignore his pointed stare.

My only contact for parts is Sienna, and she would take too long. In any case, I'm still mad at her betrayal, even if Gloriana threatened her. I don't want to ask her for anything. With Martin gone and Sienna out of the picture, I have no other way to get mythic parts, and there is a growing part of me that is relieved by this.

"I think you know what we have to do, Raf," Marix says. "Besides, it's been a while since we visited that side of the family."

He visibly pales and shakes his head. "No. No, we don't."

"What's going on?" I ask. "What do we have to do?" Rafael looks terrified, but there was a playful tone to Marix's words, and Cesar and Teo exchange amused grins.

"Oh, we have another way across the island—only Rafael doesn't like it." Marix's eyes sparkle with amusement.

"Because we don't have to do it. I was wrong. I'll fly us all there super quiet."

Marix snorts. "Stop being a baby. You know it's the best way."

"These could be my last few moments alive. Do you really want me to spend them suffering?"

"Not funny," I say, hitting his arm.

"But it's spiders, Nyia. And not the tiny ones that invade your campsite but giant, creepy mythic ones."

***

"So what do we do? How does it work?" I eye the creature with suspicion, picturing burning his drool or some other horror. I am standing in front of a massive spider. Its hairy body towers over me. Behind the spider and rising into the canopy of trees is the largest spiderweb I have ever seen in my entire life. The web sparkles and shimmers and is so finely spun, it seems impossible that it can support the weight of the massive mythic that created it.

"These gentle mythics have teleportation abilities. Imagine their web as a network of roadways that can take you anywhere," Cesar explains. His expression is almost reverent as he stares up at the giant arachnid.

The spider chitters in response, and it takes everything in me not to squeal and run away.

"The telaraña requires no verbal command. They communicate telepathically. Once you make contact with the web, simply picture where you want to go," Rafael explains from his position behind Teo. He's been hovering along the edge of our group, reluctant to come closer to the spider before absolutely necessary. I can't believe Rafael allows the creatures to live so close to his home, though I suppose he makes a point not to get close enough to the mythics for it to matter.

"Here." Marix marks an *X* on a map of the island she drew from her pocket. "We are here. And you're going here." She indicates an opposite point on the map.

"I don't need to burn anything?" I can't imagine using magic without burning an object in my hand. How can the magic be directed without my burning it?

"No, the telaraña will do all the work for you. Just picture where you need to go and touch the web to take you there." Marix leans forward to demonstrate, and in a shimmer of silver, she disappears.

I blink at the spot where Marix stood moments ago. There is the distinct buzz of magic in the air, and though it leaves familiar pinpricks of tension on my body, I can't trust it.

"Are you sure this will work on me? I mean, have you ever tried with a human before? What if it only works on mythics?" I frown up at Rafael and he takes my hand, lacing our fingers together before bringing my hand up to his mouth and kissing my palm.

"Trust me. I won't let anything happen to you—not ever. Where I go, you go. I promise."

I draw in a shaky breath but nod my acceptance.

"Envision this location. Picture yourself there. Smell the ocean, feel the breeze in your hair," Rafael murmurs in my ear. His hot breath sends shivers down my spine. "Now, you've got this."

I reach up and touch the gossamer web, surprised by how firm it is under my fingers.

One moment I am standing on solid ground, and the next I am falling. There is a cold, wet mist all around and a wild sense of vertigo, but it is over before I can be truly disoriented. I open my eyes, and I am somewhere new. There is soft sand beneath my feet, and I'm still clutching Rafael's hand.

"Well, we've made it to the southern coast. Now what?" Marix looks around, studying our tranquil surroundings as though the trees themselves are going to uproot and eat us. And perhaps they could. I don't know much about this side of the island—no one does. This is the domain of the siren queen.

"We split up," Rafael says.

I can't help the derisive snort that escapes my lips. Split up? That's the worst idea ever.

"Nyia and I will look for Gloriana and the veil. You go see if you can't make one final plea with the siren queen. Perhaps your presence will be enough to convince her to lend assistance. Teo and Cesar, alert any local mythics. Tell them what's happening and see if you can enlist their aid. Tell them . . . tell them their king commands it. And if I fail to close the gate . . ." He swallows, his expression wild.

I tighten my grip on his hand. "Hey, it's okay. We will close the gate." I do my best to reassure him, to lie to him because it's what he needs to hear.

Cesar strikes a fist to his heart, and Teo presses his fingers into a heart shape before they run off on their assignments. Marix nods once and turns to leave, but she only makes it a few steps before she is running back, rushing into Rafael's arms. Their embrace is fierce, bone crunching, and I am jealous for only the briefest of seconds before I realize this is a goodbye. If Rafael and I succeed in closing the gate, it's only because I've burned his heart. The sudden fear is all-encompassing, and once again I'm questioning my ability to do what's needed of me. How can I harm him? This man who has so quickly come to mean everything to me?

Marix and Rafael finally pull apart, and she jogs off toward the water.

I blink away tears and will myself not to think about it. To somehow forget the inevitable tragedy we are hurtling toward.

"Why did you say Marix will have better luck with the siren queen?" I ask. Maybe changing the topic will somehow make it easier to forget this growing hole in my heart. The doom that hangs over us both like a dark storm cloud.

"Ahh, well because Iara and Marix have a shared past."

"Ohh. They were lovers." I grin at the thought.

"What? No." Raf shakes his head. "Not at all. They're half sisters."

"Wait, what?" I stop trailing after him, needing a moment to process this news. Rafael once again takes my hand and hooks his arm around me, drawing me close as we begin walking again.

"I'm going to need you to explain," I say after it becomes obvious he has no intention of doing so. "How are a dragon and a siren sisters? Is the offspring of mythics left to chance?"

"No, not entirely. Their father was a sea dragon."

"Oh," I say as if his answer is perfectly acceptable. And I suppose, in a way, it is. I'm wondering if a griffon and a unicorn might produce an alicorn when Rafael draws us to a sudden halt. He looks at me and presses a finger to his lips. I don't hear anything, but then again, I don't have mythic hearing so I stay as quiet as possible, hardly daring to breathe as he interprets whatever threat is seemingly just ahead.

I don't think I could move even if I wanted to. I don't want to go any farther. For a moment I truly forgot we were marching toward Rafael's death. I forgot we were anything other than Raf and Nyia—forgot we don't have a future together.

Rafael draws a dagger from his side and brings it up to his head. For one panicked moment, I believe he means to remove his other eye, but he merely slices off a lock of his hair. He shakes his head imperceptibly and brings the hair up to his lips, blowing on it between his hands. I watch in wonder as the hair seems to take on a life of its own, writhing between his fingers and rolling into a small coil before darkening into a glistening red scale.

He hands the dragon scale to me, and I take it wordlessly, forcing myself not to gasp in surprise. I've only burned fresh dragon scale once before, but I know it will heighten my senses, make my skin tougher, my muscles stronger. It's just the sort of edge I need before confronting Gloriana and her thugs, but I feel sick just holding it. I don't want to burn a piece of him, not even something as simple as a lock of hair. He takes my hand again, giving it an encouraging squeeze. The familiar buzz of magic hums between us, heavy in the air despite the fact that I haven't even burned the scale yet.

I hear it then, a strangled yelp of pain piercing through the distant call of seagulls, the gentle crashing of waves upon the sand. This sound doesn't belong, and it sends shivers down my spine. I stiffen, drawing a sharp breath. I look at Rafael and he nods.

"Get ready. When the time comes, you'll have to act fast. Gloriana will try to take control, so you have to be quicker. No hesitation. Once you hold the heart, you close the gate, do you hear me? You close it and get to Marix. She'll keep you safe. Now burn the scale, Nyia."

I take a deep breath and reach for the essence of magic humming within the dragon scale. I feel the difference almost immediately. My vision sharpens, and I smell the acrid scent of fire, though the smell doesn't contain the sweet petrichor of the jungle. This scent is bitter and vaguely familiar—burning flesh.

I meet Rafael's startled expression as he reaches the same conclusion.

Gloriana and the gate to the veil. We've found them.

Rafael crouches low as we finish our descent to the beach. I follow his lead, squatting as close as I can to the dense undergrowth. I want to run away. I want to tackle Rafael to the ground and bury my face in his chest until the entire world disappears around us. I want to plead with him once again, to convince him we can find another way. I want to beg him to stay here, with me, and consequences be damned.

"Are you ready?" he whispers. He might not actually even make a sound, his lips just forming the words, but I lie and nod. But I'll never be ready. Not for this.

The path before us opens into a small clearing, and Rafael signals for us to stop as he squints into the distance. I want to be wrong. I want this to be a nightmare.

Ahead is Gloriana. She is just as stunning as before, so beautiful it hurts to look at her. She is surrounded by her two mountainous men, mythics—I can see that clearly now—as well as a few others I've never seen before. The dragon eye is lifted on a handspun dais made out of palm fronds and seashells. It glows with an eerie golden light, and I stifle a gasp as I realize Rafael's remaining eye has taken on the same sharp glow. I'm so mesmerized by both Gloriana and the eye that it takes me a moment to process what lies beyond both.

The air is distorted and ripples in a purple and green glowing mist, like incandescent lights in the sky lit by some unknown source. Along the length of the strange light are nearly a dozen poles protruding from the ground, and tied to each makeshift stake is another mythic. Men and women alike, stripped naked and crying, some sniffling and some stoically refusing to make any sound at all. Their skin ranges in shade, and each has long flowing hair in various colors of the rainbow. It takes me a moment to register them for what they are: merfolk. Sirens and perhaps other water mythics. Some have fins where legs should be or tentacles where arms should be, but each is beautiful. Each terrified.

A strip of fabric is tied around their mouths. She's preventing them from calling for help or singing for the siren queen. I unsheathe a dagger, grateful Marix armed me with half a dozen despite my warning that I shouldn't need them.

Gloriana sniffs the air, and a sadistic smile stretches across her mouth.

"Nyia, my favorite Burner. Have you brought me a dragon heart after all?"

34

MYTHICS & MADNESS

My eyes fly to the shock on Rafael's face. I don't know why I'm surprised. Gloriana has been able to smell me this entire time. Why should now be any different?

I give him one last lingering look, memorizing the lines of his face. I lean forward to kiss him one more time. Then I swing the hilt of the dagger as hard as I can, fueled by the burning dragon scale, right into Rafael's temple. He topples forward in an unconscious heap.

"I'm sorry." I resist the urge to reach for him, to hold him. He won't be out for long so I have to hurry. I step over Rafael and rush toward my doom.

Gloriana's smile is brilliant, illuminating in the way a smile can change one from beautiful to stunning.

"——told me you were coming. I didn't want to believe him." She gestures to a man who is vaguely familiar, though I can't place his name anywhere. And the more I try to think of it, the more difficult it is to remember.

"Don't strain too hard, dear." Gloriana runs her fingers between her eyebrows. "Wrinkles."

"Let them go." I turn and address my king. He sits upon a makeshift throne, surrounded by half a dozen soldiers adorned in their familiar red and gold. He must have faith in Gloriana's protection to come with so few soldiers. I'm surprised by the fierce cadence to my command—I almost convince myself I am threatening.

The king regards me with interest. "You must be Gloriana's Burner. She says you're powerful. Why haven't you come to claim your presence before your king? Did you think I would not have use for your services?"

"Services? What we're doing is wrong. Look at them. They're people."

"They're mythics. Batteries of power. Vaults of wealth. I tire of waiting, Gloriana. Carry on with it."

"No, you can't! There has to be some sort of agreement we can come to. You have to let them go."

"I can't do that." Gloriana makes a show of looking from side to side. "I'm assuming Rafael has finally told you everything? Hasn't your noble dragon come to save the day?"

"Why are you doing this?" I hedge closer, eyeing the captive prisoners who each look at me with varying degrees of curiosity and hope. "Let them go," I repeat.

"I can smell him on you," Gloriana continues, ignoring my plea. "It's so interesting. And I thought you would be all too happy to take your revenge on the thief who ruined your life. Tell me, when did you discover it was his eye? I myself didn't realize until after I slit your husband's throat. Imagine my surprise when the returning spell snatched the acquired eye from my hands and spirited it back to its original owner."

My blood boils at her confession and I rush forward, intent to repay the favor and plunge my dagger into her black heart. I only make it a few steps before Gloriana's magic seizes me, freezing me in place.

"No, no. You just stay there for now. Tell me, where is our dragon hiding?"

"Leave Rafael out of this." The words are strangled as I struggle to break free of her magic.

"You know I can't do that. His heart is the key. These . . . creatures"—she casts a pitiable look in the direction of her prisoners—"they are nothing but bait. It's not too late to help me. Join me and open the gate willingly, and we'll find something else for my babies to eat."

By now I must have burned the last of the dragon scale, though I can still feel traces of its magic still humming on my skin, waiting for my command. I have to act quickly.

"We'll hunt them to extinction. The island will never recover—we have to stop this. It's not too late—"

"Don't spout your preservationist nonsense at me, girl. If you've made your choice, I won't try to convince you otherwise. Just know it didn't have to be this way. Do it."

Seconds. It only takes seconds for the strange red-haired man at her side to give the signal. For the throats of each prisoner to rip open, for blood to flow down their chests, staining them red.

"Noo!"

For a moment I think the horrified cry is ripped from my lips, but it is from a woman who has run into the field. Her long auburn hair whips about her on an invisible wind.

"You'll pay for that." At her words, clouds begin to form above us and thunder cracks in the air.

Iara. The siren queen. She is a stormy sea, she is death, and she rushes toward Gloriana with the ferocity of a hurricane. But Gloriana doesn't seem at all afraid. She is triumphant. They're bait, she'd said.

For something bigger. Not for Rafael but for his substitute. For the siren queen.

"No!" I scream. But I'm too late.

Because the siren queen has already rushed forward, directly into Gloriana's trap.

35

GLORIANA'S TRAP

Magic shimmers in the air, wild with static energy and buzzing all around me. The lights of the gate brighten and blister around the veil.

"Where's Raf?" someone yells in my ear, their fingers clutching my shoulder as I finally realize I am free of Gloriana's magic.

Marix.

"He's over there. Safe. You have to get her out of here." I point at the siren queen. "This is what Gloriana wanted!" I yell over the howling wind. Because all this time, while Rafael had his backup plan, so did Gloriana. And that plan is happening now.

"Get the siren queen! You have to . . ." I trail off, eyes widening as Gloriana and the siren queen collide in a swirl of magic, teeth, and claws. Maybe I shouldn't have worried. The siren queen's reputation is well-deserved, and she appears to be holding her own. A torrent of water blasts Gloriana into the air, and she is carried briefly into the ocean.

"Whatever you do, don't take your dragon form. If Gloriana doesn't already know you're a dragon, then you can't tell her." I grab Marix by the shoulders, shaking her until she agrees.

I bolt toward the king, determined to kick every single one of his guards in the balls, but the mysterious man—mythic, whatever he is—with the red hair takes the king's arm, and they fade away in a shimmer of air.

I take only a moment to frown at his disappearance before surging toward Gloriana, determined to utilize the last of this dragon scale burning within me. But her goons are on the move, blocking my way as they wait for their mistress to rejoin the battle.

"It's a trap! You have to go!" I yell to the siren queen, but I can't tell if she hears me over the screaming wind.

The goons are on me, but I don't slow down. I can't. I pivot tightly on my heel, lifting my knee in my signature move, and goon number one drops to the ground. Before I can turn to the other—Smite—, he grabs my hair, yanking me toward him so roughly, it's a wonder I'm not scalped in the process. I kick wildly and bite at his arm to loosen his grip. The second goon is back on his feet, glaring at me with a venomous expression. He draws back a fist and it sinks into my stomach, knocking all the air from me in a harsh grunt. He draws back again but is tackled to the ground by Marix before he can connect.

I use the moment for the distraction it is and take a page from Rafael's book. I reach back and wrap my fingers around a greasy lock of Smite's hair and pull.

The hair turns to fur the moment it departs from his head, and his magic floods through me. I burn every bit of fur and reach behind me, hurling Smite over my shoulder so he slams into the ground. I swing my foot into his head, crushing his skull as the last of his magic burns away. Shit, that didn't last long. I whirl toward Marix, who's locked in hand-to-hand combat with the other goon but winks when she notices me.

"Go, I've got this," she says. I turn my attention back to the siren queen and Gloriana.

"You have to go! Get out of here!" I scream at the siren queen, and she finally looks my way, disgust curling her features.

"I will have vengeance." She glows as bright as a thousand suns, her voice echoing upon itself as silken and full as any choir.

Gloriana screams a battle cry as she dives back into the skirmish.

"No, you don't understand! She wants you to use your siren magic. She aims to remove your heart!"

"She can try." The siren queen disintegrates into sea foam, and Gloriana is forced to retreat or drown in the mess.

Then Gloriana raises a dagger, clenching it in her fist. When the siren queen reappears in front of her, she takes the moment to stab her chest.

"Iara!" Marix screams. She rushes forward, falling to her knees to catch her as she crashes to the ground.

Shit. This isn't how this was supposed to happen.

"Get her out of here!" I scream. And finally Marix heeds my words, hauling the queen to her feet. They run toward the ocean, and I say a silent prayer for their safety, hoping the ocean mythics have healing powers as strong as Cesar.

I palm a dagger in either hand and sprint toward Gloriana while she is distracted. With her goons out of the way, maybe I have a chance. Rafael is still hidden away, and Marix and the siren queen have retreated. If I can stop Gloriana now, no one else has to die.

Gloriana stares out into the distance. At first I think she is watching my advance but then I realize her focus is beyond me. What has her so distracted? Now is my chance. I raise my dagger, prepared to plunge it directly into her neck.

"I wouldn't." Her gaze finally snaps to mine. "Not when the real fun can finally begin."

Dread fills me, and I know without turning around just what Gloriana means. The dagger falls from my numb fingers. Rafael is awake.

36

HIS HEART IS MINE

"No, Rafael. No." My eyes widen when they find him. "Please, don't do this."

I don't care that we've already had this discussion. I don't care that this is what we came here to do. All I know is that now, in this moment, I'm not brave enough. I can't say goodbye. I would rather die a thousand times than watch Rafael leave me.

"Time to make your final move, little Burner." Her lips curl into a sneer at Rafael's approach. "Your Majesty, welcome. How was your nap?"

"Stay back, Rafael!" I scream as Gloriana lunges at me. I reach for another dagger, but Gloriana snatches it out of my hand; she's faster and stronger than I thought she would be. I've long since burned any lingering dragon scale, and there isn't any magic left in me. It's over for me, but Rafael can still live to fight another day.

"Please, Rafael, just run. Go!"

"Now, you know he's not going to do that," Gloriana coos in my ear. "He isn't going to leave you. He loves you." Hope blooms in my chest at her words. It doesn't matter that now is not the time to be feeling such things. It doesn't matter that we're about to die—or maybe it matters all the more because we are. Rafael loves me.

"Stop fighting your destiny." Gloriana presses her blade against my neck, drawing blood. "I wonder how long I have to keep you alive to get the gate open. You see, I have this thought that I only need your blood."

Maybe if I can reach any mythic remains strewn about, I might have a chance at fighting back, might be strong enough to kill Gloriana.

But will that truly end everything? Or will the king simply find another to take her place? Rafael thinks so. And unless I plan to spend a lifetime killing everyone who will try to open the veil, then this truly is the only way. It's what Rafael wants, but it still hurts too much to accept.

Gloriana flings me to the ground, and I fall to my knees in front of her.

"Don't hurt her!" Rafael roars. "I'll do anything you want. Just please, don't hurt her."

My mind spins, trying to see a way out of this nightmare we've found ourselves in. There has to be another way—there's always another way.

"Are you okay, Nyia? Talk to me, love." Rafael takes a faltering step toward me, but he stops when Gloriana points the knife at my throat.

"You're only making this harder on yourselves. You know what I want from you both. You, shift. You, prepare to burn."

"Don't do it!" I scream even though I know my effort is futile. Rafael will do anything for his people. For me. It was always a race against the clock between us, and we've run out of time.

"Nyia, look at me, listen to me. I want this. I'll gladly cut my heart out and watch you burn it if it means you all live a long and happy life. Live for me, Nyia. Find happiness. Because you've made me happier in these last few days than I ever thought possible. Because I love you."

The power of his words slams into me, and I might collapse if I weren't already sprawled at Gloriana's feet. It's true. He loves me. My skin prickles at the revelation, each nerve alive and buzzing. A familiar hum of magic nudges my core and blooms in my chest.

"You've said your goodbyes, and I've wasted enough time. Shift now or I kill her."

Rafael stares at me one last time. His gaze is filled with so much love and devotion I don't deserve. I blink at the tears as his image shimmers in a flash of blinding light, and he is replaced by a ferocious red dragon. He is easily twice the size of Marix, and his scales are blinding as they reflect the sun. Describing him as red is a gross substitution for his actual hue. He is the color of fire, of a perfect sunset over the ocean.

Rafael rears up on his hind legs and blows a stream of fire into the sky, trumpeting his anger for all to hear.

I should be afraid, but I'm not. Because as much as I see a terrifying creature of snapping teeth and hot fire, I also see Rafael. *My* Rafael. And I know he would never do anything to hurt me. To hurt anyone. He might be a beast, but he is mine.

Gloriana cackles, clapping her hands together in glee.

"Isn't he magnificent?"

He is. He is the most majestic creature I have ever witnessed.

"It doesn't have to be messy," Gloriana says to the dragon, to Rafael. "I can make it quick. Maybe I'll even keep your pet around. The little Burner has proven herself useful." She turns her attention to me, pointing. "You're all out of time."

My hands tremble, my fingers struggling for purchase in the sand. Out of time. Rafael and I were never given the gift of time.

"Once his heart is in your possession, all you have to do is burn it in the gate. I will take care of the rest." She shoves me forward, pressing me into the veil, into the swirling mass of iridescent magic foaming around me. "Burn his heart and open the gate!"

I blink against the tears in an effort to keep Rafael in focus. I will have to be quick, like Rafael said. I can't allow Gloriana to open the gate. I have to close it before she takes control of my body. For all she promises otherwise, I know Gloriana will kill me as soon as she gets the chance. But I won't die in vain. I will close the gate before she can wedge it open. At least then, I won't have to be separated from Rafael for long.

Burn his heart... It should be simplicity itself, but there is nothing easy about this. I can't cut out his heart. It would be like carving out my own. I want to reach for him. I want his arms around me once again, just for a moment, one last time. I can almost feel his phantom touch. That familiar buzzing still tickles my skin.

I can't do this.

Once the heart is in your possession. But my heart is breaking. It began crumbling into pieces the moment Rafael confided his plans. My heart is already his possession, just as his is mine.

I reach for that well of magic buzzing just beneath the surface. It's so familiar, so unapologetically him, and my heart aches.

Burn his heart and open the gate. Once the heart is in your possession.

But I don't need to kill Rafael to possess his heart. It's already mine. Rafael's heart is mine. At the possessive thought the magic surges, pulsing in the air between us and daring me to take it.

Rafael dips his head toward me and bares his neck, his single eye staring solemnly into my own.

I forgive you, he seems to say. *I love you.*

And I love him. More than anything in my life. I wrap either hand around his gigantic snout and bring my lips to his fangs. My monster. My heart. *Mine.*

The magic is all around me now, filling me completely, utterly. I take it all.

"What are you doing?" Gloriana screams. She rushes forward, but I brush her aside with a single flick of my wrist, the action carrying as much force as if Rafael had hit her with his tail. She flies backward, landing on her back.

"I love you too," I whisper and then throw my hands out wide, surrendering to his magic.

It's hard to keep my eyes open against the blinding light all around me. It's dazzling and impossible to see, impossible to feel anything except for the infinite power coursing through me. Is this what Rafael feels all the time? I've never known such power. It's intoxicating. I could tear down mountains, break apart the world with my fire. The gate is all around me, its magic as familiar as Rafael's touch. It's a beautiful creation, but it's corrupted, darkness twisting at its center. I can see it easily now, an easy fix. I focus on the darkness, on clearing it with Rafael's magic, with the light of his love.

I push the gate closed, then seal it off so no one can ever open it again. A flood of magic rushes out of me, and I gasp as the last of it leaves my body. My knees are weak and I stumble, not caring if I'm unable to catch myself. I did it. It's over.

"What have you done?" Gloriana shrieks.

I blink up at her, struggling to regain my footing. I reach for Raf's magic, but I can barely stand, and it slips just out of reach. It doesn't matter. Gloriana can do whatever she wants to me now. The gate is closed, and I'm so tired.

"You bitch. You're going to pay for that." Her skin begins to glow, her chest heaving as she grows larger. "I have spent too long in this human form, but now you will see the true power of my kind. I will flay the skin from your bones and—"

Whatever she was about to say is cut off as she disappears into the vicious maw of the dragon king. Rafael swallows her in one gulp.

The sky is suddenly too bright. The sounds of the ocean and distant jungle are a loud roar in my ears. My skin feels like it's on fire as every one of my senses is reawakened. There is magic everywhere.

A giant claw wraps around my waist, and I am lifted, higher and higher, until the trees are only swaths of color and the ocean a glittering jewel far below. We're leaving. I relax my body into the cradle of the dragon's massive claws. I don't worry about where Rafael is taking me, though, because it doesn't matter. I'm already home.

Epilogue

The table has outdone itself tonight, likely sensing the festive mood. The burned pig looks especially appetizing, and I sit down to load up my plate.

"Where's Nyia?" Cesar asks as he and Teo take their seats across from me.

"She should be down any moment. I don't think I can let her out of my sight. She's here to stay—for good. I trust that won't be a problem?"

Cesar shrugs. "She's growing on me."

Teo shakes his head. "If you stop giving her all my things, I don't have any problems. She's not so bad for a Burner."

"Hey, I just closed the gate to the veil, thank you very much."

Nyia, Marix, and Rosadela enter the dining room, arms linked together. The ladies have dressed for dinner, each beautiful, but I only have eyes for *her*. Nyia is stunning tonight, her curls loose around her shoulders and down her back. I want to fist my hand in those curls and

...

"Hey." Nyia smiles as she takes the seat beside me.

"Hi, love. I missed you."

"Trust me, I needed that bath. But maybe next time, you can join me." She leans in for a kiss, and a blush stains her freckles.

"Okay, where is the wine? It's time to celebrate." Marix plops into the chair on my other side, urging Rosadela to take a seat as she heaps her plate full of various greens.

"Now that everyone is here, I need the full story. By the time Cesar and I got back to the beach, there was no sign of Gloriana or the king." Teo leans forward, spinning twin daggers between his fingers.

"That's because Rafael ate her," Nyia supplies with a devilish grin.

"You saw that, huh?" I'm only slightly embarrassed. I have no idea how to kill an ancient mythic, and at the time, I did the only thing that seemed logical. In my opinion, Gloriana got a quicker death than she deserved.

"Oh, I'm not going to forget it." Nyia winks. "King Ernesto escaped though."

"The human king will be a problem," Cesar says. He steals another glance at Rosadela when he thinks no one is watching.

"A problem for another day," Marix says. She stands up and takes on the dutiful task of refilling everyone's wine goblets.

I give my attention back to Nyia and find her watching me with a soft smile. Flames above, I love this woman.

Her smile widens into a wicked grin.

"What?" I ask, leaning forward until it is just us in our tiny bubble.

"I was just thinking . . . I'm not feeling very hungry," she whispers coyly.

My dick hardens, and suddenly I'm hungry for something else entirely.

"Let's go to bed, then." I rise from my chair, taking her soft hand in mine.

"Oh, I'm not tired."

"Good, me neither. Are you ready for your first knot-tying lesson?"

She leans into me as we leave the dining room, ignoring the shouts of protest from our friends. The rest of the world can wait. I'm going to fuck the love of my life.

ACKNOWLEDGEMENTS

Like raising a child, writing a book requires a community and I will be forever humbled and grateful by the endless support I received from my friends, family and colleagues. I want to first thank my abuelita for instilling a love of stories early on, I probably shouldn't have been allowed to watch all of her telenovelas. My parents who insisted I could do anything and to never stop pursuing my dreams. My sweet baby sister, my best friend and literally the best alpha reader in the world (I know, you need the official hat) and also my husband who might not be into smutty fantasy but damn, can he make a website! To my lovely team of beta readers: Heather, Neysa, Emily, Chelsea, Stacy, Stephanie and Dyan thank you so much for giving my new story a try and for falling in love with Nyia and Raf like I did. Are you ready for Sabastian and Iara?!

About the Author

Lexi Lopez is the pen name for Alexis Marrero Deese. As an avid fan of fantasy and romance it was only natural her passion would eventually lead to writing Romantasy. This is her first adult novel and the nom de plume was created to hide from her young readers.

When she isn't writing, Lexi is probably cooking an elaborate feast, riding unicorns, slaying monsters, or simply curled up with a good book.

While Lexi plans to continue publishing adult novels, you can find her published works for children and young adults under the name A. M. Deese where she publishes books with all the magic and adventure but none of the spice.

For more information and for a full list of her titles and upcoming projects, please visit www.authorlexilopez.com

www.ingramcontent.com/pod-product-compliance
Lightning Source LLC
LaVergne TN
LVHW040046080526
838202LV00045B/3513